DEAD
BEFORE
DYING

KERRY SCHAFER

DIVERSIONBOOKS

Diversion Books
A Division of Diversion Publishing Corp.
443 Park Avenue South, Suite 1008
New York, New York 10016
www.DiversionBooks.com

For more information, email info@diversionbooks.com

First Diversion Books edition February 2016.
Print ISBN: 978-1-62681-928-3
eBook ISBN: 978-1-62681-927-6

To Ryan and Brandon, good men both,
and loved beyond the measure of words.

CHAPTER ONE

I don't care what his nametag says, the young man standing by my bed can't really be a doctor. He wears the standard medico uniform—a white lab coat open over dark slacks and a button-up shirt, stethoscope draped around his neck. His nametag identifies him as Kevin Henderson, MD.

But he doesn't look a day over sixteen.

While he natters on about my discharge instructions, all I can do is focus on the brush of baby-fine hairs along his cheekbone. Sunlight slants through the window and highlights them, a golden, delicate fuzz. I want to ask him if he's old enough to shave but he hasn't pissed me off quite that much.

Not yet.

"Now, Ms. Keslyn," he says. "You qualify for some in-home nursing care, so someone will be coming by tomorrow—"

"No. They won't."

I've been polite; I've listened. Now I'm done. From my position, seated on the edge of the bed, it's fairly easy to slide my feet to the floor. The place in my belly, the one that has refused to heal properly despite weeks in the hospital, makes itself known as I stretch, but I'm pretty sure I haven't let the pain show in my face.

My right leg is another thing altogether.

It's damnably weak despite all the hours of physical therapy I've endured, and when I put weight on it I swear to God I can feel the pins creaking in the bone. The knee buckles. When I tighten my muscles to correct the fall, the pain in my belly flares. I gasp and grimace before I can catch myself.

Damn it. Rule number one: never let them see your weakness.

Dr. Henderson puts his hand under my arm, although I've already steadied myself.

"Oopsy-daisy," he croons, as though I am a child, then calls out into the hallway, "Can I get a wheelchair in here?"

He doesn't know how close he comes to a healthy slap on that baby-soft face. My fingers itch with the impulse, but he's saved by my grasp on reality. The blow would knock me flat on my ass and they'd probably tie me down and order in mental health. I'd have to tell lies to pass their little tests, and I'm just not in the mood for fun and games.

So, I smile. Apparently my smile, at least, remains the same, because the condescension is wiped off his face and his Adam's apple bobs. Ignoring his hovering, I bend for my bag, feeling the pulling of the fragile flesh, willing my knees to hold me. I manage to straighten up, wondering for a minute who's put weights in the bag and then realizing that it's the same as it's always been.

I'm the one who has changed.

Dr. Henderson takes the bag from me. "No lifting, Ms. Keslyn, remember? No bending. I knew you weren't listening—"

"I heard every word."

"Could you repeat it back to me?"

"I mustn't lift. I mustn't bend. I can bear weight on the leg but no jogging or jumping. Watch for redness, swelling, increasing discharge, or signs of a foul odor—"

He opens his mouth to speak but I ward him off with a gesture of my hand. "Wait—I forgot the last and most important thing. I must avoid any remotely useful activity that might lead to a meaningful life."

"Ms. Keslyn, I'm sure your life can have meaning. Have you given any thought to the referral I made to counseling?"

I tune him out. I've glimpsed a figure lurking in the hallway. Black skin, black suit, black sunglasses. If I listen I can hear him pacing, just outside my line of vision. A military pace, broken by a slight hitch and drag on the left.

"Ms. Keslyn? You're not listening again."

Poor child, he's feeling unimportant and neglected, but it can only do him good. He's too young to be getting the almighty doctor treatment; it will only go to his head. Let the nurses fawn over him. I have business in the hallway.

"I'm sorry, Doogie. I've got to go."

He looks at me blankly.

"You don't even know who Doogie Howser is, do you? My God."

"Wait for the wheelchair, Ms. Keslyn."

"My ride is here."

I limp out of the room. I am not going to meet Abel sitting in a wheelchair or pushing a walker like some decrepit old woman.

He's pacing down the hallway, hands clasped behind his back. Twenty paces, then he swivels in my direction. His shaved head glistens in the glare of the fluorescents. Dark glasses hide his eyes, but I know he's seen me. There's a predatory tilt to his head, a tightening of the muscles.

He wants something.

"Well, this is a surprise," I say. "If you'd like to take my bag from the good doctor here, we can be on our way."

"You need a wheelchair," Dr. Henderson protests. "And the nurse still needs to sign you out."

"I'm walking. If somebody wants something signed, present it before I reach the door." I see freedom and I'm not looking back. Abel's car will be waiting outside. If he wants to talk, he can give me a ride home. It will be quicker than a taxi.

The nurse is almost my age, grey hair in a smooth helmet over her head, a no-nonsense green uniform. Thank the stars she's said no to teddy bear prints or other falderal. She catches me halfway down the hall and presents me with a clipboard and a pen.

No point making her life more difficult. I sign, and then I'm in the clear.

The door seems too far away, like a destination in a dream. I walk and walk and don't seem to get any closer. I hear wheels behind me and I know that infernal doctor has either sent somebody after me with a chair or is pushing one himself.

My left leg feels like rubber, the right is full of lead weights. Sweat slicks down my back, my breath keens in my chest as though I've been running for miles, and my heart is throwing a tizzy.

None of this matters. I am walking out that fucking door, and I'm doing it under my own steam.

I hear Abel's voice behind me. "Lose the chair, doc. She'll fall over dead before she'll sit in that thing." His steps lengthen and pick up speed until he's at my side, my bag dangling from his fingers like it's filled with feathers. Rage over my own predicament supplies a little extra boost to muscles thinking of surrender, and I make it out into the lobby.

"I'm parked right outside," Abel says, and sure enough I can see his car through the glass doors, exactly the car to match the suit and glasses, a black sedan with tinted windows arranged at an angle in a No Parking, Ambulances Only zone.

I'm grateful for his arrogance—I wouldn't have made it across the parking lot.

He opens the passenger door but lets me struggle in without offering a hand, and I know for sure he wants something. Abel doesn't act out of kindness and decency. Never mind that his FBI badge puts him in the good-guy camp or that he focuses his predatory nature on harassing the dark side. If he wasn't out to garner a favor he'd have plunked me into that wheelchair himself, or picked me up and carried me.

Sweat-soaked and shivering in the chill of an October afternoon, I catch my breath, corral the pain, and prepare myself for whatever it is he's going to throw at me. Abel slides in behind the wheel and puts the key in the ignition but doesn't turn it. "Can we talk?"

"Home, James."

"Care to tell me why Ed isn't picking you up?"

"He doesn't know I've been cut loose. Which brings me to a question…"

Abel starts the car, pulls out onto Division, and heads north, the direction of my house.

"I badgered the doctor," he says. "That's how I knew you were getting out today."

"Why?" It's not out of any special concern for my well-being, that's certain.

"Something for you under the seat."

"I'm not supposed to bend."

He makes a rude noise of dismissal, and I am—of course—already defying both the doctor and my body's pain messages. My fingers fumble with the edges of a hard plastic box before I'm able to get a grip and drag it out into daylight.

Rugged plastic. Black. I open it to find two items inside: my revolver and my FBI guest ID. Cold shock settles over me as I realize what it is he wants, and then I start to laugh. "Thanks for the vote of confidence, but you do realize I barely made it to the car?"

"Would have been a shame to call an ambulance before you'd even left the grounds."

I am not going to ask him what exactly it is he thinks I can do in my condition, so I shut up and watch the world go by. Only three weeks out of commission, but everything looks both new and strange—as though I've pulled a Rip Van Winkle and slept a hundred years. The world has moved on fine without me, a fact hammered home when Abel pulls into my driveway.

During the time I have been gone, the leaves on the big maple have turned to crimson and begun to fall, drifting across the lawn. Frost has touched the flower beds, and only the marigolds are still in bloom.

In the driveway, parked beside my Jag convertible and Ed's much more sober Beemer, there's a minivan. Company.

I note the minivan, but it's the Jag that draws my full attention. Doesn't look too bad from this distance, other than the bullet holes and fractured glass in the windshield and the dent in the front fender. It needs a good wash, but at least Ed's had the decency to put the top up so it's not full of leaves and dirt.

There will be bloodstains on the seat covers, though.

Memory rocks me, hard. The sluglike paranormal oozing

between me and the steering wheel, its tentacles probing into my belly through skin and then muscle, eating at my innards. Bullets slamming through the windshield. My hunger for air as my lungs fill with blood. And then nothing. The before and the after are a blank.

This sudden flash hurts more than any of the physical pain and I fight it back. Not now. Not with Abel observing every nuance of my behavior. Not with Ed emerging onto the porch.

He stands there, hands in his pockets, black hair lightly frosted at the temples. He's sixty-five and still a beautiful man. I feel like I'm looking at him backwards through a telescope, small and distant. I'm still trying to decipher the look on his face—surprise, disappointment, unease—when a woman steps out behind him, putting a questioning hand on his arm.

She sees me and freezes, mouth curved in a round O of understanding. A breeze presses the velour pantsuit over a body matronly rather than voluptuous, and she puts her other hand protectively up to hair so shellacked it won't be blowing anywhere anytime soon.

"The doctor told me you'd be released next week," Ed says.

"I'm a fast healer. Who's your friend?"

For the first time he glances back at her, as if surprised she's there. She's the one who answers me. "I'm Glenda. You must be Maureen."

Indeed I must. And this is my house, and somewhere in my kitchen there is a bottle of wine, and I am going to have a drink. As I hobble toward the porch the two of them draw together, unconscious of their own body language, but it's clear to me and, I'm certain, to Abel. They do not want me in the house. I avoid Ed's eyes, don't offer even a token kiss. This is before I realize the extent of the betrayal.

The house is no longer mine. There are crocheted afghans hanging over the back of the couch, needlepoint cushions decorating the easy chair. Plants have invaded. Someone has been burning candles in a heavy, floral scent that makes me cough.

Coughing should have been on the list of things I must not do, although I suppose even the good doctor knows there's no point warning me against this one, and when the paroxysm clears I've got both hands pressed against my belly and I'm looking around through a haze of involuntary tears.

I smell Ed behind me. Thirty years of close proximity and you learn the scent of a person. "When were you planning to tell me?" Thank God my voice is steady. I have no intention of letting him see me cry.

"I tried—"

"Funny, I don't remember any mention of this." Anger comes to my rescue and I turn on him. "An affair I can understand. Always half expected you had a woman snugged away somewhere. Moving her in while I'm in the hospital? Did it occur to you I might need to make some living arrangements?"

"You can stay here as long as you need to." The woman sounds like someone's grandmother. Ed wraps his arm around her waist, protective. Good God, she's not even young and sexy. Old-lady hair, waved and colored, magenta nails, a pantsuit that looks like it's lingered since the fifties. My chest burns and my voice is drenched in acid.

"How about you wait outside? This is between me and my husband."

She makes a bleating noise and Ed pats her, comfortingly. There is a softness in his face that I haven't seen before. "She's not going anywhere, and I won't allow you to—"

"Bullshit, Ed! This is my house. Not hers."

"Actually, it's in my name." His tone has gone logical and annoyingly calm. "Remember? You were gone so much we agreed it would be easier that way. I'm not going to be a bastard about this—when we sell it I intend to give you half. And you can stay as long as you need—"

"Fuck you."

I turn around and walk back outside. Abel leans against his car, arms crossed, waiting. He opens the door when he sees me coming and I slide in without a word.

He drives in silence for several blocks, while I stare out the window and try to come to terms with the fact that I am aging, wounded, and homeless.

"You knew."

"Ready to hear my proposition now?" he says.

"You're a cruel bastard. You could have told me."

"You needed to see for yourself."

"I can't imagine what you think I can do for you."

One hand on the wheel, he reaches behind the seat and pulls a folder out of a briefcase and drops it in my lap. I know these folders. There will be pictures—contacts, locations, things I will see, memorize, and burn when I'm through.

I open the thing and stare in disbelief. "You're insane." Right on top is a picture of smiling old people with golf clubs and Bermuda shorts. Behind them is a clinical-looking building with the words "Shadow Valley Manor" blazoned across it.

This stings. I know Abel is missing most of the softer feelings, but this—this is outright enemy territory. "Stop the car and let me out."

He doesn't even blink. "You'll be working, not vegetating. Your contact is Phil Evers."

Now there's a name I haven't heard in a while. My skin warms at the thought of him, even after all these years, and my stomach does an inappropriate little butterfly dance. I squash it.

"Lies. Phil's been out of the game for years."

"He said you'd say that. He also said to remind you that you owe him."

"You talked to Phil."

"I did. He bought the Manor. Apparently, it came with a bit of a problem." The twitch of his lips looks suspiciously like a smile.

Not surprising. Phil Evers is something of a legend in our world, the 007 of paranormal investigators. Smooth, smart, and with a voice that can melt a whole lot more than butter. If he's involved in an investigation after all these years then it's going to be bigger than an intestine-eating slug.

For the first time in my life, I'm not up for that sort of danger. I feel vulnerable and frail and have a sudden strong urge to get on a plane to someplace tropical, with a beach.

"I don't care who my contact is. I am not going to any place called Shadow Valley."

Abel is too sharp for his own good. He sees right through me. "You can handle this. All undercover. Easy. No danger."

"Do tell." Undercover is good, as it means they'll pay my expenses and I'll have a roof over my head. But there's more to this story; there always is.

"Really. That's it. You hang out, keep your eyes open."

"Who else is in?"

"Just you. He asked for you. I'm your chain of command."

"Does he know?" I gesture at my leg, my ruined body, unable to articulate the damage.

"He knows."

Damn the man. Phil could always play me with a well-placed word. With just that one phrase—*he asked for you*—I know I'm in. I feel needed. Despite my years and the distance between us I catch myself preening like a cat.

"What am I looking for?"

"He said he'll brief you himself."

"Where, Abel?"

"Small town. Perfect place for a little rest and recovery."

"Alias?"

"No need. You're hiding in plain sight."

"Shadow Valley Manor. I don't know, Abe." Better judgment is trying to make itself heard, kicking and screaming for my attention. There are two possible explanations here. One: Phil heard about my disaster and still cares enough to offer me a way to salvage my pride. Two: Phil is up to something dangerous and he means it about me being the best person for this job. Which scares me. Even in the days when I knew he loved me, he would have risked me in a heartbeat for the good of an operation.

And I'm not at all sure that I'm up to the task.

"You have a better idea?" Abel asks, and that's where he has me.

My medical bills are going to be steep. I don't have the money to buy another house. I've got about another seven years to go before I can collect what I've earned in retirement benefits. I know, and Ed knows, that I'm not going to accept a single dime from him. My savings are not going to last long if I have to pay rent, and the social security I've built up is enough for subsistence living only. In this market, it's going to take a while for the house to sell so I can get my share.

At least the ignominy of Shadow Valley offers a paycheck and an illusion of purpose.

Or death. I can't shake that cold chill that tells me I'm walking into a trap.

"Tell you what," Abel says. "Take a couple of days to think—we'll put you up in a hotel, cover your expenses."

"Fix my car."

"What?"

"You'll also get my car fixed, good as new, and hire some movers to put my belongings in storage. I'll make a list of what I want to take with me."

"Deal."

And there it is. I lean my head back against the seat and close my eyes. I always knew getting old would suck, but I'd managed to visualize tropical beaches and a continuation of good health. Maybe an arthritic knee, but still active and kicking ass into my eighties.

Anything I might have dreamed on the dark side wouldn't have come close to what I've just agreed to do.

CHAPTER TWO

Score one for Abel—his connections know their stuff. The Jag is better than ever. New paint job, black and shiny. Brand new upholstery. Not a hint of blood or trauma.

I can't say the same about myself.

A week of resting up in a hotel at the government's expense and I still feel like sentient roadkill. Ahead of me looms a future I haven't quite decided to embrace, in the form of Shadow Valley Manor. The fact that Phil now owns the place is intriguing, but not reassuring.

Abel claims it's not a nursing home, or even assisted living. More like a communal unit for elderly people with money. Meals and laundry are taken care of and a nurse and doctor come in to consult on medical issues. There's a staff member available at all hours, just in case somebody falls and can't get up. Apart from that, you're on your own.

There will still be rules, I pointed out. And I have a longstanding disagreement with rules.

"God, Maureen, you'll be working. You're only playing at being a law-abiding citizen."

Between Abel's arguments—which reek of input from Phil—and my lack of better options, I've gone so far as to pack a suitcase and make the trek to Shadow Valley. This is not an easy task in my condition, considering that the Jag is a five-speed and every time I push in the clutch to shift gears, my leg protests.

Still. It's warm for October and driving with the top down and the sun pouring in recharges something inside me that damn near drained away during my weeks in a hospital bed.

Now here I am, staring at a structure that screams retirement home, and I'm not at all sure I'm going to go through with this. I've got enough money to live on for a year if I tighten my belt. I could get a part-time job to supplement the cash flow. Walmart greeter or some such.

I've got a meeting with Phil tonight for my briefing, and if I decide to bail on the job I'll find a motel in town. So I've got time to kill and I have to admit I'm curious as to what could possibly be lurking in a place like this.

Leaning against the warm hood of the Jag, I light up a cigarette and draw the smoke deep into my lungs. Thanks to Dr. Henderson, who triggered every rebellious bone in my body, I stopped along the way and bought the first pack I've held in twenty years. You'd think the body would forget in that expanse of time, but you'd be wrong. It would seem I'm satisfying a craving I didn't even know I had.

It's not procrastination, I tell myself, it's surveillance. I need to get the lay of the land. During the Cold War the top of this hill was covered in barracks and other military buildings, not to mention the radar tower. When it was decommissioned most of that was razed to the ground. The government sold the property to a religious group, who renovated the only building left standing and turned it into the Shadow Valley Home for Unwed Mothers, known to the locals as HUM. Church ladies apparently ran HUM all the way into the early eighties, after which it shifted hands again and became the Manor.

Abel says if you walk the hilltop you can still see the footprints of the other buildings, tower and all, but from my vantage point there is nothing to indicate anything out of the ordinary, and I'm not inclined to go hiking. A concrete path, wide enough for wheelchairs, winds up through an expanse of lawn to a three-story brick building, boring and symmetrical. Flower beds, bounded by red brick, imprison purple mums in regimented clumps. A stray dandelion or two would go a long way toward brightening my day, but this is a lawn ruthlessly maintained, where no weed dares to show its face.

One cigarette stretches into two as I carry on my argument

with fate.

My leg aches. A cold breeze drives a swirl of fallen leaves around my feet. I'm about to put out my smoke and go see what's up in the Manor when a cloud of dust drifts up over the trees. I can't see the road around the corner, but someone is coming. One more moment and a panel van comes into sight. It careens dangerously close to the ditch on one side, then overcorrects toward the other, before skidding to a halt in my peaceful parking lot in a shower of gravel, leaving dust hanging in the air like a curtain.

Emblazoned on the side of the van in scarlet lettering is the legend "Frank's Full-Service Crematorium and Burial." A tasteful depiction of a flower wreath draped over a giant funereal urn illustrates the message for anybody who can't read three-foot-tall lettering.

The driver, a wisp of a girl with a waist-length braid of black hair as thick as my arm, slams the driver's-side door and stalks to the back of the van. Her eyes light on me.

"Maybe you could give me a hand." Her voice is deeper than I was expecting, throaty, the tone definitely more command than request.

"Maybe I could." I take one last drag on my cigarette and grind it out beneath my good heel. The busted leg isn't happy about either the long drive with all of the clutch work or the fact that I've been standing around.

The girl reaches into the back of the van and jerks a wheeled trolley toward her. The movement bares her lower back, revealing a stylized tattoo that looks like a man with the head of a jackal, accompanied by some sort of hieroglyph. For the first time in my existence, I'm sorry that I haven't studied Egyptian. It's not the sort of tattoo a teenage girl selects by accident, even after a night out drinking, and I'm deeply curious about what it means.

I lean against the van, watching her struggle.

"I suppose you're waiting for me to say please or something."

"Or something."

Her eyes are an extraordinary shade of green, like a glacier lake and equally opaque, heavily lined in black kohl. Skin a shade too pale, but porcelain perfect. High cheekbones, a pointed chin. Not a pretty face, although not one you'd forget in a hurry. The silver lip rings and nose stud she's added do nothing to improve it.

A black stone, set in silver, swings on a chain around her neck.

She rolls her eyes, typical teenager style. "The dead are so much easier to deal with."

"More biddable, I suppose. Not particularly useful for getting carts out of vans."

Hands on slim hips, a flash of green fire. "Look, the poor thing has been waiting all morning. Give me a hand or get out of my way."

Well said. I reach for my side of the trolley and help lower it to the parking lot. I feel the pull in my belly, sharp enough to make my breath hitch in my throat.

"So…you obviously aren't Frank."

"There is no Frank, never was. Dad came up with that— 'Lysander's Crematorium' doesn't have the right ring, he says. I'm Sophronia. Not Sophie. In case you were feeling tempted."

"Noted."

The stretcher rattles and bounces as Sophronia manhandles it across the gravel and onto the smoother paved walkway that winds up toward the building. All of a sudden I'm more interested in checking out the Manor, and I yank my suitcase out of the trunk, lifting again and paying the price in blazing pain.

Trailing my suitcase behind me, I follow in the girl's wake until she and the gurney stop in front of double glass doors. Abel said this wasn't a nursing home. He claimed it was more like a condo for retired people who didn't want to do their own cooking.

Abel lied.

I've done my share of visiting in these places and I can sniff them from a mile away. Stale urine and despair make a mighty stink. I've always hated them, but they were at least tolerable in the days when I was young and invincible and they were only a cautionary tale. A sign over the door says WELCOME TO SHADOW VALLEY MANOR. It ought to say "Abandon Hope, All Ye Who Enter Here."

"Door's not going to open itself," Sophronia says.

Stepping around her, I tug at the door on the right. It swings open easily enough and I brace it with my shoulder while the cart clatters past.

Beyond her, as expected, is a lobby and an office. Yep, same construction as pretty much every nursing home I've ever been in. What's different is the furnishings, which look more like a nice hotel. Decent, comfortable-looking chairs. As hard as I sniff I'm not catching even a whiff of urine or disinfectant.

A woman steps out of the office and blocks our progress. Long, bushy hair of nondescript brown, a shapeless brown sweater, and a skirt that reaches to her ankles. Sensible, clunky lace-up shoes. A heavy wooden crucifix hangs on a chain around her neck. Her eyes burn with the sort of fervor that belongs to the extreme zealot and the maniac.

"Betty." There is enough ice in Sophronia's voice to freeze a small city.

"I'd expected your father." Betty's mouth is set in a straight, hard line and both hands twist, twist, in the fabric of her skirt. A whiff of something chemical reaches my nostrils, but on a second sniff I get nothing. Mothballs, maybe.

"I have no idea where he is—gone off somewhere again." Sophronia's gaze flicks to the side while her right hand beats a quick tattoo against her leg. "If you'll get out of the way, I'll go pick up Dora."

"We can wait for him. I've told you—"

"I know, I know. You don't want my pagan feet to cross the threshold. But Lysander is unavailable, so what are you going to do? Dora can't wait long." The girl's words are light enough, but if looks could kill, Betty would be dead as a doornail.

"You'll need help—"

"So help me."

Betty's lips curl in distaste. "She's dead."

Again the eye roll from Sophronia. "That's pretty much why I'm here." She abandons the stretcher and steps closer. "You're scared," she says, her voice an accusation. "Of a poor old woman who never hurt a soul."

Drawing herself up, military straight, Betty thrusts out her chin. "I'm not scared. I don't hold with touching the dead, is all. Let the dead bury their own dead, as our Lord and Savior told us."

"Wow. He was one cold dude." Sophronia gestures at me. "Fine. She'll have to help me."

"Heathen," Betty mutters. She turns her focus to me. "And who are you, exactly? Come to visit one of the residents? There's a sign-in book—"

"Actually, I've come to stay."

These words, coming out of my own mouth, surprise me. They're more of a shock to Betty. Her mouth drops open, then closes with a snap. "We're not expecting any new residents."

"But I had a letter from—um, a Mr. Evers—confirming my reservation. It said I could move in today."

"I told him we didn't have any rooms." Her hands are clenched around each other now, hard enough to whiten the knuckles. There's something wrong with the skin, a scaly irritation that makes me itch. I shift my attention back to her face. Her eyebrows are drawn down in a straight line across her forehead, matching her mouth.

"I've driven a long way; there must be somewhere I can sleep tonight." I let a little quaver into my voice, easier than it ought to be, which is something I'll worry about later.

Apparent weakness on my part eases Betty a little. She shakes her head, and her voice drops into that tone people use for children and the deranged. "There is clearly some misunderstanding, dear. What did you say your name is?"

I didn't say, of course. And I don't. It's too galling, even undercover, to play to this woman's need to humiliate and control. "If Mr. Evers talked to you, as you say, then you already know." I smile at her sweetly.

"Oh, for the love of Thoth. Just put her in a room somewhere," Sophronia says. "Hey, I know what. You can both help me move Dora, and then she can have that room."

Betty gasps. "How could you? The body is barely cold—"

"And getting colder every minute," Sophronia mutters.

Betty ignores her. "Besides, the room will need to be cleaned from top to bottom, and all of Dora's belongings packed up." She shakes her head emphatically. "You're just going to have to stay in a motel for a day or two, I'm afraid, while we get this all sorted out." She takes a step toward me and begins to make shepherding, shooing motions with her arms.

I'd been intending to do exactly that, but I've changed my mind. "All I need is clean sheets and a bed. I'm sure that can be arranged—"

"What about the third-floor suite, across from Mr. Vermeer? That's empty." Sophronia's tone is helpful, but her eyes are full of malice.

"We're renovating."

"You've been renovating for, like, six months now. Have yet to see a single worker do a solitary thing."

The tension between these two sizzles and pops like bacon in a pan. Plenty of time to dig for the subtext later; right now I need to insinuate myself into this facility, and whatever her motives, Sophronia has handed me a lead I'm not about to pass up.

"Any workers scheduled to do something there today?" I ask.

"Well, no, but—"

"Good. I'll just settle in there until we can talk to Mr. Evers and get this all sorted out."

Betty opens her mouth to argue, but stops as an old woman barrels down the hall toward us.

"Run. This is a house of death." Saliva sprays my cheek. Twisted, arthritic hands grab my wrist.

"Alice, leave the lady be." Betty grabs her and tries to pull her away.

A macabre little tug-of-war ensues, Betty tugging, Alice holding on to me like grim death. Her breath is fetid and heavy, her glasses smeared thick with fingerprints and splatters of food. A thin white scar cuts through the wrinkles on her chin.

Betty plants her feet and leans back, using her weight. Alice grunts softly, with pain or effort, her fingers digging into my arm. "Please," she says, "don't let them kill me."

Her whole body is trembling, her pupils so dilated that there is only a thin rim of grey visible around them.

"Sure," I say, just wanting her to let go. "I won't let anybody hurt you."

"Promise."

"I promise. Let go of her, Betty. Just give her a minute."

I've all but forgotten Sophronia, in the hallway behind me with the gurney, but at this point her voice knifes through the proceedings. "If nobody wants to help, I'll go get Dora by myself. But you're all in the way."

Alice begins to wail, loudly and incoherently, a high keening sound that chills my blood.

Betty's own ears must be ringing, because I see her wavering. This sort of thing can't be good for business, and I keep expecting the hallway to fill up with other hysterical geezers. Finally she shouts over the racket, "Can you go with Sophronia?"

"I don't see why not." This is exactly what I've been wanting all along, of course, but there's no need for Betty to know that. Chances are good that in a place like this a dead body is simply a dead body, but there's a reason why Phil wants me here, and it's unlikely to be a problem with accounts receivable.

Betty tries again to detach Alice, and she cinches her arms into a death grip. I take her wrists in mine and tug, easing my windpipe enough to draw breath and say firmly, directly into her ear, "Listen, Alice—I'll come up to your room later and make sure it's safe, okay? We'll check the locks and the windows."

She moans, but her hold loosens a little. "Betty will go to your room with you now, to make sure it's safe. Okay? Come on now, let me go."

Her arms fall to her sides, limp. When Betty takes her hand and pulls her forward she goes along, on autopilot, still wailing.

Sophronia nudges me with the gurney and I step aside to let

her roll on ahead.

She stops at the open door of the office. It's disordered and cluttered. The filing cabinet is unlocked, the top drawer half open; the desk is covered with file folders and papers. A Bible lies on top of the mess, open to Deuteronomy. While Sophronia rifles through the drawers I check out Betty's reading material. She's not one for uplifting psalms or verses of forgiveness and hope. A passage on the open pages is highlighted in yellow:

> Let no one be found among you who sacrifices his son or daughter in the fire, who practices divination or sorcery, interprets omens, engages in witchcraft, or casts spells, or who is a medium or spiritist who consults the dead. Anyone who does these things is detestable to The Lord…

While I flip through the Bible, finding other similar passages marked for emphasis, Sophronia rifles through the desk. She surfaces at last with an old-fashioned brass key and presses it into my hand. "You'll need this for your suite."

And then she rolls away again and I fall into step behind her, dragging my suitcase. I'm slower, limping, no matter how hard I try to ignore the pain, and can't keep up with her brisk pace.

In this hallway we pass four rooms, two on each side. Each has a nameplate. Some are decorated or have welcome mats. Others are just plain doors. At the end of the hallway we pass through a central lounge—huge stone fireplace, velvet drapes, Persian carpets. The five occupants of the room fall into suspended animation at sight of the gurney, so utilitarian and truthful in this place where death is gilded and glazed over with ostentatious elegance.

All I get is a quick glimpse of a scene that looks like something out of a wax museum. Three women playing cards. Two gentlemen peering over the tops of newspapers. All eyes are fixated on the cart. I have memorized a dossier that sums up their various histories in a few hard words and I have a name for every face in the room.

Down the hallway a little further we stop in front of an elevator. Sophronia rolls on in and stands there, staring at me while I keep my feet firmly planted on solid ground. I'm not fond of elevators.

"There are stairs," she offers.

I weigh the idea of a steep, narrow stairway against my aching leg, take a deep breath, and step in. When Sophronia punches the second-floor button the whole thing shudders, creaking and groaning through its ascent. Despite my misgivings, the elevator arrives at its destination, although it stops off-kilter. When we open the doors the floor is six inches below us.

"They should fix that. I keep telling them." Sophronia steps down and yanks the cart toward her. Again I lift the other end and wish I hadn't.

Across from us, through an open door, is a library. Comfortable-looking chairs, shelves of books from floor to ceiling. One of those odd, wheeled ladders rests against the far stack. A faint change in the temperature sends a shiver up my spine. Sophronia's gaze focuses on the top of that ladder and she gives an almost imperceptible nod.

I can't see whatever it is, but it follows us down the hall. I know by the little chill on my back, the fine hairs standing on end. It doesn't feel like a hostile. Just curious, maybe.

Dora's room is a cozy little suite with a living area, bathroom, and separate bedroom. A crocheted afghan folded precisely across the foot of the bed. A basket of knitting beside a cushioned rocking chair. A glass on the bedside table containing a couple inches of water and a set of false teeth. Several pictures hang on the walls— watercolor landscapes. The antique dresser holds a crocheted doily and a jewelry box. No clutter of framed pictures, no trinkets from grandchildren and children, or even friends. One window, closed and latched. No sign of a disturbance.

The dead woman lies flat on her back, hands folded across the blanket, which is drawn neatly up almost to her chin. A silk scarf is knotted loosely around her neck, turquoise and crimson, garish and harsh against the pallor of death. Her mouth sags open, collapsed inward over toothless gums. Her eyes are open and staring, not up at the ceiling, but turned to the side as though she'd been looking at somebody or something when she died.

The trolley is a tight fit in the small space, but Sophronia wrangles it around and wedges it tight against the bed, brakes set. She strokes a strand of hair off the dead woman's forehead.

"I'm sorry you had to wait, Dora darling, you must have been so frightened." She leans down and plants a kiss on the pale forehead. With her black hair and pale skin, so white it glows in the dim room, Sophronia looks otherworldly, a dark angel come to collect a soul. I remind myself that said angel in black is an obnoxious teenager who drove here in a panel van. Still, my fingers fumble more than they should as I locate the light switch and turn on a harsh overhead light that makes everything normal. Just an old woman, dead of natural causes, an eccentric undertaker's daughter, and an aging operative who sees the supernatural where there is none.

"How do we get her on the trolley?" My voice sounds harsh to my own ears.

"Don't you feel it?" Sophronia asks, one hand still resting on Dora's forehead.

"Feel what?"

"She's terrified."

"Don't be ridiculous." But there is a creeping in my flesh and my heart has speeded its cadence. Every beat of it throbs in the broken place in my belly. Sophronia gives me a look and my eyes almost drop before I catch myself. No teenage bit of a thing is going to establish dominance over me.

"Look, even if you can feel what you say you can—fear—it's not surprising, is it? Say she had a heart attack, or a stroke. She'd have time to think, 'Oh my God, I'm dying. I'm not ready. I don't want to be alone...'"

My own words trigger a memory flash. *It's so dark. Pain everywhere. Can't breathe. All alone, going to die...*

"Hey!" Sophronia glares at me from across the bed. "We need to get her out of here to somewhere safe."

"She's dead," I manage.

"Exactly. She can't move herself. Come on." She pushes back the strand of raven hair that has escaped from her braid. "We can roll her or slide her. Do you have a problem touching the body?"

Bodies don't bother me. God knows I've handled enough of them. I let Sophronia issue orders. We roll the body one way and then another to get a transfer sheet beneath it. The old woman is an awkward, ungainly dead weight. Her skin feels like putty. Rigor has set in and she's stiff, which is a good thing—the task would be more difficult with flopping arms and legs.

The trolley is broken. It's an inch taller than the bed and I have to tug upward on the sheet as I pull Dora toward me. I feel a sharp pull in my belly, followed by a sudden wet heat. Hopefully it's only blood and my insides aren't about to spill out onto the gurney. I put one hand over the wound to hold everything together. Just in case.

"Are you all right?"

"Fine." It's hard to speak with my teeth clenched around the pain. Also hard to focus. Something about the body is wrong. The blood should have settled and pooled, but there is no lividity at all.

Sophronia expertly fastens the straps to belt the body in place, then lays her hands on either side of the still white face. "Dora, I need to cover you up now. It's only for a few minutes, so the others won't be frightened. And then a little ride. I'll be there all the time, all right? Here we go." She pulls up a white sheet and tucks it in.

Dark spots dance in front of my eyes and the room has begun to spin in a nauseating way. I lean on the bed to hold myself upright, and through my rapidly fading vision I think I see a dark-colored splotch that doesn't quite blend in with the flowered quilt. I could be imagining this, or it could be one of the spots increasingly filling my vision. My ears fill with a rushing sound and the darkness completely obscures my sight.

When I can see again, I'm staring up at a high ceiling, something hard underneath me. The floor. A pointed face peers down at me. "I thought you said the dead don't bother you."

"They don't."

"You're bleeding." Sophronia's gaze settles on the front of my T-shirt, which is, in fact, showing a big red splotch.

"It's nothing."

"Bullshit." She gets down on her knees and pulls up the fabric despite my rather feeble protest. It's not as bad as I'd envisioned. Already the blood flow has slowed to a trickle. No gaping hole. No loops of bowels spilling through, thank God.

But the shirt is ruined. Worse, the belt of my small-of-the-back holster is visible. Sophronia says nothing about the holster, just surveys the wound with a professional eye.

"What did that?"

"You don't want to know."

"Maybe I do."

"It's good to want things."

"You should have said something." She gives me her hand and pulls me up to standing. Thank all the powers that be the floor remains steady beneath my feet; the room spins only once and settles.

"I'll show you your room," she says. No fussing or fretting, no awkward questions or offers of wheelchairs or further assistance. She unlocks the wheels on the gurney and rolls it out into the hall and toward the elevator.

Once again I'm not crazy about getting into the elevator, but it's very clear I'm not doing stairs at this point. We take Dora with us, as Sophronia has no intention of leaving her alone, and we make quite a procession down the third-floor hallway. Faded carpet muffles the sound of the trolley wheels. As for me, the momentary weakness has passed and the pain has eased again to a dull throbbing. I feel mostly deadened, almost two-dimensional, as though part of me is missing.

"This one is yours," Sophronia says, stopping in front of a door. "And that belongs to Mr. Vermeer." As if her words are a cue, the door across the hallway opens and I get my first glimpse of my new neighbor.

CHAPTER THREE

My neighbor is a shriveled-up old bastard, eyes hidden behind a pair of dark sunglasses. His skin is an unhealthy shade of pale that speaks of anemia or illness, but his lips, caved in over toothless gums, are redder than an old man's lips have any right to be. He leans forward, sniffing like a hunting dog, his head turning from side to side.

I know who he is, thanks to the basic info I got from Abel. Gerald Vermeer, ninety-three years old, former tax accountant, widower. More significantly, the man harbors the delusion that he's a vampire.

"What if he is?" I'd said to Abel when I leafed through the dossier on my new housemates.

He snorted. "And I'm an incubus."

"That's not so far off—plenty of soul sucking coming from you."

"Phil vetted him. Vampires don't age, and no self-respecting vampire chick is going to bother to turn an old fart like that one. He doesn't even have any teeth."

Vermeer does not look like a vampire, sure enough, but he also doesn't look psychotic or senile. He levels an index finger at Sophronia's heart.

"You."

"Yes, me. And Dora, in case you hadn't noticed. Died suddenly in the middle of the night." Sophronia's body is a line of tension, green eyes cold as winter.

"A shame. Was she ill? And more importantly, what is she doing up here, taking the scenic route?"

"Asshole."

He grins. "Are you going to introduce me to your assistant?"

"Can't. She hasn't told me her name yet."

Even on assignment, I am not going to play anybody's assistant anything. All I want to do is get into my room, close the door on the three of them, and lie down. But I take a breath and stay on task. "If you need to call me anything, Maureen will do."

I turn the key in the lock and the door swings open.

Sophronia presses up against my shoulder, breathing down my neck. Vermeer rolls up on the other side. Both of them are craning their necks to peer around the half-open door.

"Do you mind?"

Apparently they do. Sophronia shoves past me and into the suite. Vermeer crowds closer, rolling over my foot with his wheelchair, not seeming to notice he's hit a live speed bump. The addition of an aching foot to my tally of injuries does nothing to improve my mood.

The suite is a little unexpected, but not enough to inspire this level of interest. Floor-length velvet curtains that can only be described as the color of blood are half open to reveal a multipaned window. Dark hardwood floor, softened by thick Persian carpets. An enormous four-poster bed, a couch, several old-fashioned chairs with needlepoint upholstery. An antique wardrobe and a chest of drawers. Whoever lived in this room before understood luxury. They also didn't have a taste for the modern.

Sophronia, hands clasped behind her back, stares at a closet door. Her jaw is clamped tight, and in the gloom her eyes glow like a cat's.

"Please—could I have a look?" Mr. Vermeer is parked in the doorway, damn near breaking his neck in an effort to peer around the corner.

"Be my guest," I mutter, with full sarcastic inflection, well aware that he is a self-professed vampire. If there is a shred of truth to this tale, the easiest place to stake him will be right here, away from curious observers. If he's stupid enough to try anything.

The old man smirks, reminding me that he's not stupid,

whatever else he may or may not be.

An instant later he too is obsessed with the closet door, parking his chair right smack in front of it and laying his palm against the wood.

"Do you suppose it's true?" Sophronia murmurs. She looks like she's in a trance.

"All things are possible, if not probable," he says.

"What's true?" Neither answers. Forcing myself between them, I grab the closet doorknob and twist. It's stuck. I rattle it, give it a tug, and it swings open.

Revealing nothing more exciting than a walk-in closet. Shelves line the right side, floor to ceiling, all coated in a thick layer of dust. Clothes hangers dangle from two long rods. And that's it. No mystery here, other than why whoever does the cleaning doesn't ever dust in here, and I know the answer to that one. Most humans aren't going to do more than the minimum requirements. It's a closet. Nobody's using it.

Conscious of a small pang of disappointment, I turn to Sophronia. "I thought you were worried about Dora."

A quiver runs through her, and she looks at me as though I'm miles away, unfocused and vague. "What?"

"The dead woman, currently decomposing in the hallway."

It's like watching somebody wake from sleep. I can literally see her gaze sharpen, her face firm into decision. "You're right. I need to get her away from here." She gives the old man a scathing look. "Him first. Back to his room."

Vermeer gums a smile at her. "I've got all day and nowhere to go. Scurry off, imp, and ferry the poor old dear away."

"Out. Both of you—out now. Surely there must be something more interesting to do than sit and stare at an empty closet."

"In this place?" Vermeer makes no move to go. Sophronia gets behind his chair and gives it a shove.

"Hey—"

"Stow it, Gerry. We're leaving."

"All right, all right. But I go under my own steam." He wheels himself toward the door. Sophronia looks back over her shoulder. "If you're smart, you'll lock it," she says. The door closes behind them, and I'm alone.

Much as it irks me to do anything Sophronia has ordered me to do, I didn't live to be almost sixty without learning a few things, one of them being that petty spiteful actions usually hurt yourself more than anybody else. I'm not at all sure that the man across the hall has even the most rudimentary understanding of privacy and boundaries. Plus, it's a matter of habit. I've spent most of my life watching my back for enemies both human and supernatural.

I lock the door. Digging through my luggage, I locate my silver cross and hang it over the knob. Tomorrow, when I feel human, I'll get it up above the doorframe. Somehow. Next I unfasten my holster, pull out the revolver, and check all of the chambers. Two silver bullets, one cadmium, the rest lead. Because you never know what's going to come at you.

Sophronia strikes me as a girl who doesn't miss much, and I hope I haven't blown my cover. She knows now that I'm packing heat and that I've got a belly wound that has nothing to do with a gallbladder surgery. What's done is done, though, and there's no point wasting energy on it.

It's a messy scar. Now that the wound is mostly healed it could pass as the result of an encounter with a rabid dog. I'm relieved to see that I've done no serious damage. The bleeding is due to a disruption of fragile scar tissue. Nothing serious.

I wash away the blood and toss the shirt in the trash.

The bed calls my weary body, but knowing that once I'm in it I'll never want to get out, I lie down on the couch. I have exactly two hours before I'll need to leave for my rendezvous with Phil.

Before I let my eyelids drift shut I check my revolver again and tuck it under the couch where it's ready to my hand.

Only then do I let sleep come and take me.

CHAPTER FOUR

Phil is late.

To be perfectly fair, so was I. By the time I woke from my nap, dark had already crept across the floor, the sun ready to sink behind the hills.

Even after all these years, a part of me wanted to prink a little, to take time over choosing clothes and do something with my windblown hair and maybe even put on makeup. I squelched that little voice. This is business, not leisure, and unless he's somehow managed to go bald and fat, Phil is the sort of man who is going to be reeling in women half his age.

This meeting will be business only.

So I ran a comb through my hair, put on a tank top and loose-fitting button-up that would conceal both holster and gun, and showed up fifteen minutes late, expecting to find Phil waiting for me.

An hour later he has yet to arrive. My two-drink maximum has been reached, I've consumed a basket of chips and salsa and have resorted, out of boredom, to counting the piñatas hanging from the ceiling. Twenty-seven, in bright purple and yellow and green. Also, fourteen velvet sombreros, embroidered with gold and silver thread, stuck around the walls. My guess, assisted by the highly Americanized menu, is that the owner of Banditos has never been anywhere near the southern border.

Little by little my anger fades into worry. Phil might have issues with commitment, women in general, and me in particular, but he is a consummate pro when it comes to work. This is not a date; it's a business meeting. And in this business, when your contact doesn't show up it means something is wrong.

All manner of things can happen to cause delay. I know this. A last-minute phone call. Lost car keys. Colliding with a deer. But this is the age of technology. If he's merely running late, or been delayed, he would call. I try his home phone, his cell phone. Both go to voicemail.

"Are you ready to order yet?" My teenage waitress, underdressed for the weather in a halter top and a frilly, flower-patterned skirt, shivers visibly. There are goosebumps on her bare arms.

Cursing myself for my stupidity in sitting here this long wallowing in irrelevant emotions, I pay for my drinks and the time I've occupied a table, and head out to my car.

I know the patrons are staring at me as I leave. My little waitress gives me a pitying look, like she knows what it feels like to be stood up. And she probably does, poor thing. Hers is not a face to launch a thousand ships.

Once in the car I plug Phil's address into my GPS.

I half expect he'll be entirely off the grid, and it's a relief to find his address on the map, even though it's way the hell out of town. By the time I pull into a gravel drive that winds through the trees and into a rough yard, it's utterly and completely dark, and my sense of foreboding has risen.

First off, this is not Phil's usual choice of accommodations. He's got a taste for luxury, and this split-rail cabin in the middle of nowhere is primitive and far from whatever amenities the little town has to offer. The yard is surrounded by trees and makes both a great hiding place and the perfect spot for an ambush—miles away from town, full dark, no neighbors closer than a mile. My headlights illuminate a grey hatchback, empty, and nothing else. Light spills out of a window in the cabin, revealing a rectangle of table and chairs framed by checkered curtains.

Nothing moves.

I stand by my car for a long moment, listening, sensing the darkness around me. No clear and present signs of danger, so I pick a path across the dark yard, all systems on high alert.

An automatic spotlight flicks on as I approach the door. A

congregation of insects swarms around it. At the edge of the circle of illumination I can just make out a small garden shed.

My knock echoes loudly. Way off in the distance a dog barks. There is no response. By now my stomach is a vast cavern of unease. I've got a small, homemade set of picks that I always carry with me, and I pull it out and jimmy the lock. This is way easier than it ought to be. Phil has gotten lax and I'm prepared to lecture him, just as soon as everything turns out to be okay.

The door opens into a neat kitchen. Clean dishes are stacked in a drainer. The dishcloth hangs neatly over the faucet, precisely folded. A single woven placemat shares the table with pepper and salt and a napkin holder. A clock hanging over the kitchen sink punctuates the otherwise profound silence, measuring off the seconds. *Tick, tock, tick.* One empty coffee cup.

Nothing out of order, nothing to account for the cold that runs the length of my spine. A deep breath to steady my nerves, then I walk through the kitchen and into a neat sitting room, revolver in my hand. Here, too, everything is neat and in order, and I see hints of the luxury enjoyed by the man I knew. A soft leather couch, bookcases neatly lined with books, flat-screen TV, sound system with speakers everywhere. A huge orange cat yawns, stretches, and uncoils from a corner of the couch. If danger lurks in the house the cat is not concerned.

I step lightly down the hallway, past an empty bathroom. A towel hangs on the rack, precisely folded, damp. A scent of aftershave lingers and in one breath I'm remembering looking up into those ice-blue eyes, drinking in the smell of him, waiting for his lips on mine.

The bedroom is sparsely furnished. One chest of drawers, a nightstand, a bed. The covers are rumpled and tossed back. Both pillows are indented. There's been more than one person in this bed. Besides, Phil always makes the bed in the morning, even in a hotel when he knows the maids are coming in. The untidiness bothers him.

I keep moving. At the end of the hallway an open door reveals a study, dimly lit by a desk lamp. Phil sits in a leather office chair at the desk, bent forward, his head resting on folded arms.

"Phil?"

I'm reluctant to wake him, but call his name again.

He doesn't sit up, bleary-eyed and rubbing the back of his neck. Doesn't look at the clock, now pointing to eight fifteen. Doesn't say, "Shit, Maureen. I must have fallen asleep."

My heart is hammering, but I can't go to him, not yet. Old habit takes over and I look first. The room is tidy. No signs of either a struggle or a search. The blinds are open. A small lamp on the desk sheds a circle of light on a book, turned upside down to mark his place. His laptop is open, pushed back to make room for him to lay down his head, as if in the course of work he became too weary to hold it up any longer.

He's not sleeping.

I know this before I walk across the rough plank floor and put my hand on his shoulder. Not my first dead body, and I know what one feels like. Still, knowing it pointless, my fingers seek the pulse in his throat, the signal of warm life still coursing through his veins, but he has no heartbeat. His skin is cold and feels rubbery and wrong. Too late to call an ambulance, too late to do anything.

Probably a heart attack or a stroke. The only set of footprints down the hallway belongs to me. The window is closed. He looks peaceful.

If I hadn't waited, if I hadn't tried to be patient, if I hadn't let my damned emotions in where they had no business, maybe I'd have been in time.

Grief wars with both logic and training. My gut twists uneasily and a lifetime of reliance on its warnings shouts at me to pay attention. I'm missing something. It hovers at the edge of my awareness, taunting me.

Don't touch anything. Don't disturb the body.

But it's not a body, it's Phil, and there's no protocol for this. There's a tightness in my chest that won't let me get a full breath of air.

Focus, Maureen. You'll only get one chance at the scene.

A large photo hangs on the far wall, the only decorative touch. It's a desert, with scrub trees and a wind-sculpted sandstone structure. The only furniture is the desk and office chair. His laptop is locked and password protected. The book is a paperback spy novel, the sort of thing he was forever reading even while complaining bitterly about the stupidity of the characters. I pick it up and skim through the pages it's open to, but there's nothing that leaps out as a clue. I can't get into the center desk drawer without moving the body, and since I'm not at all sure I have the strength to put him back if he falls out of the chair, I satisfy myself with a quick rummage through the side drawers. Paper, pens, blank notepads. A little too neat, maybe, but other than that there's nothing.

It strikes me that the entire house is a little too sterile, a little too clean. Phil always was organized and precise, but even he generated clutter. Bills. Groceries. Of course, he hasn't been here long. According to Abel, the house is only cover. He was here to work, and to make it look like he'd come to stay.

I've already delayed the phone call to 911 far too long. It's past time to summon police and ambulance, but once that's done I can't come back here. No more opportunity to try to piece together his last minutes, to look for more memories in the few belongings he has stowed away.

There seems to be a shortage of air, and it's hard to breathe past the tightness in my chest. Grief is a luxury, though. It will wait.

I snatch up the laptop and carry it out to my car, sliding it under the front passenger seat.

The night air cools my aching throat. An owl hoots off to the right, and is answered by another. Stars spread above like an extra dimension, a sky you could get lost in if you tried. Once, in the oh-so-long ago, Phil and I lay together on a blanket spread out under a sky such as this. Young then, bulletproof and certain nothing could harm us.

There's no cell phone service here, but there's a landline in the study. I make the call to 911, saying out loud for the first time the truth that Phil is dead.

Half against my will I sit down on the other side of the desk to hold vigil for this man who has been, at different times, my lover, my partner, my friend. The cat meows, sniffs around his master's feet, then leaps up into my lap and settles there.

My hand smoothes his fur, over and over, a rhythmic, sensory experience that grounds me here in this now.

"Fine mess you've left me with," I say at last.

Phil doesn't answer, just continues to rest silent, his cheek pillowed on his arms.

"Why did you bring me here? What am I looking for?"

A siren wails in the distance, growing closer. Tires crunch in the gravel outside the window, bright light flashing the room. The cat twitches, lays back his ears, and leaps down to the floor, melting into shadow.

Getting up, I brace myself on the desk and lean down to kiss Phil's cold cheek.

I hear the front door open. A deep male voice calls, "Sheriff."

"In here," I answer.

The sheriff is tall and lean, his hair silvered, his face tanned and deeply lined. He wears his uniform like a second skin, and the look he turns on me registers a deep suspicion. "Who are you? And what exactly are you doing here?"

The knot in my throat eases a little. A fight is exactly what I need right now. "You tell me who you are and show some ID, and I'll be more than happy to answer your questions."

His jaw tightens. "I'm the sheriff."

He doesn't say, "And I own this town," but I figure he means it. I reign myself in a little. The man knows things. If I antagonize him too much he'll never cooperate.

"Begging your pardon, but I know this how?"

He gives me a long, cold stare, not missing a thing. "You have a permit for that weapon?" He nods at the .38, which I've set on the desk beside me. Yet another oversight that shows I'm not thinking straight. I should have holstered it as soon as I heard him coming.

I shrug, knowing this will annoy him. "I do, actually. Look,

Sheriff, I don't care if you're the king of the world. I don't answer questions unless I know who I'm talking to."

"And I need you to turn over your gun until I know what is going on here."

His hand is on his own service weapon and he's got all the power. Last thing I need is to get myself arrested, or even detained by small-town law enforcement. If he searches my car he'll find the purloined laptop. If he searches my wallet he'll find my FBI badge, and I don't want him to know about that, not yet. So I stand back as he picks up my beloved revolver and empties the chambers, brow furrowed over my collection of ammunition.

Only then does he turn to examine Phil.

"What time did you find the body?"

There it is again. He's not a body. He's Phil. Even if I wanted to answer I find I can't. That horrible tightness in my chest has spread to my throat and my voice is trapped in there. Again the man stares me down, and then finally hands me his badge.

As usual, I ignore my own good advice about cooperating with him. Digging in my coat pockets for the reading glasses that I don't really need, not for this, I clean them before I put them on, then peruse the badge as though it's a complex legal document. Once or twice I look up to compare the photo with Jake Callahan, Sheriff. The living version has eyes that match his hair, shark grey, and his steady stare raises the heat of guilt in my cheeks, makes my heart beat a little faster.

"Satisfied?" he asks.

"As to your identity? Yes." I give him back the badge. "Now— what did you want to know?"

"First, that permit."

Moving slower than I'd need to, as if grief is molasses and has rendered me about thirty years older than I am, I dig it out and show it to him.

"Satisfied?"

Two can play this game, and he reads every word before handing it back to me.

"Are you the one who called 911?"

"Yes."

Pulling out a small notebook he flips through the pages, taking his time. "Maureen Keslyn, is that right?"

"That would be me."

"And this is how you found the body?"

"No, I found—him—hanging from the ceiling, cut him down, dragged him across the floor and hoisted him up into the chair. All by myself. What do you think? Yes, this is how I found the body."

"Look, Ms. Keslyn, are you trying to be difficult?"

"I have answered all of your questions, Sheriff."

He flashes a cold smile. "How about if you tell me what happened tonight—specifically, how you come to be here, how you know the deceased, and what you found when you arrived."

That's specific enough, and frankly, I am weary of the game. A headache is building behind my eyes. The constant pain in my leg and my belly are gnawing at me. I give him answers as straight as I can make them without giving away the fact that I'm really here on some sort of operation so covert I don't even know what it is.

"Phil is an old friend. I needed a place to stay for a while, and he suggested I come stay at the Manor. We had a date tonight..."

To my horror, tears force themselves into my eyes, my throat thickens. I take a deep breath. "He didn't show up, he didn't answer his phone. This isn't like him, so I came to check. He was dead. I called 911."

"Did you touch anything?"

"The cat. The phone. I might have jimmied the door."

I try not to think about the laptop.

His eyes narrow. "Okay, so you broke in."

"It's not B&E. I was worried."

"How did you get in?"

"I already told you. It was an easy jimmy—he should have had a better lock. Look, Officer, he was my friend. I found him dead. This has been quite a shock. If you're done grilling me, I'd like to go home and rest."

"And where is home, Ms. Keslyn?"

"I've come to stay at the Manor."

He gives me a smile full of white teeth. "Now that I find hard to believe."

"What is that supposed to mean?"

"The residents are—let's just say you're a bit of a misfit. And I have a few more questions before I let you go. Do you know if Mr. Evers had a will? Who his executor would be?"

"No."

Headlights glare through the window, but neither of us looks away. Footsteps in the hallway, lighter this time, the clicking of heels rather than the thud of boots. A woman pauses in the doorway, leaning against the frame in a way that exaggerates curves that need no help. In one hand she holds a black bag, with the other she pushes a fall of salon-blonde hair behind her ear. "Jake."

"Charlene."

The greeting is stilted and brittle, full of an unspoken tension.

The woman pales when she turns her gaze to Phil. She swallows. "What on earth happened? I saw him at Saveco this morning—he looked healthy."

Callahan makes a display out of flipping backward through his pad. "At 8:56 p.m., a call was received at dispatch, allegedly made by this woman, Maureen Keslyn, who reported that she found Mr. Evers dead. I arrived on the scene at 9:20 p.m. The house was as you see it. Ms. Keslyn alleges that he was dead when she arrived, that they were friends, and that there was no bad blood between them. I see no sign of a struggle or any evidence of foul play."

Charlene removes herself from the doorframe and turns to me. "I'm so sorry for your loss." I can't imagine why a coroner responding to a late evening call would show up in a tight skirt and a clingy blouse with a plunging neckline, not to mention the heels, but the ways of womankind often elude me, so I let it go.

I'm seized with the need to be away. Away from the body and the empty house. Away from this sexually charged coroner and angry cop.

"He looks very peaceful," Charlene says, touching Phil's cheek. "Like he just drifted off to sleep."

I find myself wondering what Sophronia would have to say about his state of peacefulness. "Will you be doing an autopsy?"

"That depends on what the preliminary shows, Ms. Keslyn—"

"Maureen. Please."

The bowed lips curve in a smile. "Maureen. I'm sure you realize we can't do autopsies for every death. The deceased has to be shipped to Spokane; it's very expensive and time consuming. We only do it when there is some irregularity."

"I'd sure like to know cause of death—" I stop myself, realizing I sound like every bereaved person everywhere. Stage one of grieving: shock and disbelief. *This can't be happening.* Anger is supposed to come later, but I've never been much for the rules. I want to throw something, or maybe just kick the sheriff in the shins.

"Can I have my gun back? I'd like to be going."

He hesitates, then hands me my .38. Empty. "Don't leave town."

"Oh, for heaven's sake, Jake. You sound like a B movie," Charlene says, pulling out the liver probe. "There's not a thing here to indicate foul play."

Jake pockets my ammo. "What about the cat?"

Charlene is busy now, taking pictures of Phil and the room, and I turn to Jake, bewildered. "What about the cat?"

"Since you're a friend of the deceased, I suggest you take the cat home."

I look from the sheriff to the cat to Charlene. Surely he must be joking.

"What a lovely idea." Charlene looks up and smiles.

"I don't think so." Animals and I don't get along. Mostly because they expect to be fed and patted and otherwise nurtured, and I haven't got a nurturing bone in my body. I'm pretty sure the sheriff came up with this idea out of sheer malice.

But he picks up the cat and hands it to me, then goes off on a quest for cat food and the litter box. I follow, objecting all the way.

"Cats don't like cars. I'll find a carrier and come back for him tomorrow."

"It's a short trip. I'm sure he'll be fine. I'll walk you to your car."

The tone is total lawman and I decide not to see what will happen if I argue. As he follows me to the Jag the purloined laptop blazes in my mind like a beacon. But the dark is my friend. He stows the cat's baggage in the back and stands at the driver's door, waiting, while I maneuver myself and the cat into the car.

I don't want to leave Phil here, dead and alone with strangers. And I need to spend more time going over what I can't help thinking is a crime scene. But Jake stands outside my car, waiting for me to betake myself off the property. Besides, whatever secrets Phil brought me here to uncover are much more likely to be back at the Manor than here in his empty house.

CHAPTER FIVE

The front door to the Manor is locked.

A handwritten note reads, *Push button for after-hours entry*. My hands are occupied by a cat and a litter box but I manage to give the button a good hard shove. And then another two or three, just for good measure.

Betty emerges in the dimly lit hallway and stops short when she sees who is asking to come in.

The cat meows and starts to struggle. I push the button again and hold it.

Flinging up her hands in a universal gesture of annoyance, Betty strides down the hallway, skirt swirling around her ankles, hair blowing out behind her. She looks for all the world like a dark witch bent on mischief but I'm so in need of a fight I'd be willing to pay for one, and I welcome her malice.

When she opens the door she wedges her body into the opening, forehead creased into a forbidding frown. "You really do need to sleep in a motel tonight, like I told you earlier." She tries to close the door, but my foot is in it. I've taken care to make it my good foot, or at least the less bad one.

"All of my things are still here. Let me in."

"I've taken the liberty of packing them up for you." She opens the door a little wider and I see my suitcase parked in the hall. I'm wondering what she made of all the paranormal supplies I carry with me, and am grateful that I was smart enough to dispose of the dossier after reading and memorizing what I need to know.

"If you don't go, I'll call the police." She's in a quandary, because if she moves to grab the suitcase or go to the phone, she'll have to let go of the door and then I'll be in.

"Just finished talking to them. They're busy."

I take a perverse pleasure in watching her flounder. Her gaze zeroes in on the cat, now turning himself inside out in an effort to get free, and her chin sets in firm defiance.

"You cannot bring that creature in here."

"I'm coming in. The cat comes with me."

"I'll call Phil—"

"He won't answer. He's dead."

All of the blood rushes out of her face at once and I am touched, just for an instant, with remorse. Maybe I've gone too far.

"Dead…when? How?"

The cat uses his claws on my hand and I drop him. He lands right-side up, lightly, and squeezes through the door and past Betty.

"Hey, you!" She makes a grab for the cat. I take the opportunity to open the door and walk in.

"When did you see him last?"

She gives up on the cat, now far down the hallway, and turns back to me. "What?"

"When did you last see Mr. Evers?"

She blinks, dazed. "He came here last week to meet with the new cook. Tell me how you found out—"

"What happened to the old cook?"

I'm walking now, rolling my suitcase behind me.

"She up and quit. No reason given."

Betty gets ahead of me and plants herself in my path. A sick triumph has overtaken the shock of the death. "There's no room for you here. Mr. Evers will not be able to override that now, whatever you say."

"We've had this conversation. I have a room—all of my stuff was in it."

"There's a waiting list! Someone signed up for Dora's room over a year ago! You can't just walk in here and—"

"Apparently I can." I detour around her, but she doesn't give up.

"There's paperwork! Just because this is a private operation doesn't mean the government doesn't have its hooks in us. Protocols. Forms. Data entry."

"Best get on it." This morning I'd been planning on fleeing as fast and as far as I could get. Now I know I'm not going anywhere. Not until I figure out what Phil was looking at. Why he bought this place, why he has allowed this woman to continue working here.

She trails along at my heels. "I'm already here on overtime; Cathy didn't show up for her shift."

"Life's tough. Do the paperwork tomorrow; I'm sure nobody will care."

"I'm telling you to get out! You are trespassing. I can have you arrested."

God, she's like a yipping little ankle-biter dog, trying to get her tiny teeth through a layer of jeans and boot leather.

"Look. It's late. I'm tired, you're tired. How about I just go to my room. If you want to call the cops, let me know when they show up."

I leave her there, seething.

Right now, bed is definitely in order. I'm pretty sure the good sheriff won't evict me tonight. The laptop is still in the Jag, which worries me, but smuggling it into the Manor is a job for tomorrow. The cat food is out there, too, but that can also wait, especially since I don't see the cat.

He reappears just as the door swings open, and follows me into my suite. I can't help smiling a little as I lock the door behind us. Whatever tomorrow holds, it's not going to be boring.

• • •

I wake with the sensation that I can't breathe and that somebody is watching me. I'm buzzing in full adrenaline mode before I can get my eyes open.

Phil's cat sits on my chest, staring down into my face. Seeing me awake, he bats at my cheek with a paw, just enough claw included to let me know he means business, and meows. With a sinking feeling I remember that his food is all the way downstairs and out in the car.

I feel like I've been worked over with a meat tenderizer, my muscles an interesting combination of stiff, jellied, and painful. Dragging myself out of bed, working the kinks out one by one, I hobble across the room and look out the window. The Jag is right where I left it, parked alongside a blue Toyota pickup. Behind it, the mountains are bathed in a wash of pink and gold. The sky is clear and blue.

It ought to be beautiful, but in my current state of mind it's just bright and annoying. And it's looking like a long way to the Jag.

Both cat and laptop are going to have to wait.

What I need to do first is set up basic communication operations—far safer than venturing out of the relative safety of my room before my brain decides to get in gear.

People are all too ready to believe that anybody over fifty is a technological moron. I encourage this useful perception, carrying an old flip phone as camouflage, fumbling with it and pretending I don't know how the damn thing works. Truth is, I embraced computers for what they could do when they first made their appearance on the scene, and I've kept up ever since. My current tablet fits inside a hardcover sketchbook that locks and looks like a diary. It's tiny but powerful, thanks to some customizations I've added on my own.

The Manor has wireless but it's locked. Getting the password would be a hassle, so I just hack in.

First thing once I'm up and running is to get a face-to-face connection with Abel. He's neither very happy nor very awake. Not that he's ever happy, but I know the range of inexpressiveness of his face, and this morning he radiates darkness like a deep black cloud, as though his skin has sucked in a storm.

"Let me get coffee first," he mutters, the first time I've ever heard him mutter. This does nothing to improve my own mood, acting as a reminder that I have no coffee of my own. He leaves his laptop open and I watch him move about his kitchen, pouring himself a big mug from the pot on the counter. Apparently when he sleeps he swaps out the sunglasses and the trench coat for a pair of sweatpants and a tank, but even in his jammies he looks lethal—all smooth muscle and underplayed strength.

I let him take one good swallow before asking, "What have you got me into here, Abel?"

I can see him checking out my surroundings and I pick up the tablet and scan it around to give him the visual tour.

"Interesting decor. Circa 1800s? The brochure looked a little more updated."

"They weren't expecting me. No arrangements made. Nobody uses this room, apparently."

"What did Phil Evers say?"

"Phil Evers isn't saying anything. He's dead."

I've caught him in the act of swallowing and if he were a lesser man he would have spluttered and coughed. Instead, there's just a longer pause. And another long swallow.

"You're sure?"

I know that look on his face and that his brain is running a high-speed risk and recovery profile. He's also in a state of shock. Phil Evers was supposed to live forever.

"What happened?"

"Looks like natural causes."

"You're not buying that."

I shrug. "There won't be an investigation."

"Not an official one, anyway." He gives me a long, calculating look. "I want you out."

I ignore that. "The woman who runs this place really doesn't want me here—particularly in this room. Something feels off."

Abel sets down the coffee mug and leans forward, enunciating every word. "Mission over. Abort. You get in your car and—"

"Phil never did anything on a whim, Abel. Never. This wasn't some fun little game he was playing. He bought a fucking nursing home. He went to the trouble to get me here. There's a reason for that, and I'm not leaving until I find out why."

"I can't support that."

"Fine. I'll go up the chain. I'm not leaving. Who do I need to talk to?"

He goes quiet for a little too long, thinking about whether to tell me what he knows. At last he sighs, deeply, and pushes the mug away as though coffee no longer appeals to him. "There is no chain."

"What?"

"There's nobody, Maureen. Phil was solo on this. He pulled me in to get to you and I went along."

As the ramifications of this sink in my body buzzes with adrenaline. "So you sent me in, without backup, without resources, on a rogue assignment."

"I'm sorry, Maureen. When he called, I—truth is, it went straight to my head. He's the stuff my bedtime stories were made of. This is why you need to come back, now. I'll find you something to do—"

I hold up my hand to cut him off. "Stop right there, before you ruin it."

"What?"

"I'm savoring the moment."

The fact that both Phil and Abel thought I could handle an assignment like this, beat up and battered as I am, mends something inside me that was broken and rattling around like Legos loose in a box. No cotton wool here, no caretaking of the fragile old lady.

"Maureen—"

I lean forward and look directly into his eyes. "I'm not going anywhere, Abel, and neither are you. You got me into this, you're in for the duration. Understood? I'll check in tonight."

Definitely not happy. His face sets in hard lines and I figure I can expect a visit sometime soon. But he knows me and stops trying to order me home.

"I've got a tracker on your phone—"

"As I have one on yours."

At that he almost smiles. "Of course you do. Fine. If you get in trouble I'll know where to find your body."

I give him a middle-finger salute and disconnect before he can get out another word. The cat meows and wraps around my legs, reminding me that he still needs breakfast. Time for me to grab a shower and go in search of cat food, Phil's laptop, and my delinquent coffee.

CHAPTER SIX

Gerry Vermeer's door is firmly closed and when I stop to listen I hear snoring. Farther down the hall the elevator lurks, maw open, hoping to tempt me in, but I bypass it in favor of the stairs. They will hurt, but the leg needs to get over itself and the best way I know to make that happen is to actually use it.

First things first. I make my way out to the Jag, propping the Manor door open with a stick to be sure I can get back in. The cat food bag serves as good cover for Phil's laptop, not that I need it. I make it all the way back to my room without seeing a soul.

Cat fed, laptop tucked out of sight under my mattress, I go in search of the kitchen. I find the dining area first. It's a low-ceilinged, dingy room that does its best to appear classy, despite the dim walls and scuffed linoleum. Five round tables are spaced at regular intervals, each covered with a white tablecloth and laid out with real china and silverware and coffee cups.

No coffee. But I catch the scent of the magic brew and follow my nose to the kitchen.

The cook has his back to me, chopping onions. I slow my footsteps and quiet my breathing at the kitchen door. Not that I want to sneak up on him, as such, but I do want to observe for a minute, undetected. I swear I make no sound, but he spins around, a cleaver in his right hand, center of balance low and ready.

"Quite the startle response you've got there." According to Abel's intel, Matt hasn't been back from Iraq for more than a year, and that would account for him being jumpy. Still, his response puts me on high alert. This young man has combat training.

"Sorry about that." His voice is easy and affable, his body looks relaxed, but he's still holding that cleaver and he doesn't feel the need to explain himself.

His photo in the dossier didn't do him justice. Shoulder-length, wavy hair, almost black but with copper highlights. Eyes the color of good dark coffee, and a face that could have been copied from a Greek statue. There's a cleft in his chin and just enough hint of stubble to make him look casual.

"What can I do for you?"

"I'm suffering from severe caffeine deprivation."

"Help yourself." He jerks his chin toward the coffee pot on the counter. "Made that pot for myself—hope you like dark roast. There's cups in the cupboard right above. You need cream?"

"Black." Cream just gets in the way of the caffeine, and I like bitter just fine.

While I take the first burning swallow he swivels back to his task, dumping diced potatoes and onions into a frying pan, spitting hot. His motions are graceful and easy, the ballet dance of someone comfortable in the kitchen.

"You must be new." He pulls a giant package of bacon out of a stainless steel fridge and lays it on the counter. Just the sight of it makes my mouth water, and I suddenly remember that I missed dinner last night.

"I didn't think we had any rooms," he says.

"I'm in the third-floor suite for the moment."

There's no hiccup in the action as he lays the bacon out onto a griddle. "Rumor has it that room is haunted."

"And yet I saw nary a ghost."

I'm not going to mention the ghost that followed me to Dora's room yesterday. People are already inclined to dismiss older people as slipping a gear or two. Best not to bring up the paranormal to the uninitiated.

"Heard you were new, too. I'm Maureen, by the way."

"Matt," he says. "And yep. Brand spanking new. Just started last week."

"What are you doing here?"

Betty's voice is like fingernails on a blackboard. It might be early, but she looks perfectly rested. Just like yesterday, she's wearing a long skirt and shapeless sweater, her nondescript brown hair loose on her shoulders. Apparently the woman never sleeps.

"I needed coffee." Enjoying antagonizing Betty, I refill my cup and take another long swallow. Good. No almond-flavored roast or anything designer. My brain is waking up. There's a stool over on the far side of the kitchen and I perch on the edge of it, resting my leg.

"Coffee is for residents only," Betty says. "Besides, it's too early."

"Are there hours where the natives are confined to their rooms?"

"Matthew doesn't need the distraction of residents wandering into the kitchen. Or nonresidents, for that matter. When are you leaving?"

"I didn't see any rules posted. No sign that says *no old people past this point*."

Matt snorts, turning it into a cough.

Betty frowns. "As we discussed last night, you don't belong here."

"And yet I have a letter from Mr. Evers saying that I'm expected."

"Since Mr. Evers is dead, your letter is invalid."

A spatula clatters to the floor.

Matt doesn't bend to pick it up, or start cleaning up the bacon grease now splattered all over the kitchen. He just stands there looking from one of us to the other.

"Maureen here claims she found him dead last night," Betty says, although Matt hasn't asked. "This has not been confirmed by any authority."

"My God. What happened?"

His tone is right for shock and surprise, but that doesn't mean it's real. I shrug, watching him. "Just dead."

Betty gets between us, demanding my attention. "So you say. I'll be checking in with the sheriff this morning on that. And I'll be telling him about you. You can stay for breakfast but then I expect you gone. Sorry, Matt, extra work for you."

He still looks shell shocked, but shrugs this off. "Same number we had yesterday. How do you like your eggs?" He retrieves his fallen spatula and drops it in the sink. Then he lifts the coffee pot and gives me another splash to top off my mug.

"She'll take them scrambled," Betty says, as though I am a small child making demands in a restaurant.

I roll my eyes at her in my best imitation of a teenager. "Benedict would be good."

"You got it." Matt manages a smile. Raising the coffee mug in a salute, I leave Betty on the battlefield and walk back into the dining room. Best to let her believe she has vanquished me. There's plenty of time to skirmish. I wonder if she's going to fire Matt for the sins of being new and nice to me. I hope not, but there's little I can do here beyond doggedly refusing to leave.

• • •

Breakfast is more than just a meal; it's my first assessment of the inmates of this madhouse.

I come in a little late, partly on purpose, partly because I've failed so far at figuring out the password on Phil's laptop. The entire crew is assembled and waiting, five round tables with five residents at each, except for one table with an empty place. All of their names and faces are safely stored in my memory, but documents are one thing, reality another.

Sheriff Callahan was right: I am a misfit. Even at this hour, the residents are all dressed to the nines. Some of the finery is outdated, mind you, but these are expensive people.

They are also old.

I am neither.

Conversation dies as they all turn their heads to stare at me. It feels like entering the cafeteria at a brand-new high school, an experience I'm not happy about repeating. Even at my age, the weight of all those critical eyes is daunting.

Careful not to limp or show any sign of weakness, I make my way to the only empty chair. Dora's. It's at the table farthest from the door, closest to the big bay window. If I could have chosen the least defensible seat in the house, this would be it. I'll have my back to a picture window, a perfect target for any blood-hungry paranormal that can come through glass. There are twenty-four slow, old people between me and the only exit. Add my limited range of motion and it doesn't even take experience and training to know that if something were to go down, I'd be toast.

Fortunately, it's broad daylight and this is, no matter what Abel said, a nursing home. Not much is likely to happen. My biggest problem currently is the ordeal of spending an hour with my tablemates. Dora's chair feels awkward and wrong. I'm actually relieved to see crazy Alice. She sits directly across from me, and like me, she doesn't belong here. Half of her hair is flattened to her head; the other half sticks straight up in the air. She's wearing a yellow sweater and purple stretch pants. Lipstick is smeared around her mouth and on her teeth.

Next to Alice sits a man who might have been good-looking once and firmly believes he still is. His nose is fleshy and red, with a visible network of broken blue veins that looks like a roadmap to somewhere. When I try to shift focus I get stuck counting chins, none of which is as closely shaved as he would like to think. His belly forces him to sit back from the table, which he doesn't seem to mind, as it displays his suit, tailored to fit his awkward frame, along with the gold watch chain and the expensive shoes. His right hand rests on the table next to his coffee cup, displaying a fat gold ring inlaid with diamonds.

"Welcome to table number four," he says. "I'm Chuck. And this is Virginia, Julia, and Alma." He nods at the others. I note that he excludes Alice, and this does nothing to improve the impression of him that I've already formed. Thanks to Abel's dossier, I've memorized all of their names, along with those of the rest of the population, but I welcome the introductions even as I flip through what I know of them in my mental files.

Chuck, for example, was in sales, and the big money he came into had some questionable tie-ins with insider trading.

I already don't like Chuck.

"Please, it's Ginny," the thin, elegant woman says. She's the polar opposite of Alice and reeks of money. A linen jacket in a tasteful beige, cream-colored linen pants, pearls, the sort of face paint that must take her an hour to apply. She's had plastic surgery, too, I'd be willing to bet. Her forehead doesn't move when she smiles, but then that smile doesn't go anywhere other than the corners of her lips, so maybe my assessment is unfair. Her dearly departed husband was a plastic surgeon.

"Can I pour you some coffee?"

Alma sits on my right. She's heavy, but carries her weight neatly under a loose-fitting shirt and slacks. The fabric looks expensive, but there's no jewelry, no fuss, and her steady gaze suggests intelligence and a certain sharpness that makes me think she might be capable of a cynical turn.

"Please."

I note approvingly that she drinks it black.

"Welcome to the zoo," she says. "What can we call you?"

"Maureen will do. Thank you." The cup is hot, the coffee smells rich and good, and it gives me something to do with my hands while I assess the neighborhood.

"I do wish they would make some sort of real coffee," Ginny says. "Almond-flavored, you know? Or at least buy some decent creamer."

Alma earns more approval from me by filling Alice's cup for her and giving her a smile.

The other woman at our table, Julia, is in a wheelchair. She is young, at least comparatively, forty-four last month. She holds her cup in both hands, as though one is not sufficient to the job, and there's an obvious tremor when she lifts it to her mouth. Catching my gaze on her she looks at me over the cup, blue eyes hostile and defiant. "I've got MS."

She says this in the tone a person might use to remark that they've won an Oscar, and I very nearly reply, "How nice for you." Since there isn't really a more appropriate social response, I don't make one, noting instead that although she's limited her makeup to foundation and powder, something that can be managed with limited dexterity, her hair is obviously salon material and she's sporting a French manicure. The sparkling dangles in her ears are, I'm willing to bet, diamond and not cubic zirconia. Julia is a trust fund baby, and her presence here confuses me. She could be pretty much anywhere in the world she wants to go.

Unless I make up a story to explain myself as an eccentric, it's already clear that I belong in this crowd about as much as Alice does. I've got my hair cut short, a product of the long hospital stay when it was too much trouble to maintain anything more than a brush cut. I'm wearing non-designer jeans and a button-up flannel shirt. Lacking the costuming, I fall back on my usual personality. I've already antagonized one of them; what's left to lose?

I look at my watch. "So, will there be breakfast, or do we fast in memory of the deceased?" Truly, I am ravenous. My early trip to Matt's kitchen primed the hunger pump and that was hours ago. It's now three minutes after nine.

"Poor Dora," Ginny says. "She seemed so healthy."

"And active," Julia adds. "Very active. Hard to believe she would just die in her sleep."

There is venom behind the words of both women and I wonder what Dora did to piss them off. Chuck jostles Alma with his shoulder. "Died happy, maybe, eh, Alma?"

The woman keeps her calm, but there is a bite to her voice. "I doubt that anybody really dies happy."

"Alma writes fiction novels," Julia says. "Romance. Happy ever after and all that."

"Erotica," Ginny corrects her. "Very explicit sex," she says directly to me, as though I don't know what erotica is.

"A woman has got to do some research," Chuck says. His mouth is wet and he wipes it on the back of his hand. "If you need some help, give me a call. Want to contribute, Maureen? What's erotica without a threesome?"

This is why I don't like people. It's the cafeteria all over again. Chuck is the bully. Ginny is the queen bee, Julia her second-in-command. Alma is an unknown quantity, but at the moment I want nothing to do with any of them.

It's work, I remind myself. I'm here for a reason, even though I don't know what it is yet.

Betty appears in the doorway, wheeling a cart, Matt close behind her with another. They begin handing out trays at the table farthest from us. Scrambled eggs, toast, bacon, hash browns, orange juice. Pretty standard breakfast fare, which smells heavenly. Chuck dives right into his, loading up his chin with a glob of egg on the very first bite. My plate is delivered personally by Matt and the eggs are not scrambled. I also don't get bacon, which is a sadness. What I do get is a perfect eggs Benedict complete with restaurant presentation.

Matt waits while I take the first bite, a taste explosion that wakes up my taste buds and makes my stomach growl.

"Do I pass?"

"Straight to the top of the class."

Special treatment. The others are all giving me looks of dislike now, even Alma, who might have been an ally. The whole thing is so ridiculous it almost makes me laugh. I take another bite, savoring it. The hollandaise is creamy and tangy, the English muffin crispy, the egg perfectly poached.

After the third bite, I make an overture of peace by opening the door to gossip. "So, what's with Gerald Vermeer? He doesn't come down to breakfast?"

Julia lights up like I've given her a diamond. "He's so creepy. I bet he killed Dora. In the night."

Chuck snorts. "That wimp? Not unless he shot her." He leans forward. "You saw the body, right, Maureen? Was she shot?"

"Just because he's in a wheelchair doesn't mean he's weak and stupid," Julia says. "Somebody creepy like that? You never know."

"Maybe it was sex and her heart gave out." This from Virginia. Her thin cheeks are flushed. She licks her lips.

Alice's lip trembles. Before I have a chance to head her off she begins to sob and all possibility of conversation is over.

CHAPTER SEVEN

Frank's Full-Service Crematorium and Funeral Parlor stands just outside of town, across the river and screened from view by a thick stand of cedars. Heavy black smoke belches from a brick chimney and I shudder, picturing Phil's body burning, flesh and blood and bone.

I can't afford to think about these things. When I scramble out of the car the air smells of cedars and wood smoke, and I'm pretty sure that even in Shadow Valley the health department would have something to say about human ashes drifting about over the town. Probably an ordinary wood fire needing to have the dampers opened.

Despite my hearty breakfast, there's a hollow spot in my belly as I follow a brick pathway up to the two wide front doors, part wood, part glass, and step inside. A low chime announces my arrival as the door thuds behind me. I smell candles. Artificial flowers adorn several glossy wooden tables. Two armchairs in a floral pattern flank a love seat probably meant to look Victorian. The flowers are dusty. The love seat has seen better days. I'm oddly relieved by the general tackiness; it lets me revert to my usual sardonic sense of humor.

Until Sophronia appears in the doorway. Her hair is loose over her shoulders. She's wearing a floor-length white tunic that isn't as opaque as it ought to be. Silver bangles jingle on her wrists; the heavy silver chain with the large black stone hangs around her neck. Her eyes dominate her thin face. Too big, too green. She's emphasized them with a dark kohl liner that would have done Cleopatra proud.

"You're here to see Phil."

Not a huge guess. Why else would I be here? It's a small town. She will have heard that I was at his house, that I found him.

"Shouldn't you be in school?"

"Waste of time. You're too late, by the way."

"For what?"

"To talk to Phil. He's already been done."

"What do you mean, done? Did they do an autopsy after all?"

"Cremated." Her voice trembles on the word, a reed flute keening loss. "Craig did him this morning."

I seem to be missing my words. My whole body pulses with the shock. I can't get my mind around the idea of him gone, just like that. Not so much as the husk of the man left to help me grasp his passing.

Sophronia shakes her head. "Instructions from his daughter. Very specific."

"His daughter called you?"

"No, Charlene talked to her."

"And Craig cremated him."

"I don't do cremations." Again the grief spills out of her voice with the word. "Craig doesn't mind."

Something occurs to me. "And your dad? What does he do?"

Behind those luminous eyes a barrier slams shut. "He doesn't mind doing cremations either. I assume you don't want to commune with Phil's ashes? You can if you want."

Communing wasn't what I had in mind. What I really wanted was a chance to go over his body and look for signs of trauma. Needle marks, say. I still can't believe that he would be cremated so quickly, that his daughter would demand something like that. Wouldn't she want to see him first?

It's like Sophronia reads my mind. "Jill is in France. It will be a while before she can get home. She told Charlene we should just get it done, and she'll pick up his ashes when she gets back. The memorial will be whenever she can be here."

I'm having trouble with my breath. There is a tightness in my chest and an ache behind my eyes.

"Look, are you sure you don't want to see the remains? I can't release them to you, because you're not next of kin. But you can look at them."

This is Phil we're talking about. Phil, who was always the whole enchilada, who was never the *remains* of anything. I want Sophronia to be quiet, to go away, to leave me alone. But I'm in her territory, not mine.

"I don't like the word *remains* either," she says. "Imagine how Phil feels about it? Listening to everybody talk about him like that? It just makes the transition harder. I think he'd be comforted by having you hold him, though. Hang on."

She vanishes through a door and I would make a run for it, but the logical part of my brain is overriding my emotions. If Phil was murdered, then this quick cremation is part of a cover-up and puts Dora's death in question. I need to have a look at her body, which means I have to pull myself together.

Sophronia returns a moment later with a cardboard box. She holds it out to me like a gift.

"Still warm," she says.

And it is warm, a gentle heat that would be pleasant on my cold hands if I didn't know its source. It's a plain cardboard box, sealed with packing tape, heavy for its size, but not if you consider that it represents all of a human being I once loved.

"The soul is forced to leave the body at cremation," Sophronia says. "His wasn't ready."

My hands are shaking. The weakness annoys me, as does the prickling behind my eyeballs. I know about ghosts; I've hunted them and helped to expel them. I never stopped to wonder how they felt about the whole thing.

"How well did you know him?"

"Phil?" She shrugs. "How well do you ever know anybody? I saw him around. He asked me questions about the Manor before he bought it."

"And you told him what?"

"Just what everybody knows. Are you done? Because I have things to do." She reaches for the box. For just an instant I catch myself playing tug-of-war with Phil's ashes, but I let it go as if my fingers are burnt.

"Take care," she says, not meaning it. The implication that I should leave now is clear, and I turn as if I'm going to do just that. A glance over my shoulder shows a flutter of white vanishing through the interior door. I follow her, after a long enough pause that I figure she won't be expecting me. There is no glimpse of her as I traverse a short hallway and pass through another door into a small, square viewing room.

I've been to viewings, but I've ever seen one that looked like this.

Dora from the Manor lies in state, clothed in a long, flowing white gown, startling against the scarlet satin lining of the casket. Four tall ironwork candelabras, each holding three black tapers, stand at head and foot on each side. Her folded hands clasp a single white lily. Incense smolders in a brass bowl, a heady fragrance that makes my limbs feel heavy, my brain slow.

As my eyes adjust to the contrast of darkness with the flickering light of the candles, I begin to notice other things. A bottle of wine. A loaf of bread. A small heap of jewelry.

"You shouldn't be here," Sophronia says behind me. My skin prickles.

"I'm not sure Dora should be here either. What the hell is this?"

"For the journey—to help her on her way."

"I hardly think all of this is necessary. People die all the time and go wherever they go without this."

She comes up beside me, candlelight flickering over her face. "How do you know? Have you ever been dead?"

Technically, yes, though I'm not going to tell her this. No white light for me, no tingling warmth, no sense of peace. No fear either, if I'm honest. Just confusion, uncertainty. Okay, if I'm strictly honest, yes, I saw a light, but I wasn't convinced that it meant me any lasting good and I didn't move toward it. Maybe I'm not the best candidate for reporting back from the other side, but I very much doubt that Miss Sophronia has been there at all.

"Dora's still frightened. She needs comfort, support, so she can move on."

"What happened to her?"

"Not sure. But it was terrifying, and she wasn't ready to die. I found this."

She lifts one of the candles from its holder and moves it to shed a clearer light on Dora's neck, beckoning me closer. A wound mars the skin. No blood, just two jagged puncture wounds.

"The scarf," I murmur. It had been bothering me all along, that scarf, I just hadn't realized it. What sort of woman puts on a nightgown and perfectly knots a scarf around her neck before climbing into bed?

The girl nods. "Right. Charlene didn't even look. She just called it a heart attack. Which is fair enough; Dora already had two."

"Did you tell her?"

"I showed her this morning, when she came in about Phil. She said it was interesting, but not something that could have killed anybody."

"And what does Dora say?"

Sophronia gives me a withering look. "She's dead. She doesn't talk anymore."

Clearly I need to brush up on the rules of what the dead can and cannot do. "What about the sheriff? Did you say anything to him?"

"What? That I noticed a mark on the dead person, which the coroner says is unimportant and irrelevant? Yeah, he's gonna just come running over here to see what the crazy undertaker's daughter is up to."

"Sophie, about Phil? Did you notice anything unusual about the—body?"

"It's Sophronia. You can't call me Sophie."

"I can, actually. So—did you?"

She shakes her head. "He was...angry. He felt unfinished, undone." Her whole body shudders.

"So Charlene didn't just call this morning to give orders about Phil—"

"No. She came in, about six a.m. Asked to be alone with him."

"Isn't that a little unusual?"

"Not really."

"So what happens with Dora?"

"Her family is coming for her."

"And they'll be okay with this?" I try to imagine an ordinary family showing up to say goodbye to grandma and running into this scenario.

"By the time they see her, she'll have crossed," Sophie says. "She'll be in her own clothes and all of this will be put away."

"Does your father know you play dress-up with the dead?"

Her eyes flare. Two spots of color burn in her cheeks. "Is that what you think I'm doing? Playing dress-up?"

Half of me thinks yes, that's exactly what she's doing. Another part of me acknowledges that whatever it is she's doing, play has nothing to do with it. I also note that she has once again deflected a question about her father.

Sophie turns her back on me. "You need to go now. Dora needs my attention—you've already disturbed the process."

"Look, Sophie—"

"Get out!" No shrill screaming from this girl. Her voice is low, menacing. There's nothing to be gained from antagonizing her, and on this occasion my wishes lie in tandem with hers. There is nothing in the world I want more than to get out of this place.

CHAPTER EIGHT

As I step out of the candlelit room and into an ordinary hallway, worn carpet under my feet, dim lighting overhead, I feel like I've passed from one realm into another, as though nothing is quite real. Before I have time to acclimatize, I run smack-dab into Sheriff Callahan.

Both of us let out a grunt of pain. He steadies me, his strong hands on my shoulders while I gasp for air like a floundering fish. He's got to be as old as I am, but this is not a man sliding down the death slope. He burns with life force and passion; I can feel it radiating off him like a wood stove in a cold room.

"Maureen Keslyn. You do get around."

"Is next-day cremation standard procedure in your county, Sheriff?"

Something in his eyes flickers. I'm not sure if it's anger or uncertainty, and he's not going to give me a chance to figure it out. He gestures at the door. "Let's talk outside, shall we?"

It's not a question. He opens the door and holds it for me. As I brush past him I catch a whiff of soap and cologne that is like a strain of half-forgotten music. Outside, the sunlight glares, driving all lingering strangeness out of my mind.

"So—is it standard procedure? Do we even have a cause of death?"

"How about you tell me what you're really doing here."

"I planned to say goodbye to my old friend Phil. I was permitted to hold a cardboard box full of ashes for a couple of minutes, which wasn't what I had in mind. I'd really like to know what killed him."

"Ms. Keslyn. I've asked you before, and I'm asking again. What are you really doing here?"

"Staying at the Manor. I'm recovering from an—accident."

"You hardly look like a woman who needs the Manor, and you certainly aren't a woman who wants to be there. Surely you have a home to go to."

"Unfortunately, there is currently another woman in it." Now why in hell did I just spill that turd into the punch bowl? Since I've already launched it I try to look pathetic. His face doesn't soften.

"Tragic."

"How do you know I don't have money?"

"Do you?"

"I don't understand your hostility."

"You have asked me to look into the death of Phil Evers. You are the one who found the body. As a matter of routine, I have questions for you, and you persist in putting up roadblocks rather than answering."

There is nothing routine about his questioning, though. I can feel it—the man actually suspects me of murder. I'll admit to a warm little glow at that. Not quite washed up yet, if I look like a woman capable of killing a man like Phil.

"Did you know that he put you in his will?"

"He—what?" Too late, I realize my mouth is hanging open and snap it shut.

"Left everything to his daughter, except for one thing." He pauses, watching me. I'm not sure what it is he's expecting to see, but I have a sudden and horrible presentiment of what he's going to say next.

"This is all very interesting, Sheriff, but I'm sure there's some confusion. I have no idea why Phil would will anything to me."

"Ms. Keslyn, are you honestly telling me you didn't know that Phil Evers willed you the Manor?"

I close my eyes to block out his face and the sky and the sight of the funeral parlor looming behind him.

Oh, Phil. What the hell were you thinking? And why didn't you tell me?

"Ms. Keslyn?"

There is no escaping this reality, and I open my eyes and use them to stare down this man who has begun to seriously annoy me. "'Maureen,' please. Whatever you choose to believe about me, let me make one thing clear to you: I do not want the Manor."

He barks a short laugh. "Right. Worth a lot of money."

"And it's a pain in the ass."

"I'm sure you can appreciate my problem," he says, looming over me. "Here you are in Shadow Valley—you show up on the same day Phil dies. Incidentally, there's a death at the Manor as well, but I understand that took place before your arrival, not after. Betty insists that she had no idea you were coming, but you install yourself in a room anyway. Not just any room, but specifically a room that is off-limits. And then Phil dies, suddenly, and you're the one who finds the body. As it turns out, you have a lot to gain from his death…"

Tears threaten, but I manage to push them back. How many operations have I navigated over the years? And I've let this man push my buttons like a two-year-old with the TV remote.

Much as I curse the tears, since they've showed up, I might as well use them, and I make a point of wiping my eyes with the back of a hand. "You're picking on me. If you think there's something suspicious about Phil's death, how about you answer my question? Tell me why there was no autopsy or any sort of investigation done before he was cremated."

He's silent for too long. Either he doesn't have an answer or he's thinking of a lie. Either way, I'm done with this conversation. I grit my teeth and launch my body toward the parking lot. Maybe, if I really focus, I can keep from limping, although the leg is complaining bitterly today—a fierce ache with every step.

Callahan saunters along beside me, effortless, and I want to pound him with my fists.

"Any criminal record? Ever been in jail?"

The answer happens to be yes, but that has been deeply sealed and he's not going to find it no matter how hard he looks, so I just give him my most annoying smile and keep silent. When we reach the car, first thing I do is pull out the package of cigarettes and light up, blowing the first lungful of smoke into his face.

His jaw tightens; his nostrils twitch. "I'd still like to know what you're doing here."

I blow another lungful of smoke, wondering how I managed to work for so many years without the luxury of a habit that gives me so much time to think before I answer. "Hiding from my husband, if you want to know the truth. Plus, I really did just get out of the hospital and need some recovery time. Manor seemed like a likely spot."

"Give me one of those smokes, will you?"

I hand one over, and after a brief hesitation pull out my matches and light it for him. He inhales with the desperate gusto of a drowning man surfacing for air, blows a stream of smoke over my head, and then his face breaks into a grin.

"How long?" I ask him, savoring my own.

"Five years. Seems like yesterday."

"Are you going to arrest me for corruption of an officer?"

He just grunts, and we smoke companionably for a minute. "What do you know about the Manor?" he asks, at last. "It has a bit of history. A lot of rumor and speculation, too, but the facts are interesting. Since you're going to own it, you might want to know."

"I heard it was haunted." I do know its history, but I'm curious as to what he'll tell me.

I expect a snort of derision but he just takes another drag on his cigarette. "It was part of a radar installation during the Cold War, but it did most of its time as a home for unwed mothers. Opened in the sixties, closed its doors in 1983. They brought those young women in from all over the country and isolated them up there on the hill. Private adoptions arranged. All legit, according to the paperwork. Doctor and a nurse and a bunch of caretaker types on staff—they delivered the babies on-site, so the hospital was never involved."

"Plenty of unwed mothers still. What shut it down?"

There was a story recently on PBS about the homes for unwed mothers, and I figure I know the answer. Too hard to isolate young women and keep them quiet in this age of electronic communications. Especially when the secrets started to leak out about all of the babies buried in back yards, the forced adoptions, the unnecessarily invasive and painful medical procedures and deliveries. Historically, the sort of home he's talking about tended to be more of a house of horrors than a refuge.

"Nobody knows for sure," the sheriff says. "One day everybody's just gone, or mostly gone. If there's an extra baby or two adopted in town, there's nothing illegal about that. Nothing the police would look into. The Manor sat empty for about a year, and then a company bought it, renovated it, and started renting out rooms to the senior population."

"And then Phil bought it."

"Right. Which was sudden and unexplained. Why would a private individual spend that kind of money to take over the place? I'm sure it generates an income, but enough to be considered an investment property?"

"At the time he bought the place, I was in the hospital," I tell him. "Unconscious and likely to die. So if you're thinking there was some conspiracy on my part, you're off-target."

He looks at me, a long, slow, burn of a look that makes me realize this is a man to be reckoned with. He's smart, he's perceptive, he's tenacious.

"Mind if I confirm that?"

"Would it matter if I did mind? Save yourself some trouble. Holy Family. Spokane. Feel free to investigate."

This is safe enough, I figure. The doctors at the hospital have no idea what really happened to me and have pieced together a story built out of what they want to believe. He's welcome to that if it gets him off my back.

My cigarette is done. The air is cold this morning, despite the sun, and shivering hurts. "So, you didn't tell me if the Manor is actually haunted." I use a teasing tone, but he doesn't laugh.

"Some strange things have happened in this town, Ms. Keslyn. Things I can't account for by logic or science."

"What kinds of things?"

But he doesn't answer. He grinds out the butt of his smoke

beneath his heel. "Whenever you feel inclined to tell me what you're really doing here, give me a call."

Halfway to his car he stops and looks back over his shoulder. "Thanks for the smoke. I feel like a goddamn sixteen-year-old kid sneaking around behind the school." He breaks into a teenage swagger for a couple of steps, then reverts to military precision, driving off without so much as a wave or a backward glance.

Time to go, but I linger just a moment more, letting reality sink in. I now own Shadow Valley Manor. Just like Phil to will it to me, ensuring that I'll have my finger in this pie, even if he's gone. Now, besides trying to unravel a mystery with a very big piece missing, I'm going to need an attorney and an accountant and to get my mind around how to run the bloody Manor. I wish I wasn't alone in this mess, and that Phil was still here to watch my back.

Wishing never did any good for anybody.

CHAPTER NINE

The average password takes only a minute to crack, especially if you know anything about the person involved. Names of grandchildren and pets, birthdates, that sort of thing. But Phil was never the average anything and I've been at it for a couple of hours. There was a time when I had access to some of his passwords and could have made a good guess at others. But that was more than thirty years ago.

Phil's cat, I'm convinced, knows this information perfectly well. Hell, maybe the password is his name, whatever that is. The creature insists on perching on my lap while I try to break the code. He doesn't curl up in a ball and purr, but sits upright, staring at the screen.

I've removed him to the floor multiple times but he won't stay put. Every time he leaps up there are claws involved, which jolts the busted leg. So I've succumbed to terrorist tactics and allowed him to stay.

I try various permutations of *goddamn cat* but the computer still refuses to talk to me.

Time is breathing down my neck.

This is a small town. If the good sheriff's suspicions about me are strong enough, he'll be able to pull in some favors and get a warrant to search my room. This would be bad. I've broken laws, protocols, and professional courtesies by spiriting the laptop away. Even if I showed him the FBI badge at that point, he'd be a pain in my ass.

Of course, I can argue that the laptop belongs to me, but the welcome screen that blazons the words "Phil's Property" is a giveaway. Also, somewhere in this town there is a woman who has warmed Phil's bed. I'd be willing to bet on that. And she may be a woman who pays attention to detail, who can testify that he had a laptop. Or who could sneak in and search my room for it without the need for a search warrant.

Doesn't matter that the man was nearly seventy. Some things just don't change.

Right. I'm being paranoid. Nobody is investigating Phil's death. Natural causes. Old people die. Not every death has a sinister component.

But I keep coming back to the fact that he was investigating something. The idea that death just happened to come along before he could tell me what he was up to seems a little too ironic. I know I'm missing something, some clue. My mind keeps running through his house, looking for the nagging little detail I know I've missed. I picture the kitchen, the hallway, the study, the body, over and over again in an endless loop.

I've got nothing.

My leg aches. My belly isn't bleeding anymore but I'm not entirely certain I didn't break something yesterday with the lifting program, and every movement involves pain. The cat is heavy and seriously annoying me.

"Enough," I tell him, finally. He doesn't know this word, or pretends he doesn't, and I pick him up and lock him in the closet.

It's a big closet, and I add his food and water bowls plus an extra pillow off the bed, but you'd think I've committed him to live burial by the ruckus he stirs up. Clawing, scratching, howling at the door.

If he thinks that's going to get him released he doesn't know me very well.

"Howl away, old man," I mutter. One by one the old passwords Phil and I shared slide back into my memory, each one leading to another, and I try them out in varying permutations.

Nothing works.

What if he's done something simple and ordinary, like other people do? I try *Shadow Valley* with a bunch of number combinations.

Important dates, his daughter's name, the town where she was born. Even, in desperation, my own name and the date we met. But the welcome screen just continues to blink at me and tell me I've entered the wrong password.

Bleary-eyed and frustrated, I finally shove the blasted laptop away. My muscles have frozen into this sitting posture and it's not an easy thing to get them moving again.

I'm out of ideas.

Time to go do something else and let my brain percolate. Maybe I'll unpack. Not that I've brought much with me, but living out of a suitcase is an extra layer of hell and there's no need to deliberately pile up misery.

Things have gotten very quiet in the closet and it seems the cat has accepted his lot in life and settled down. But when I open the closet door to hang up my shirts, he has vanished.

Orange hair on the pillow case, water spilled on the floor. The carpet just inside the door is shredded. But there's no sign of the cat. He's not curled up on any of the shelves or hiding in the shadowy corners.

I know damn well I put him in here. And I know he didn't come out through this door. I wasn't that focused on my project.

Grabbing my penlight, I shine it over the floor and all the walls. Nothing. Zip. Nada. But this is not my first barbecue and I know there's nothing supernatural about this cat. He didn't vanish into thin air, which means either he's in the closet or he's found a way out.

My pulse picks up a little at the thought of a hidden door. Maybe I'll forgive Abel and my dearly departed former lover for getting me into this if I find a secret passage.

Sure enough, at the back of the closet, left-hand side, I find a tuft of orange fur, caught on the edge between two panels. In the semidark the crack wasn't obvious, but I see it now. There's just enough of a gap to get my fingernails behind it and the door swings smoothly inward without so much as the creak of a hinge.

When it comes fully open a light turns on, revealing a stairway. Nothing fancy. Just a stairwell, with four stories' worth of ordinary concrete steps. It's been swept recently. No cobwebs or spiders, all of which is a little disappointing. This is no mysterious dungeon or cellar full of paranormal creatures; it's just an ordinary, boring basement.

It smells like all basements everywhere, a little damp, a little musty. A lot like concrete.

The orange cat is at the bottom of the stairs, sniffing at the base of a door.

"What's in there?" I ask him. He doesn't answer, just shoves a paw into the crack and meows. Fine. I have hands and door-opening abilities. I turn the knob, which isn't locked.

The cat dives into the room in search of something invisible, leaving me to stare at a water heater and a bunch of pipes. About as mysterious as finding French fries in a greasy spoon cafe. Since I'm down here, though, I take the opportunity to look around.

A row of storage units, fenced in by mesh, lines one wall, containing furniture, cardboard boxes, a bicycle. Unless there's something in one of the boxes, it's just the usual flotsam and jetsam that ends up stowed away, mostly junk that didn't sell at the yard sale. Each unit is labeled with a room number and I locate Dora's.

The belongings here are pitiful and few. A cardboard box that has seen better days holds a baby sweater and blanket and a couple of photograph albums. Feeling like I'm trespassing where it's not my business, I flip through the books. Photos of a younger, much slimmer Dora holding a baby. In one of them the chubby-faced kid is wearing the sweater in the box. The pictures stop in the middle of the book—no more baby pictures, or Dora pictures, or any kind of pictures. Other boxes hold vinyl albums, paperback romance novels, and a selection of mismatched power cords. There's a bag of linen tablecloths, a box full of china.

And that's it. No clues, no information, just evidence of a personal tragedy and the dregs of a life.

There's a whole truckload of such treasures in a storage unit under my name somewhere, if Abel was true to his promise. In that moment I do some rethinking about my possessions. Whatever becomes of me, I don't want this kind of legacy. Best to get rid of the shit now.

No point searching all of the storage. It would take a long time, and already I regret the few boxes that I've shifted in order to see what was beneath. If I have reason to suspect anybody then I'll come down for another look. The only other unit that might have been of interest, the one belonging to Gerry Vermeer, is empty except for the mother of all dust bunnies.

My leg is not happy with the exercise of the morning, the calf muscles going into a full-on spasm that threatens to drop me. When it eases I tell myself I'll look around for just a few more minutes, and then I'll go back to my room and rest a little, maybe find the solution to my password problem.

The only other visible door leads to a room full of old medical equipment. Bedpans, patient gowns, hospital sheets. And a tray full of what looks an awful lot like speculums. This I give a long, suspicious look, recalling what Callahan said about the Manor as a home for unwed mothers.

Where did they do the actual deliveries? I've seen nowhere in the Manor that would work well as a delivery or surgical suite, but then plenty of renovations have happened here. It occurs to me that there isn't enough basement. Letting the floor plan run through my brain, I cross the room and walk a wall that ought to have something on the other side, looking for a door. There is none.

The cat reappears from behind a jumble of furniture, dust draping his whiskers and a mouse dangling from his jaws. The thing is limp, but breathing. Playing dead. Just a mouse, and the cat is doing the world a favor, I suppose. Still, when he drops the little creature at my feet as some sort of misguided gift, I pick it up, meaning to put it where the cat can't reach it and give it half a chance of survival.

No good deed goes unpunished.

It bites me.

Cursing, I drop it and the cat's back on it in a heartbeat. My finger is bleeding and I squeeze it to encourage the flow. Maybe it will cleanse out bacteria and I won't get rabies or tetanus or whatever mice carry. A few drops of blood fall on the floor.

In that instant a cold draft swirls past me, tugging at my clothes, lifting my hair. The cat drops the mouse, howls, and heads for the stairs, all of his fur standing on end and his tail three sizes too big.

I know how he feels. There are no open windows down here, no excuses for a flurry of wind. If I had fur it would be standing up too. As it is, my body is all over gooseflesh and my thumbs are pricking.

The wind is gone, the air settled back to its musty basement self.

But I am not alone. The goosebumps are still with me, and even as I watch, the blood drops vanish from the floor, one by one, as if lapped up by an invisible tongue.

My brain flicks through a list of known bloodlusting paranormals. Vampires and shifters are the most common, but I've never known one to be invisible. And all the creatures I know of that are invisible, mostly the denizens of the spirit world, don't care about blood or any lust of the flesh. So I don't have the slightest clue what I'm dealing with.

I can't shoot what I can't see, so I draw my knife from the ankle holster. Not an easy thing, but adrenaline helps mask the pain of bending over.

And then I wait, long enough to begin to think I imagined everything.

No wind, no movement. No smoke or fog, no wavering of the light. Holding my breath turns out to be a bit of a challenge but I manage it, listening. The water heater kicks in, startling me.

A strange tingling sensation in my bitten finger turns to cold. It begins at the bite, spreading first to the finger tip and then the whole finger, as if somebody is pouring cold liquid through the wound and filling up the flesh. The skin turns dead white and bloodless. I jerk my hand upward and it feels like suction breaking. The rush of blood back into the skin is visible.

Whatever was sucking at it is not.

Knife in hand, I take a step backward. Another. At this speed it's a long way to the stairs and I tell myself I should run for it, but I can't make myself turn my back on whatever is stalking me. Which is ridiculous. It could be anywhere in the room, including between me and the door. It also could have made its way up the stairs and into my suite, or the rest of the Manor, for that matter.

Panic never solved anything. Three controlled breaths and an attempt to figure out what I'm dealing with. Stretching out both arms, I wave them around my body, feeling for a dense or cold patch, half expecting slimy fingers to grab my arm and cling.

Nothing.

Another deep breath and I force myself to turn and walk toward the stairs with slow, confident steps, although I very much doubt I can trick the thing into thinking I'm not terrified. It's not a fair fight when you can't even see what's trying to kill you. One step. Two.

And again the cold, nibbling at my finger. Extending upward into my hand.

This time I use the knife, slicing through what looks like air just above the bite. The blade catches and drags. My clenched fingers brush against something cold and jellylike. It quivers, then retreats.

No more shuffling for me. Knife in my good hand, shaking the other spasmodically, I sprint across that basement, bad leg be damned. Up the stairs, as fast as my protesting flesh will take me. Through the secret door and into the closet, which I slam shut, panting, heart racing. I have no idea what will keep that Thing out of my room if it hasn't already followed me in, so I use the entire arsenal at my disposal.

I have a special mixture for situations such as this—salt, iron filings, and silver dust—and I shake it out in a half circle around the door. On second thought, I add another half circle to the door leading to the hallway. If the Thing is in my room, I don't want it getting out into the general population.

Then, when there is no sign of any further danger, I sink down in a chair with the knife in one hand and my revolver in the other.

Nothing happens.

Just as I'm about to relax enough to at least shift position, the dust ruffle on the bed ripples and sways. I'm on my feet in a heartbeat, ready to fight. A nose pokes out from under the bed, attached to whiskers and then a pair of ears. Apparently the coast is clear, because the cat emerges from his hiding place, making a point of nonchalance and the fact that he ran because he felt like it, not because he was scared. He leaps gracefully up onto my bed, where he settles himself and begins licking his paws.

"Well, I guess you're good for something after all."

Clearly the wretched little beast can see whatever came after me and it's not here in the room with us, so I follow his example, minus the paw licking. A tentative stretch and a head-to-toe examination reveal no visible harm done. My incision is intact and healing. The leg aches viciously but shows no evidence of any further damage. My finger looks and feels normal. Just to be sure I inspect myself in the mirror. Still visible, no strange intelligence looking back at me. Despite the dregs of a really good scare I feel fine, better even.

Fear has always been good for me.

My mind goes back to Phil and all of the paranormals we fought together. A long way back, to the one thing we agreed to never talk about.

Opening his laptop, holding my breath, I think for a minute, then type in *Project Paranormal*. Too obvious, and sure enough, it doesn't work. So I turn it around. *Lamronarap Tcejorp*. After a brief hesitation I add the classic Evers password specifier, the one he says nobody ever thinks of.

Shit.

Then I add a number made up of the month of my birth and the day of his and hit enter.

The screen goes dark for just long enough to make me think he's encoded a self-destruct program in case the wrong person gets too close. And then a graphic of a handgun comes up, tumbling end over end across the screen. A single word pops out of the barrel:

Bang.

A cold shiver runs through me and my vision narrows down to a tunnel. He's written the word in red caps, as if he thought I'd lost my edge and would need to be shouted at.

But there's nothing wrong with my memory, even if my body is a mess. Some things you don't forget.

"I want to go out with a bang," he'd said once. "Not just a little bang, Maureen. A Big Bang. Remember that, will you?"

Phil didn't consider little things like a stabbing or a gunshot wound worthy of *bang*. He was talking some sort of huge supernatural extravaganza. And if this operation is connected to Project Paranormal, the shit is much, much deeper than I can handle on my own.

CHAPTER TEN

Phil might have wanted to go out with a bang. Me? I don't want to go out at all. Shaking my head, I murmur out loud, "Thanks so much for the warning. A little late, old friend. Now—what have you gotten me into?"

The man was always annoyingly prepared for any eventuality. The gun stops spinning, and a series of files opens automatically. I assume he wants me to look at them in order, so I follow the breadcrumb trail he's laid out.

The very first document is a schematic of the Manor. This fits what I have already seen—the layout of residents' rooms, the dining area, the staff's office, the kitchen, a small medical room I have yet to visit. Even the basement, including the main entrance and the secret one from my closet.

Behind it is another, older, blueprint. Same basic shape and size, but the rooms are different. There's another passageway leading down from Vermeer's room. And downstairs is a network of tunnels and rooms so tiny they look like cells.

There's a big discrepancy between the two, I realize, clicking back and forth from one to the other. I knew something was off when I was down there, but didn't exactly have the luxury to think about the problem. The basement area I accessed is not even half the size of the Manor. Which, I realize with a little thrill of excitement, means something has been purposefully walled off and hidden.

The rest of the files are straightforward—a dossier on the residents of the Manor. He'd only gotten started on this and much of the information is rudimentary, little more than I've been given by Abel. Names, birth dates, employment history, family connections, legal records for a couple of people, although only for petty misdemeanors. I'm interested to see that Chuck did a year of prison time in his youth for breaking and entering and was charged with assault, although this didn't stick.

Another file has information on staff. Of the current and recent staff—the former cook, cleaning staff, nighttime relief—there is only basic information. Betty and Matt have more extensive notes. Betty, legally Elizabeth Cameron, was born and raised in Shadow Valley. Her parents, a physician and a nurse, are both deceased. She's been the manager of the Manor for the last five years and has no legal record. Also no known living realtives.

Matthew Pennington completed one tour of service in Iraq, where he distinguished himself with valor. Prior to Iraq he graduated with a culinary arts degree from Kitchen Academy in Seattle. His record is also squeaky clean. Again, no family. His parents are dead. No known girlfriend or close friends of any kind. I find this suspicious, for a good-looking and charming young man, but war does things to people and I won't be too quick to judge. The boy makes damn fine coffee.

Phil has also included Charlene Rivers, MD, who works at the clinic and provides medical care to residents in addition to her duties as coroner. She grew up in Shadow Valley, went to medical school at the University of Washington, and came back on a rural program that paid her student loans in exchange for time worked. She does have family here, both parents still living. Her father is afflicted with Alzheimer's, and her mother lost most of her memory and cognitive abilities following a severe heart attack. Community people love her and she has no legal record.

Storing all of this info away for further thought, I move on to the next folder. This one is a list of names, all former employees of the Manor. There's a notation at the top that reads, simply: "Find them. Talk to them."

At the end, in case I was in any danger of forgetting, is another picture, only this one is different. This picture also hangs on the wall at his house, and this is what has been nagging at me. It's just a picture of a desert, without even an interesting cactus. Scrub brush, dirt, and sky. And in the distance, a wind-carved sandstone formation. Only this version, unlike the one at his place, has the two of us Photoshopped into it, his arm around my shoulders, me laughing, my head leaning just enough to graze his shoulder. Even with the alteration it's generic and nondescript, unless you know where it was taken.

I need very much to talk to Abel.

He doesn't respond to Skype, home phone, or cell phone. This is not like Abel and the excuses I can come up with are pretty thin. Being in the shower or on the toilet wouldn't keep him from the phone; he's too conscious of the need to respond if one of his people is in trouble. The only other option I'm willing to entertain is that he's on an operation and had to disconnect.

My tracking software shows him at home, and this fills me with even greater unease. If there's no chain, he's got no backup. Nobody to check in or rescue him if he's gotten in trouble. And he could be in a hell of a lot of trouble.

Need drives me, and I dial the Unit. I know damn well this is an independent op but it's gotten out of hand. We need help here. I'm still smart enough to use one of the disposable cells I always carry with me. If things feel off, I don't want to be tracked. I also remove the tracker Abel put on my phone, and flush it down the toilet. He knows where I am if he needs me.

The secretary sounds young, but voices are deceiving and she could well be an experienced old battleaxe whose voice didn't keep up with the times. Still, she's a croaker, and that's a modern trend that puts her in her twenties.

I keep my own voice bright and young, clipping all the vowels and sounding like I'm impatient and driven and on my way up. "Abel Galloway, please."

A hesitation tells me everything I want to know. She's young, inexperienced, and about to lie to me.

"He's not available right now. Can you leave a message?"

"When will he be in?"

"I'm not sure. If you'll just—"

"I really need to talk to him. Cell number?"

"You'll really need to leave me a—"

"This is too important for messages."

Again the hesitation. "Look, just give me your name and number—"

"You, young lady, are about to go down in infamy. Trust me, if you don't put me through on this, you're going to lose your job and be remembered as the one responsible—"

"Just a minute. I'm putting you on hold—"

"Don't you dare hang up on me!"

"I'm going to transfer you."

A moment of silence, which means she's explaining the call before putting me through.

Another woman's voice comes on. Nancy. "This better be good." No croaking here, and she means business.

I slide a piece of paper between me and the receiver. If this call is recorded and goes to voice recognition it's not enough, but if I add an accent and lower my voice a little she might not recognize me. "I need to talk to Abel."

"Who is this?"

I picture her, sitting across the clear expanse of her desk. Dark hair twisted in a tight bun, glasses perched on her nose..

"I need to speak with Abel. It's important."

"I'm sorry. Abel is on vacation. How can I help you?"

Her lies are as smooth as honey, but still lies. Whatever Abel is doing, he's not on vacation. I tell myself he might be on assignment, but there's something in her voice that bears watching.

"No help needed." I keep my voice matching hers, calm and matter-of-fact. Then, trusting my gut, I hang up before she can say more or have time to trace my call.

Removing the battery from the phone, I grab another disposable cell from my suitcase and step out into the hallway. Nothing stirring that I can see. No visible cameras. I plan to get myself to the river to dispose of both cell phones, but just as I start for the elevator Gerry

Vermeer's door flies open.

"Neighbor!" he says, leering at me. "What are you about, I wonder? Would you care for a cup of tea?"

I hate tea. It's like drinking hot water with milk and sugar. Also, I'm tired and miserable. My leg feels like an invisible dog is gnawing on the bone. I should dispose of the phones sooner rather than later.

But there's a good chance Vermeer is involved in nefarious deeds, so I dredge up what I hope is a pleasant, nonthreatening smile, and lie. "That would be lovely."

CHAPTER ELEVEN

The layout of Vermeer's suite is the same as mine, but that is the only resemblance. Where my curtains are crimson velvet, he has state-of-the-art blinds. French doors lead out onto a small railed veranda. The furniture is light and airy, the floor is covered with woven mats that look a lot like tatami. The puffy down comforter on a low bed looks much more appealing than the high four-poster monstrosity in my room.

A grouping of three living room chairs surrounds a square coffee table. Something seems missing until I think *wheelchair* and I understand what he's done. Lots of wide open spaces for him to get around, and the chair fits neatly on the empty side of the table.

He rolls off to the kitchenette and returns with an old-fashioned tea tray balanced on his knees. Delicate china teapot and cups, sugar bowl, cream jug. So there I sit, a moment later, with a cup of tea in my hand. It's fragile and awkward to hold and I'd be more comfortable with a solid mug, but I'm civilized enough to sip away while trying to think of small talk.

"What brings you to the Manor?"

Vermeer's question sounds a lot like Callahan in both tone and phrasing, but when I shoot him a glance he is only a little old man, toothless as a newborn baby and just as bald. His hands are distorted with arthritis, bony ankles sticking out of too-short sweatpants. It's hard to keep in mind that he might be devious.

"I didn't see you at breakfast."

"Can't stand the mindless drivel. Groceries are delivered weekly—microwave meals, mostly." He lifts his cup, violets and green grass with a gold rim around the top, and then puts it back in the saucer without drinking. "You don't seem the type for mindless drivel."

And this is my opening. If he wants to be direct, I can do that.

"I'm surprised to find you drinking tea. I heard rumors about you—that you like a stronger beverage."

"I like tea, actually," he said. "But yes, I drink blood most days. Comes in a bag—I buy it from a guy who drains himself for me on a regular basis."

"That is—"

"Disgusting?" He licks his lips and grins.

"I was going to say dangerous. Anybody willing to regularly sell blood—"

He laughs, a dry, painful wheezing that sounds more like asthma than mirth. "So he's got AIDS, or hepatitis, or yellow fever, or the plague—what's it going to do, kill me?"

He's got a point. Guy's got to be at least eighty. I'm trying to remember the actual age on the dossier. As if he can read my mind he grins, his shrewd little eyes sparkling. "Ninety-three at last count," he says.

"Mr. Vermeer—"

"Gerry."

"I'm not sure that openly expressing your sanguinary tastes is a great idea."

"Not breaking any laws."

"Funny thing. The woman who died—"

"Dora. Fancied herself an enchantress."

"Yes, well, your enchantress had marks in her throat, like somebody bit her. You wouldn't know anything about that, would you?"

The room seems to darken. Shadows expand, becoming more defined, almost solid. As he leans forward a little in his chair it takes all of my will to hold myself in place, to not flinch or quiver or back away.

But you never show fear to a vampire, and instead I take a sip of tea.

And then he's laughing, all toothless gums and bald head.

"With what would I bite her?"

He's right, of course. The idea is ludicrous, but I know what I felt and I've been in this business too long to entirely discount such things. I take another sip of the tea, which, as expected, tastes of milk and sugar with a slight bitterness. It's also lukewarm.

"What did you do before you wound up here?" I ask him, watching to be sure that he is actually drinking his tea before I take another sip of mine, waiting for him to tell me what I already know. Or not.

He opts for the truth.

"Tax accountant." He laughs, but he isn't amused. For the first time I see past the liver-spotted head and wrinkled skin to the bleakness in his eyes. A gold wedding band hangs loose on his finger.

"When did she die, your wife?"

He blinks, pauses. "A year? Ten? Time plays tricks with me." His hands shake a little as he toys with his cup, turning it in the saucer, back and forth. A wave of tea sloshes onto the table.

In his grief he is dignified and reserved, and I suddenly feel guilt for coming here and harassing him. I have a job to do, though, and I'm not letting a few emotions get in my way. "Why the Manor?"

"Why not?"

I can think of plenty of reasons why not, but he has effectively blocked my opening. I swallow the rest of my tea, cold now, the metallic tang of tannin stronger on my tongue.

"I'd better mop up my mess." Vermeer backs his chair away from the table, rolling over to the sink for a rag.

Taking advantage of the opportunity, I get up and snoop.

On a credenza by the wall there is a record player and a rack of vinyl albums, stored with precision. His modern taste in furniture apparently doesn't extend to his choices in music. A cabinet holds curios collected from all over the world—carved jade elephants, a Russian Easter egg, a Buddha that looks like it might be gold plated. There is also a large bookcase, mostly full of old leather-bound books—the classics. *Oliver Twist, Jane Eyre, Dracula.*

Dracula forms a boundary line between these old books, worn and cherished, and a row of glossy new paperbacks—comprising both mythology and lurid vampire romance. *Vampires in the Modern World. The Myth of the Vampire. Vampires and Werewolves through History. Vampire from Hell. The Vampire's Bride.*

I hear the chair rolling behind me, feel the lifting of the hairs on the back of my neck, and spin around to see a sickly old man holding a fragile china teapot in tremulous hands. "Care for another cup?" he asks.

"Interesting selection of books."

He gives me his toothless smile. "Lots of sex and beautiful women, and I'm a dirty old man."

I accept the cup of tea he hands me, but I don't drink. "Some of those books look a little heftier than vampire romance."

"Got curious. Is a vampire made or born? How did this fate fall to me?"

Just talking about vampires makes my skin crawl. I've dealt with the diabolical monsters, and know full well they are neither handsome nor beautiful, and that they don't feel love for their human victims. I pull one of the romances off the shelf and barely resist the urge to throw it at the wall. The damn things are dangerous, lulling poor idiots to sleep. A dark shadow looms, cold and calculating; it's reaching out from my past, from the graves of friends, and I shiver. Vermeer may or may not be a vampire, but I'm pretty sure he's involved in Phil's mystery one way or another.

"What's with the closet in my suite?"

"I'm not sure what you mean."

"You were pretty interested in it last night."

"Myths and legends. Every kid in town knows there is a secret passageway that leads to hidden treasure somewhere in the Manor. That suite is always locked—nobody goes in there, except to clean. Made me curious, is all."

He makes too much of a point of looking at me directly, and I know he's lying.

"There is a door in that closet, Mr. Vermeer. It leads down into the basement. Furnace room, storage lockers. Nothing exciting."

At least not if you discount a bloodthirsty invisible Jelly Thing.

Vermeer turns his back to me, busying himself with straightening papers on his coffee table, and says, lightly, "Well, that's a lifelong daydream crushed."

"What about the closet in your room?"

"What about it?"

"A secret passage in one room, why not in the other?"

No more manufactured smiles or laughter, and when he speaks again his tone is faintly menacing. "You should go now."

"Aw, we were just starting to have fun." He tries to cut me off with the chair but I'm quicker and already in the closet before he gets there.

"You're trespassing. I'll call the sheriff—"

"Now why does everybody keep threatening that? But go ahead. I'm sure he'd be quite interested in this."

Some people have very little imagination. The panel is in precisely the same place as the one in my room. All it takes to make it open is a little pressure in the right spot. A click, and a crack appears in the wall.

I stand on the first step, looking down. A long way down, my leg reminds me. Vermeer sits in his chair, blocking the door of the closet. His face is in shadow. He says nothing. No reaction of surprise, no further attempt to hold me back. If he has a gun or a knife he could get me in the back, but hell. I'm already committed.

One slow step at a time, I make my way down. Like the staircase leading down from my room, there's a door at the bottom of the steps. It's locked, but it takes only a minute to pick it. Then, for a long moment, I stand on my side of it, listening, sensing. I draw my knife in one hand, the gun in the other, just in case of attack.

And then I give it a shove.

The missing delivery room is on the other side. There's a delivery table, a surgical light, a cabinet for medications and equipment. It's dusty and inhabited by spiders and a little creepy in the dim light.

A hallway leads off to the right and I follow it. Phil's map indicates that this is a tunnel. Several doors lead off to left and right, opening into empty rooms. Storage, maybe.

Or isolation cells.

Past a door at the end of the tunnel, a large room holds a row of six metal tables. Familiar equipment sits on a counter that runs the length of the far wall. A centrifuge for separating blood components, a high-powered microscope, an autoclave. All old-fashioned now, and out of date. The wall to the right is all closed cupboards.

At the center of the room the cement floor slopes toward a drain. Rust-colored splotches under the tables look like old blood stains. Iron in the water could make stains like that, but I think more has been spilled here than water.

The tables are wrong for delivering babies. No mattresses. No stirrups. They look more like autopsy tables than anything else, except that they have leather cuffs attached, four per table.

Dead people don't need restraints.

And filling the wall to the left, from floor to ceiling, are plexiglass cubes, each sealed from the outside.

I don't scare easy, but those cubes make my blood run cold and my flesh shiver. I've seen something like them only once before, and the sight of them sets off all of my alarms. Long-suppressed memories flood through me, and I have to consciously slow my breathing and my heart rate.

Phil cups my chin in his hand, tilting back my head so he can look into my eyes.

"This is the last time," he murmurs, tucking a wayward strand of hair behind my ear.

"Why?"

"Because we know, and they must believe we have forgotten."

"I'm not scared."

"You should be scared. You should be so goddamn scared that you forget this ever happened. You never mention it to anybody. You don't mention me to anybody. You don't even dream about it, understood?"

"Phil—"

He silences me with a kiss, long and gentle, then walks out of my door and out of my life.

I realize I have one hand over my heart, that there are tears on my cheeks. I did what he said. And while I've been staying safe, he's been working behind the scenes on his own. Risking the danger, trying to make things right.

Why bring me back in now?

It's a very good question, and I intend to find the answer. I will also finish whatever he's started, even if it kills me—the chances of which, I'm thinking, are higher than not.

No matter how valiant my intentions, though, my body isn't with the program. I start up the stairs okay but on the last flight my legs just quit. The muscles of the broken one go into a spasm that won't stop, and the other feels like a wet noodle that refuses to bear my weight.

Being stuck here and requiring a rescue is ludicrous and unthinkable, and in the end I sit my butt down and lever myself up with my hands, one step at a time. When I get to the top I fix Vermeer with my best ice-cold stare.

"If you ever tell anybody—"

Seeing the look on his face I break off midsentence. "You know what's down there."

He doesn't acknowledge yes, nor does he deny. Instead, he asks, "Who are you, really?"

"My name, as I told you, is Maureen Keslyn. I'm a curious old bat and tend to get myself in trouble."

"Will you be talking about this?"

"Just a basement," I tell him. "Nothing but spiders and dust bunnies." He'll either know I'm lying, or not. If nothing else, I've stirred him up a little. Now I just need to watch and see what he does.

Extricating myself from his room is easy now. The old man clearly wants me gone and can't wait to open the door and usher me out. Limping is inevitable, but there's not time to rest now. Dragging my leg and ignoring the looks from the few residents I pass, I take the elevator down and head straight for my car, dialing my old home number as I walk.

Glenda answers. "Maureen, how lovely—"

"Just give the phone to my husband, would you?"

A hitch in her breathing, and then a shuffling sound and Ed comes on.

"What's up?" He sounds abrupt, but a little guilty.

"I think you and Glenda should take a little vacation."

"What?"

"Now would be good. Get out of the country."

"Maureen—"

"I didn't call, okay? You haven't heard from me. I hear Mexico is lovely this time of year."

At the moment I feel like I don't care much what happens to him, but we've spent long years of life together and he deserves this much at least.

I hang up and take the battery out of the phone before I shift the car into gear.

The road winds along down the side of the mountain, through town, and to the river. Which is where I stop and toss both disposable phones into the current. Not that this will save me. If they really want to find me it won't be all that hard—I don't have even a rudimentary cover. But I'm not going to wrap up the information and hand it over like a birthday gift.

Let them come for me.

I'll be ready.

CHAPTER TWELVE

Phil's house looks ordinary and normal. No crime scene tape. By daylight I see that the front yard is full of weeds. The garden shed is shabby, green paint peeling. Tall grass grows around the door.

I stand on the porch and have a good look around before entering. If anybody followed me, something I've definitely been watching for, they are either damned good or have chosen not to follow me into the yard.

The front door is locked, but that only takes a minute to fix.

Already the house has begun to take on a slightly neglected smell. It's familiar. I've been away from my own house more than I've been in it, and Ed was prone to frequent and long vacations. I wonder, idly, how many women he's taken with him over the years, or whether it's been Glenda all along.

Nothing at Phil's has changed, at least that I can see. The dishes sit in the drainer in the kitchen where Phil left them, except for the coffee cup on the table. I want fingerprints, DNA, and an analysis of the contents, but I have no way to get them. Yet. Abel can pull some strings if and when I catch up with him. I bag the mug in a plastic baggie from the drawer and set it aside to take with me.

Next step is to sweep the house for bugs. I'm not a pro at this, my specialty being the para creatures and not the humans, but I've been around and I'm not an idiot. I don't find any hidden mics or cameras. Nothing, in fact, that would indicate that Phil was anything other than an average citizen, quietly living out his life in the woods.

Now that I've figured out what's involved in his project, though, I have a better idea of what to look for, and go methodically through the house.

In the bathroom all is in order. Nothing in the medicine cabinet but aspirin, ibuprofen, and a box of Band-Aids, all precisely lined up on the center shelf. The drawers hold a razor, toothbrush, toothpaste. A pair of scissors. A nail clipper.

This means he's got a hiding place somewhere for the real first aid kit; I just haven't found it yet. It wasn't in his study, which leaves the bedroom.

I should have given this room much more than a cursory glance the night he died, but emotions got in the way and I failed. There are so many memories connected to Phil and bed, and investigating the scenario where he was apparently engaged in a sexual romp while I was waiting for him at the restaurant was too much for me.

Now I force myself to look at the room dispassionately. Or at least I try. As intrusive and creepy as it feels to be investigating the scene of an old lover's last sexual tryst, I steel myself to go into the room and gather evidence, but all my courage goes for nothing.

The bed is neatly made.

I actually doubt my own memory for a minute. I was distraught, in shock. But I know damn well what I saw. The rest of the room looks the same to a casual glance, and since that's all I gave it I can't tell if anything else has been altered.

When I pull back the covers to check the sheets they are smooth, unwrinkled, and smell of fabric softener. They are the same color as the sheets I saw before, but they are cotton. Phil was always crazy about satin. Tastes change, and it's been years since I knew him, but I'm still suspicious that whoever made up the bed also put on clean sheets.

I take another good sniff. As a clue, the fragrance is not much use; probably half the residents of this little town use the same fabric softener. Still, you never know which piece of the puzzle will be the key to solving a mystery.

Nothing else in his room catches my attention. There's a picture of Phil's daughter on the bedside table. His alarm is set for five. His drawers are full of ordinary clothes, neatly folded. Nothing under his mattress. One suit, a windbreaker, and three dress shirts hang in the closet. Nothing to indicate he's anything other than an ordinary man, retired and living a simple life in the country.

The back of the closet is solid; there are no pictures on the walls that could be concealing a safe, so I move on to the study.

This room I did catalogue thoroughly the night Phil died. Everything is present and seems untouched. If there's been a search, it's been done neatly, with every item returned to its rightful place. Only difference I can see is that the wind-up clock has stopped. It sits silent and blank on the shelf.

Because I didn't want to move the body, I haven't investigated the middle drawer of his desk. Here I find his revolver, fully loaded. I empty the chambers and line the bullets up on the desktop—silver and lead, mixed, like mine. Further searching in the drawer yields a heavy silver cross on a chain and a coil-bound sketchbook.

I know this book. He was working on it already when I knew him, and the first few pages are familiar. On each page is a detailed sketch of a paranormal creature, along with a secondary sketch of internal anatomy where this is known. And next to each sketch is a list of agents that will hurt, bind, or kill. He's been adding to it all these years, and I flip through the pages with a sense of wonder. All the easy ones at the beginning—different breeds of vampires, werewolves, and some of the lesser-known shifters. Your average ghost.

From there things get a little more freakish.

These are truly the stuff of nightmares. If people only knew what really is floating and crawling and oozing about in the world, they would sleep with the lights on and never laugh at their kids about the monsters under the bed.

At the back of the book are the truly dark creatures for which there are no names—I'm pretty sure even Phil didn't want to take the chance of calling one into our reality.

On the very last page he's etched in an empty square, maybe because he just got started and didn't have a chance to finish. But he's gone so far as to write "Killing Agents" in his neat block letters. Underneath, where the list ought to be, there is nothing. I only realize I've been staring at this page for a long time when my hands start to cramp from holding on way too tight, and I take a few deep breaths and remind myself this may have no relation at all to the invisible thing in the basement of the Manor.

And if it is, standing around woolgathering won't do anything to stop it.

Now that I'm looking for it, the location of the safe is obvious. The desert photograph is on hinges, and there, right behind it, Phil has installed a built-in safe. I spin the numbers we shared on operations and the door clicks open.

There's not much here, not for a man like Phil. A passport, in his real name. A thousand dollars in cash. Some extra ammo, some of it factory, some specially designed silver, some amalgam. The medical supplies are here: a standard first aid kit with the addition of sutures, antibiotics, and a selection of his own concoctions designed to counteract the more common supernatural injuries. There's a copy of the will, which makes his daughter his executrix and leaves her everything but the Manor, which he has indeed left to me.

There's nothing else here other than a set of car keys. He ought to have a cell phone, but there's been no sign of one. Of course, he doesn't get cell service out here, so maybe it wasn't a thing he thought he needed. Either that or it was taken by whoever made the bed. Which means somebody out there has my number.

Somewhere he must have weapons, and my best guess is in his car. Scooping up his keys, I head outside. By light of day I can see that his ride is a Subaru, aging and a little worse for wear. I'm pretty sure he's got an expensive car more to his taste stashed away somewhere. Spokane, maybe.

The glove compartment contains insurance and registration, neatly bundled in a clear plastic sleeve. Receipts for tires and an oil change. A small LED flashlight.

Nothing under either the driver's or the passenger's seat. An empty coffee mug in the cup holder.

And a key in the ash tray.

Looks like it belongs to a padlock, and I limp over to the garden shed at the edge of the parking area.

A few rusty garden implements lean in a corner or hang on a pegboard wall with hooks, but it's pretty clear that Phil wasn't interested in gardening.

He's got all the weapons here, laid out neatly on workbenches. Some are recognizable, some obviously experimental. Rifles, shotguns. A grenade launcher. Flamethrowers large and small. Ammo boxes full of silver and compound loads. Stakes of iron and wood, a selection of throwing knives. There are a couple of items I'm not sure about. One of them looks like a *Star Trek* stun gun.

I'm as buzzed as a teenage boy let loose for the first time on the firing range. I love weapons, and I can't wait to play with the new toys. I've got the stun gun in my hands, checking out the dials and making guesses at settings, when I hear a creak of wood behind me and spin around to find myself looking straight into Sheriff Callahan's shark-grey eyes.

I'm also pointing an unclassified weapon in his general direction. Not good.

Give the man credit—he doesn't blink or show a sign of fear. He's smooth and quick, has his service weapon aimed and ready to fire before I have time to draw another breath.

"Drop it," he commands.

Don't mess around with a cop on high alert or you'll end up dead. I know this. Since I'm not inclined to shoot him at this point, I go as far as to drop the weapon, but my mouth is another thing entirely.

"You're no fun. I was just about to see what it does."

"Step out of the shed. Keep your hands where I can see them."

He steps to the side of the doorway to let me exit, then makes me put my hands against the shed wall and pats me down, taking my revolver once again. He misses the knife in my ankle sheath and I have to bite my tongue to keep from pointing out his oversight.

Can't say I blame him, and I'm happy to comply with his instructions to move away from the building. I'm not quite sure what that dial was I just moved. For all I know I've set a timer for the shed to blow up, so I step back with my hands at half-mast, palms out, in the universal sign of "Don't hurt me, I'm harmless," and let the good sheriff walk into the shed and take a good look.

I do offer up some advice. "I wouldn't touch anything."

"Why's that?"

He's got his hands on the stun gun and actually turns around to look at me. It takes him a minute, since I've now got the length of his car between him and me.

"Because Phil made that."

"What does it do?"

"I was about to find out. For all I know, it makes soup out of anything organic."

"Guns aren't good enough?"

"Depends what you're shooting at."

He's not a stupid man, thank all the powers that be, and he replaces the weapon and picks up the sketchbook, which I'd set down to free my hands. A moment of silence as he turns the pages.

"Ms. Keslyn, you have not been honest with me."

"Are you calling me a liar? I'm wounded."

"I'm going to ask you one more time: what are you doing in my town?"

"And I told you the truth. I am staying at the Manor while I recover from injuries. Do you need to see the scars?"

"You were friends with Mr. Evers, who was clearly not what he said he was—a businessman here to retire. And you are not the average Manor resident. I'm listening."

My brain is spinning. I need an ally. If I can trust the sheriff, even a little, he could be of great use to me.

I need a cigarette. Amazing how fast that habit creeps back up on a body.

"Just a second." I head for my car.

"Hands where I can see them," he says. He means it. That calm thing he's got going on doesn't run much deeper than his skin.

"Permission to smoke, sir."

"Oh, all right. I'll take one if you're sharing."

When I turn around with the smokes he's right there, ready to shoot if I step out of line.

"You don't trust me."

This is a point in his favor. First things first. I get us both lit up and wait until he's had a drag or two before I show him my FBI creds.

"Where have you been all my life?" he says in a slow drawl, and gives me a grin.

"Pardon?"

"I told you there's been some strange happenings in this town. I didn't begin to tell you how strange. Nobody in the law enforcement world wants to hear it." His face takes on a focused intensity and he's not smiling anymore. "People have died. I can't protect them, I can't bring them justice. If you're telling me you're here to do that, then I've been looking for you for a very long time."

"Phil was the one to do that, Sheriff. I'm just—I was supposed to be undercover at the Manor."

"Well, then, you still are. Or does owning the damn thing blow that sky-high?"

I take a long drag and consider that. "My cover wasn't great to start with. A few things you should know about Phil: He was a mastermind. In the paranormal world people actually called him 007. If he didn't die of natural causes, then whatever we're dealing with—well, you should know what you're getting into."

"Hmmm." He blows a little cloud of smoke into the air and sucks in another lungful, contemplative. "And what is that?"

I can't say I don't know, so I shrug and play the evasive card. "There's some critters up at the Manor. We think some of the deaths up there haven't been from natural causes."

"Right. And nobody cares to look into it because they're old and who gives a damn." There's a bitterness in his voice.

"You're the sheriff." I can't keep the hint of accusation out of mine.

"Yes, I am. And when the coroner looks and tells me cause of death is old age and I'm imagining things, what can I do about that?"

We smoke in silence for a minute and then he asks, "So what's the plan now? Where's your team holed up?"

I want to trust him. I think I can. But some built-in caution kicks in and I shrug. "We're still figuring that out. Nobody ever planned for Phil's demise. That was never in the cards. It will take a little time."

"Do we have time?"

I don't answer that one. He follows it up with, "What can I do?"

When I tell him, he doesn't object. Just nods understanding. And then he blows it all. "I'm confiscating the weapons."

"I wish you wouldn't."

A hesitation on his part. He's weighing the odds, my badge against the lies I've told him.

"Sorry. It's my job." He hands me back the book. "Have you met any of these?"

"Plenty. You?"

To my surprise he nods his head in the affirmative. "Look, is that book top secret?"

"I don't think so."

"Maybe sometime we could sit down and you could let me have a better look."

I sense a trap but I can't see it. "All right."

"Perfect. Tomorrow at eight, for breakfast? House of Joe makes a great cup of coffee."

"Hey, if the coffee's good, I'm in."

I stand by, smoking, while the sheriff gingerly loads the weapons stash into his truck. He salutes as he drives away, flashing me the sort of smile that gets me wondering whether I've just agreed to a business meeting or a date.

Once he's gone I go back into the shed, hoping he's missed something, but there's nothing left but garden tools and a medium-sized flashlight.

The flashlight hangs side by side with what looks like a handheld seed spreader, the two of them separated from all of the other garden tools by both space and newness. No rust here. There's a drawing of the seed spreader, glossy green paint and all, in the sketchbook. It's actually used for spraying salt at susceptible paras. As weapons go it has limited uses, but if I'd had one the night of the fateful giant slug attack I'd be a healthier woman today. As for the flashlight, I have hopes that it's something lethal disguised in a mundane package, but when I switch it on, taking care to point it well away from me, it does nothing more than create a warm yellow circle of light on the floor of the shed.

Even so. It was Phil's, and carrying anything of his makes me feel closer to him. So I clip it onto a carabiner hanging from my belt.

"Well, Phil," I say to the darkness and the trees, as I lock up the door to the shed. "Last chance if there's anything you want to tell me."

An owl hoots off in the distance. Wind murmurs through the trees. Phil says nothing. I didn't really expect him to. The rest of this puzzle is going to be up to me.

CHAPTER THIRTEEN

Even while it's unfolding I know it's a dream.

I'm alone, standing in the middle of a green field of alfalfa that stretches away around me on all sides, an endless vault of blue sky arcing overhead. Birdcalls fill the air, combined with the whirr of grasshoppers and a buzzing of bees.

A peaceful scene, but I am alone and frightened, overwhelmed by a horror that roots my feet to the ground and keeps me from moving so much as a finger.

On the ground in front of me, a single leaf of alfalfa turns brown and drops off. For no reason I can see, the rest of the plant withers and dissolves into dust. The blight spreads outward in concentric circles, at speed, until the whole field is brown. A crow falls at my feet, dead. A sere wind begins to blow, carrying with it a dust made of all of the dead plants. If suffocates me, stifling my breath. My hands go to my throat, my mouth open in a fruitless attempt to suck in oxygen but there is none. And then my body begins to crumble, skin turning brown and drifting off flesh, bone following. I try to scream, but without breath this is impossible. A pain lances through my side and I'm awake, sitting upright in my bed and gasping for air. My skin, my bedding are soaked in sweat, my heart is thudding against my ribs.

I feel short of breath and can't get enough, as though I've been swimming under water. Maybe I'm having a heart attack. I'm old enough for that. It could happen. It actually occurs to me to call 911 and to wonder where my cell phone is, but by then my breathing is easing, my heart is slowing, and I'm ready to believe it is only the fear from the dream.

I flick on the lamp at the bedside, letting the warm glow push back the darkness. The closet door is firmly closed, still locked, with the line of salt intact. The cat is sound asleep at my feet, curled up into a furry ball and making a small *mrp* of objection as I jostle him climbing out of bed.

Probably just the dream, then, that makes me feel a cold wave of evil oozing from under the closet door.

Cold water on my face wakes up my brain, settles my nerves. Still, when my phone rings I leap half out of my skin. For a minute I think it's the closet, that whatever is in there is demanding to be let out. But it's my ringtone, I realize at last. Somebody is calling at three a.m., which can't possibly mean anything good.

By the time I get my hands on the phone it's too late. Abel's number.

I hit call back, but there's no answer.

"Come on. Where are you, Abel?"

The feeling from my dream is still with me, oppressive and stifling. This is bullshit. I don't have time for emotions to slow me down, and I brush the mood off and focus. I get to my tablet and check the tag I put on his phone.

What I see makes no sense. It puts him within a couple hundred feet of me. A quick inspection of the Manor floor plan gives me a location.

Cursing my slowness, I get my jeans on. The flashlight is still attached to my belt loop. I don't bother with a holster for my revolver, readying it in my hand.

When I step out into the hallway Vermeer's door stays shut, thank God. No attempts to follow or make conversation. As fast as my stiff muscles will let me, I traverse the hallway, take a sharp right, and knock on the second door down. A minute passes before I hear footsteps and then Chuck appears in the doorway.

He's wearing a robe, loosely tied at the waist, exposing drooping, furry pectorals and an expanse of white belly, unexpectedly tattooed.

Chuck positively leers at me. "Come in. You're more than welcome."

Oh God, no. Disgust comes close to drowning the adrenaline. Against my will my gaze is drawn back to the ink, undoubtedly meant to be a sexy, naked young woman, lying on her back with one arm trailing down inside the band of his boxers. Either he was much thinner when he had it done or his artist sucked. The girl looks bloated and distorted.

"I'm looking for somebody," I say, trying to peer past him into his room.

"Me too." He strokes my arm with the backs of his thick fingers.

"Unless you're hiding a young black man in there, I'm not interested."

His leer gets wider. "Not tonight, but if that's what you're looking for, it can be arranged."

He grabs my arm and pulls me toward him.

"Don't touch me. Just tell me—"

"Come on, sweetheart, don't be like that. I've got wine, I've got—"

Reflex comes easy. I stomp on one bare foot with my boot and then knee him in the groin. Once he's doubled over making inarticulate noises I'm able to look over his head into his room. It's small and crowded with stuffed furniture. No hiding places. The bathroom door is open, the shower curtain pulled back.

I was sure Abel was at this location and am about to start tormenting Chuck for more information when I realize I haven't taken the floors into consideration. Abel is down the ever-loving stairs.

This time I take the elevator.

Downstairs, everything is dark. The common areas are all empty. Following the diagram in my head, I take the requisite turns and wind up outside a door. I don't bother to knock, just fling it open.

Abel lies spread-eagled on the floor with Matt kneeling over him.

A deep cold numbs me, leaching away all emotion. Fear, anger, grief, all dissipate as I phase into a focused detachment. Crime scene. Man down.

102

"What happened?" I sink to my knees on the other side of Abel.

He's not breathing. His heart isn't beating. It's automatic to fall into CPR but I know even as I begin that there's no point. His skin is ice cold and the color of ashes. No blood to be seen anywhere, not even a drop.

"Call 911." So far Matt has been about as useful in this emergency as a wild rabbit, but at least he has opposable thumbs and the dexterity to dial a phone.

Maybe. He looks nearly as drained of blood as Abel, and his hands are shaking so badly that he drops the phone twice before he manages to complete the call. Meanwhile, I continue with the CPR, because that's what you do until the ambulance comes. The compressions are hell on the broken place in my belly. Abel is a muscular man and it takes all my weight and strength to compress his sternum enough to do any good.

"You're going to have to take over."

"I don't think he has any blood in him."

At that I stop and look up at Matt. Then back down at Abel. His eyes are wide open and staring. Mouth twisted in what looks like a silent, ongoing scream. He's not coming back, no matter how many chest compressions I do, how much of my breath I pump into his lungs.

My own breath has a hitch in it.

"Tell me what happened."

"I—heard noises in the hallway. I opened the door and this guy, he—he was standing there, bleeding. I opened the door and he staggered in—" Matt swallows hard and scrubs both hands through his hair.

"And the blood started to disappear."

Matt shudders. "How did you know?"

"Keep talking. What happened next?"

"He sort of gasped, said something like, 'Oh, shit, it's got me,' and then he collapsed. I thought I should try to stop the bleeding, only by then there wasn't any." Matt swallows. "I swear to God when I first saw him there was blood."

"How long ago did this happen? Why didn't you call somebody?"

"It just happened. I mean, he just stopped breathing and then you were here…"

If this is true, the body is colder than it ought to be. There is a neat little slice through Abel's shirt. No blood. There was no visible blood in the hallway, either. I undo the buttons to expose the wound, surprised by the steadiness of my own fingers, always aware of Matt in my peripheral vision.

Between the second and third ribs on the left side I find the wound. It's a clean slice, made with a sharp blade. Putting all thoughts of Abel out of my mind, I explore the hole with my fingers. It runs deep into the chest, but when I withdraw there is no blood. Something clear and viscous clings to my skin.

His white shirt is pristine, save for the cut in the fabric. No bloodstains in the hallway or on the floor around Abel's body. It bothers me that he's lying on his back. The trajectory of collapse would make more sense for him to be facedown.

"Tell me again," I say to Matt, pacing around the body.

Don't think about it being Abel, don't let on that you know him. Stay sharp. Everything is a clue.

While Matt repeats his tale, pretty much word for word as the first time, I take in the details of his room. Much smaller than my suite. Not much bigger than a college dorm room, in fact. Single bed, a twisted mess of sheets and blankets. The wall at the head is a collage of black-and-white art photos. Bedside table, cluttered with magazines and a couple of books. Dresser, also cluttered, the drawers not quite closed. A bookshelf. Dirty clothes in a heap on the floor. Two pairs of shoes, one muddy.

"Did you move the body?"

He blinks. Swallows again. "Was that wrong? He fell on his face—I thought I should do CPR or something so I rolled him over…"

The door bursts open.

First through is Sheriff Callahan, followed by a couple of guys in ambulance uniform. There's a gurney in the hallway. One of them drops to his knees beside Abel and checks for a pulse. "Cold already," he says.

"Yeah," his partner agrees. "We should call the coroner."

"You think? It's the middle of the night. Maybe just transport to the morgue."

"Does that look natural to you?" I show them the wound in Abel's chest.

The guy blinks. He has a steady, open face, and looks a little sick as the reality hits him. "No blood. Somebody cut him after he was already dead. Looks like he's been dead awhile, judging by the body temperature."

"Coroner then. I'll make the calls." The partner steps out into the hallway and speaks into his radio. The first responder starts repacking his equipment.

"Want us to take him into the hospital and have him declared there?"

Jake looks at me, and then at Matt. He kneels down and examines the body. "Hang on just a sec. What happened here?"

"Ask Matt."

Suddenly I'm so exhausted I can barely hold myself upright. Now that the reinforcements have arrived I want only to flee to my room and weep like a child. But there are miles to go before I sleep, and the reality is harsh.

Abel was my only remaining backup. He's gone. And the fact that he was stabbed before the Jelly Thing took him means my life isn't worth beans and I've got nobody to watch my back. I need to find the phone he called me from—last thing I need is to be tracked from the last phone call he made.

While Matt recites his story, again, I make myself useful, digging through pockets for belongings.

"Hey, don't—" Jake starts. Too late. I've compromised his crime scene and we both know it, but I play stupid and he doesn't blow my cover.

"Name's Abel Galloway," I say, thumbing through his wallet as though I don't know perfectly well who he is. "No obvious next of kin or emergency number." Being helpful with the ID of the body is a nice cover for sneaking his FBI creds and cell phone into my pocket.

"I'll take that," Jake says, reaching for the wallet. He's got a cloth in his hand so as not to leave fingerprints. I can't quite read his face but I have a suspicion he might not have missed my little sleight of hand after all. Which is fine. I plan on telling him all about Abel. Later.

"He was packing heat," I say, still with the pretense of being an ignorant civilian. Like me, he carried a revolver. So much less to go wrong when you're dealing with the paras. I don't touch the gun, but I do make a note that he didn't draw it. Which indicates to me that either he knew his attacker or it was somebody he wasn't scared of.

I want a proper autopsy done by somebody in the Paranormal Unit. But that isn't going to happen, or if it does I'll never hear an accurate report. I have a sick, sick feeling building in the pit of my stomach that Abel's death is a result of my phone call. I shouldn't have tried to go up the chain; I should have trusted that he'd get in touch with me sooner or later. Technically it was the para that killed him, but he'd have been dead anyway. Whoever placed that blade knew precisely what they were doing. His chest would have been filling with blood. Cardiac tamponade, collapsed lungs. No good death that way, either, although the horror of the Thing overtaking your body was worse.

I know.

Phil and Abel both dead, which means that any one of the people in this room, this building, this town, could be gunning for me next.

I'm about to retreat to my room, a slightly more defensible position, so I can try to get some perspective, when the door flies open again and Sophie dashes in.

And stops short as though she's run headlong into a sheet of plexiglass.

Her face goes dead white and she puts one hand to her heart. Given her exposure to death and her attitude toward it, I'm pretty sure it's not the sight of Abel that's giving her the problem. For a minute I think the invisible Thing has attacked her, but she's still breathing and moves forward, at last, dropping to her knees beside the body.

"Soph," Jake says, warning.

"What in hell," she mutters. Her hands are shaking. But she's a suspect, like all the rest of them, and I harden my heart.

"What do you see?"

"It's gone," she whispers.

"What's gone? What do you know?" Jake's voice shifts from sympathetic to interrogation.

Sophie's shoulders shudder once and then her face hardens. She lifts her chin and enunciates very clearly.

"His soul. It's gone."

"Isn't that what's supposed to happen?" Matt looks stricken. He's not much older than she is, I realize. Babies, both of them, in way over their heads.

Her huge green eyes meet his. "I'm not saying he's crossed over. I'm saying his soul is gone. Missing. Lost."

"Soul stealer, you think?" I say to Sophie, forcing her to pay attention, to break away from her fixation on Matt.

"Has to be." Her gaze measures me with a new respect.

"There are such things?" Jake asks.

"Such things, and such people." If the Jelly Thing is also a soul stealer we are dealing with a particularly horrible para, a thing I don't know how to fight. Abel's spirit should have either crossed or be floating around here in a ghost form. If it's gone—well, I'm not sure what happens to the balance of things when something is completely destroyed. I'm not sure I want to know.

"But what does that mean?"

Sophie answers. "There's a—fracturing. It hasn't been erased, it's still…out there somewhere. Trapped."

CHAPTER FOURTEEN

Jake meets me right on time at Cup of Joe, but his face is lined with fatigue and I doubt that he slept last night. Both of us are exhausted. I'm still in a healthy stage of denial. I know that Abel is dead, but the pain of it still circles and hasn't come in for a landing yet.

"You brought the book?" Jake asks.

"I said I would."

"People don't always do what they say."

I let that pass, but only long enough to take a healthy swallow of coffee. "Which sort of person are you?"

Jake's face hardens and that predatory light comes into his eyes. "I did what you asked; spent all night looking up the records. I don't like what I found." He takes a swig of the orange juice he ordered and makes a face, looking at it doubtfully. His bowl of oatmeal has gone pretty much untouched.

"If you don't like it, why do you drink it?"

"Vitamins."

"You can get those out of a bottle."

"Sucks getting old," he says, after another meditative sip of the orange juice. "Takes more energy to stand up straight. My joints ache. Doctor is always preaching."

I lean forward, taking a big swig of scalding black coffee and grin at him. "All the more reason to eat what you want."

"You're not into the theory of extending your life by healthy eating and exercise?"

"I'm into the theory that life is precious, and chancy. What if you eat oatmeal and orange juice—which you appear to enjoy about as much as a poke in the eye—and then you get hit by a car in the parking lot? Or stabbed, or have the soul sucked out of you by a paranormal?" I take a bite of chicken fried steak and gravy, savoring the greasy crunch and salt of it.

"So every meal is like a last meal for you."

"Pretty much. The more there is in my body that hurts, the more I figure I deserve a reward for getting up and dealing with the day. Are you going to share the bad news?"

He's staring at my plate, almost drooling. There's no way I'm going to eat all of this, despite my chatter, so I cut off half and pass it over, laying it on top of the despised oatmeal.

A moment, and then he picks the thing up in his fingers and takes a good healthy bite. "You win." He waves at the waitress. When she shuffles over he grins at her. "Coffee, please. Bring cream and sugar."

After he's downed about half the mug she brings him, he pulls a sheet of paper out of a battered soft leather case and puts it on the table in front of me. I scan through it, then look up at him in disbelief. "All of them?"

"Those are the employees that worked up at HUM during the last five years before it shut down."

"And they're all dead."

"Seems a little improbable, I agree."

I go through the list again. Automobile accidents, heart attacks, a house fire, a drive-by gang shooting. "More than a little. There must have been other employees; the Home was open for ten years."

"People didn't quit. I was around here then, even if not as the sheriff. The place was up on the hill and we just…left it alone. But I'll dig deeper. Might be some under-the-table workers." He finishes his coffee, slams it down, and leans toward me, hands on the table. "Are you ready to tell me what you know?"

I'm all out of food and wish I had a cigarette. I look around. The table next to us is engaged in loud chatter. The man at the next one over is Skyping with somebody, completely oblivious to his surroundings.

"Best for you not to know," I say slowly. "If it's what I think, me telling you could be worth your life."

"And you don't think that's my decision to make?"

My throat feels tight, shrunken, and I swallow another mouthful of coffee just to be sure it will go down, despite the fact that my stomach is now unhappy.

"Phil's already dead," I say carefully. "And Abel. Not to mention all the people on that list."

"Who else is on your team?"

When I'm silent, he nods. "You're in this alone. Your teammates are dead. It's a rogue mission and you've got no backup." His voice roughens. "It's my goddamn town. If people keep dying I'm not doing my job. Now—you let me in or I put you in jail."

"You wouldn't."

"Try me."

One long look at his face and I have no doubts. I'm going to have to tell him something and he'll know if it's not the truth. "Not here," I say.

"Where, then?"

"Driving. Not my car, not yours. And not now." I heft the sketchbook out from under the table and hand it over.

Clearing himself a space, he begins paging through it. I watch from upside down. He pauses at the page labeled CHAMELEON VAMP and looks up at me.

"Chameleon?"

"They can appear human. Not all vampires can."

"Old man Vermeer claims he was bitten by one of these."

"Too many *Buffy the Vampire Slayer* episodes," I say lightly. "Most people don't know about the Others."

Jake turns the page and his face darkens.

"What?"

"Ugly bastards."

There's more than that, I think, watching his face, but he's not going to tell me and I let it go.

He keeps turning pages.

"Looking for something in particular?"

He shrugs. "Lots of unexplained deaths in this town. Guy with his throat torn out—got blamed on the neighbor's pit bull, but I doubted the story. A couple of deaths at the Manor seemed off. There's plenty of ghosts." All true, I think, but he's also not telling me something. Which is fine, for now. I have my own secrets.

When he gets to the end he hands the book back. "What's next?"

"I want to talk to Gerald Vermeer."

"Vermeer? Whatever for?"

"Dora had fang marks on her neck."

"You do know he's not really a vampire?"

I shrug. "I know that chameleons don't generally masquerade as little old men. But nothing is impossible."

"Oh, come on."

"He's lived in this town forever and now he lives at the Manor. And, Dora did have puncture wounds on her neck."

For a minute I think he's going to refuse, but then he nods, pulls money out of his pocket. I let him pay for both meals, reminding myself that this is not a date and the man has a budget. Meanwhile I secure the book, taking a minute to look through the last drawings one more time. The soul suckers draw my attention. None of them are invisible.

It's just possible we're dealing with something entirely unprecedented, something that even Phil had never encountered.

And that, all in itself, is disturbing.

CHAPTER FIFTEEN

There's no answer to a knock on the door. Even when Jake calls, "Police! Open up!" there's no sound from within.

"You think he's okay?"

We're both a little jumpy after last night. It must show in my face.

I've got my lock kit in my pocket and it only takes a minute to open the door.

"This I did not just see," Jake says, but he doesn't try to stop me.

Once more, extra loud for the benefit of advanced age and deafness, he shouts, "Sheriff Callahan here! I'm coming in!"

He opens the door, both of us covering with drawn weapons. The main apartment is empty. Jake signals that I should take the bedroom and he'll take the bath, which is clearly the source of an ongoing thudding. I'm not about to miss out on the action and follow right behind.

Vermeer is hanging from the shower rod by a thin cord tied in a slipknot around his neck, pulled so tight it's embedded in the skin. He's mostly naked, wearing only a pair of boxers, his knobby arthritic knees bent a little, feet dangling. He's growing bunions on both big toes and his nails are yellow and clawlike. Every time his body spins the tips of his toes thud against the edge of the tub.

His face is purple and swollen, the eyes open and staring at me. Really staring at me. Focused.

His face crumples into a grimace and his lips move. Of course there's no sound, since his windpipe is completely cut off by the rope, and it takes me a couple of tries before I'm able to lip read what he's trying to say.

"Cut you down? Give me one good reason why I should do that."

But Jake has already surged into action before he truly becomes aware of what it is he's seeing.

"Call dispatch!" he barks at me, grasping the old man about his scrawny naked waist and hoisting him up so the rope is no longer choking him. In theory, anyway. The cord has drawn so tight it doesn't release when the pressure is off.

I make no move to obey, taking note that the skinny chest is not expanding or contracting, there is no heart beating, but those lips are still moving and the eyes are only bulging because of pressure. It's a matter of professional interest. Vampires behave in a predictable fashion, and turning an old man is so far outside their bounds of behavior I don't know what to think.

I'd rather Jake didn't know about my knife, but I suppose we need to cut the old man down. The blade is silver, and the temptation to stick it right smack into that unbeating heart is huge. But we need information, and dead vampires can't talk. So I get out the knife, taking my time, being old and infirm and all, and cut through the cord.

Vermeer and Callahan tumble to the ground in a heap, and the sheriff fumbles at the cord, trying to release it, while the old vampire flails around trying to get up. They are at cross-purposes, which, I confess, I find amusing, so I simply step back and watch them, not intervening.

Jake is not a stupid man, just conditioned by a kind heart and humane responses. He'll cotton on to the truth eventually. It takes longer than I would have thought.

Vermeer manages to extricate himself from beneath his would-be rescuer and gets to his feet, the cord still embedded in his skin. He's clearly not breathing, even as he fumbles at the knot with his crabbed, arthritic fingers. He's standing right in front of the mirror, but there's no reflection.

Jake takes this all in, then shoots me a look of pure venom. "You knew about this."

"I suspected this. I didn't know."

As the truth dawns more fully a new set of emotions washes over him. It's easy enough to see what he's thinking. First, the "If he's really a vampire then he's a threat and could kill us" thought, illustrated by the hand twitching toward his service gun.

This is followed by another glance at the bony, scrawny, naked old fart and the recognition that it's ludicrous to believe the old guy could possibly be a threat. And then the realization that people are dead, and that somebody or something with fangs bit Dora's neck around the time that she died.

Meanwhile, Gerry has managed to free himself and turns to face us—at bay and on the defensive. "Something wrong with knocking?"

"We knocked. You were—busy."

"You might show some gratitude that we saved your sorry life—" Jake catches himself, remembering vampires don't die. I'm beginning to feel sorry for him, remembering the first time I found myself in a situation that defied belief. "Who strung you up?" he says, reverting to the known and familiar, and pulling out his notebook. "Someone in the Manor?"

He still hasn't seen it, and it's time for me to step in. "More to the point," I say, "where are the teeth, Gerry?"

Vermeer grins toothlessly. "Don't have any."

"Old liar." I start my search, beginning with the bathroom drawers.

He blocks them with his body. "I don't see a search warrant."

"Vampires have no rights," I say, casually. "Step aside, or I'll put a bullet in you."

"Hang on just a minute," Callahan says, laboring to catch up. "Didn't somebody try to kill him just now? Although I suppose you can't kill somebody who is technically undead."

"I welcome your bullet!" Vermeer says, spreading his arms wide. He looks so frail standing there, but I remember the shadow I felt, the moment of power, the first night I visited him here.

"It's a silver bullet and I plan on missing your heart. Not sure if you're fully up to date on the discomfort of having a silver bullet lodged in your vampire flesh, but it's not the quick death your were hoping for."

At that, Vermeer stands a little straighter, but doesn't say anything. I take this as permission and leave the bathroom to search a little wider. It's not hard to find what I'm looking for. He's actually soaking the dentures in a little cup by his bed, with one of those effervescent packets open beside it. An act so normal, so expected, for a man of his years.

The teeth, however, are not.

I fish the top plate out of the water, trying not to recoil from the touch of somebody else's slimy mouth leavings on my fingers, and show them to Jake. For the most part, they are normal, ordinary dentures, with one notable exception. The eyeteeth are long and needle sharp.

"How do you keep from getting your own tongue with these?" I'm genuinely curious.

Jake is all cop now. "Do you think these match the marks on the body?"

"Possible. Sounds like a visit to Sophie is in order." I turn on Vermeer, not that I've ever had him out of my line of sight. I'm honestly not sure how fast he can move, how much of this old man act of his is legit.

He's sitting in his wheelchair, looking ancient and tired, his chin sagging on his breast as though he lacks the energy to hold it up.

"Did you kill Dora, Mr. Vermeer?" Callahan is past the mercy stage, but he still can't bring himself to be rude to an elder. I don't have this issue; I can be rude to anybody with aplomb.

"Well, Vermeer? Did she scream while you were sucking her blood?" Both hands planted on the arms of his wheelchair, I lean right into the old man's face. He doesn't have his fangs in, and I'm trusting that Callahan will back me up if some other superpower comes into play. "Or are you going to tell me she liked it?"

"I didn't kill her! I bit, I tasted, I left her alone. I never suck them dry."

For sure, I thought there was nothing in the world that could still make me shudder in revulsion, but those words from his chapped, old, toothless mouth make me want to gag.

It's enough to bring Jake into the new reality, though. "What about Mary Sanders? Two months ago, now, she died. I never thought to look for a vampire bite."

Vermeer shakes his head, vehemently. "No. She was alive when I left her."

"How many 'snacks' are you taking?" I lean forward a little more, just enough so that the silver cross I wear dangles close to his face.

He shrinks back. "I drink blood from a bag—you know that."

"But it's not enough, is it? Doesn't quite satisfy the craving?" A thought comes to me, a memory. "I noticed Alma wearing a scarf yesterday at breakfast. She's not exactly a fashion princess. What did you do—go in while she was sleeping?"

At that he sits up a little straighter in his chair. "Alma is doing research for one of her books. She likes to play."

"Dear God, your wife must be rolling over in her grave." Jake doesn't bother to hide his disgust. "How long has this been going on? Did she know?"

"You leave Lucille out of this—you hear me? It has nothing to do with her!"

"Unless you killed her too. If we exhume her body, what are we going to find?"

"Don't you dare."

Vermeer is on his feet. He's still old and gnarly but that dark power I sensed is no longer hidden. He seems to expand to fill up more space, hands reaching out for Jake's throat. The world darkens.

"Oh, for God's sake. What are you going to do, gum him to death?" I step between them, and give Vermeer a shove in the chest. "What do you expect us to think when you go around feeding off old women?" I was going to say "defenseless," but then Alma comes to mind, and the mental image of well over three hundred pounds of erotic romance writer makes me drop the word.

The old man crumples back into his chair. Tears fill his eyes, faded and rheumy once again, and leak out over his cheeks. "I didn't kill my wife. I loved her—"

I want to believe him. He's still wearing his wedding ring; the tears look genuine enough. But I've never known a vamp to retain a soul. "Vampires don't love." I keep it matter-of-fact. Watch him. He doesn't bother to protest, but the tears keep on flowing. Watching an old man cry is not a lovely thing, not at all like a fresh-eyed young girl spilling tears on TV and looking even more beautiful for her sadness.

Nope. Vermeer was an ugly old man to begin with, and the crying just makes it worse.

"So who tried to hang you?" Callahan demands. "Can't imagine any of the women you've been bleeding have the strength. Did somebody talk? Family, friends. Betty? God, you haven't been putting vampire moves on Betty—"

"Nobody strung him up," I say, looking into the bathroom again. "He did it himself."

"What?"

"This is an elaborate suicide setting. Note the music and the flowers and the bottle of wine."

"But he can't—"

"Precisely."

Vermeer doesn't answer. Just sits in that chair looking miserable and wretched. And naked. I toss him a blanket and he huddles under it but he's shivering. His skin has gone dead white and I know what he needs.

"Where is it?"

"Fridge."

"Where is what?" Callahan is in over his head and knows it, but he doesn't throw a fit when I locate a bag of blood in the fridge, fill up a large tumbler, and hand it over to the old man.

Vermeer's hands are shaking so badly he can't hold the glass without spilling, and I help him drink. One glass down and the shakes resolve into a mild tremor. His chin is stained with blood and there are dribbles over his chest.

I pour him another helping and let him drink it himself.

"What are you going to do with me?"

Fair question. I look at Jake. He looks at me.

Not much you can do with a vampire, besides stake him. We have no grounds to arrest him. Although we could make a case for insanity by telling a truth nobody would believe, he'd be a danger to others in a mental hospital.

"Suppose we just all pull up chairs and Mr. Vermeer explains to us how and when he came to be a vampire in the first place."

"Don't care to talk about it."

"Talk anyway."

The old man's eyes glitter with something far from tears. Even so, I sense the echoes of grief and try to be polite.

"Have you ever been married, Maureen?"

"I have. Not that it's any of your business. Why?"

"Just wondering what sort of poor bastard would sign up for that life."

Jake snorts, and I feel an itch to shoot the pair of them, mostly because they have a point. I'm not prime marriage material, and it's no big surprise that Ed found himself a new woman. It's the type of woman that's the biggest problem—that and the fact that his timing is totally off.

"Evasion will get you nowhere, Mr. Vermeer. Please proceed."

He sighs, heavily, and his body sinks in on itself again so he looks like a pile of rags huddled into an expensive wheelchair.

"Long, long ago, there was this woman…"

I've stopped listening to the words, other than picking up the general *blah, blah, blah* of a man seduced and turned by a vampire. His body language is screaming things that have nothing at all to do with what's coming out of his mouth.

Fear. It's written all over him. But there's something more than that. When he opens his mouth to speak there's a catch in his jaw, a hesitation on his lips. Almost like watching a movie where action and speech are slightly out of sync.

"So she invited me to her room, and that was when—"

"Now how about the truth?"

Vermeer jerks like a puppet whose operator has just suffered a seizure.

Jake grins, teeth white and sharp. "All lies, Gerry. Aren't they?"

The old man passes a shaking hand over his face, slow motion. "What am I…" His voice trails away. He reaches for the sheriff's arm with a palsied hand. "Jake. Who is this woman? Why are you here?"

Jake's gaze shifts to me, brows lifted in a question.

"Still faking. He's scared. Tell the truth, or we'll lock you in the basement."

Just like that, the palsy stops and his eyes flare red. "You wouldn't dare."

"Wouldn't bother me in the slightest. You doubt me?"

"What's in the basement?" Jake's sudden intensity is a little alarming and the old man laughs at this.

"That's got your interest, doesn't it, my boy?"

"Cut the bullshit," I tell him. "You're already in as much danger as you're ever going to be in. You know that, right? Besides, you're wanting to die so maybe you tell us, and maybe we help you."

A moment, and he sags back in the chair.

"Fine. You win." He's quiet for a minute but I leave him be this time. His face has the look of somebody going back in memory, searching out the story line.

"I was a tax accountant," he says finally, as if the point is self-evident.

"What's that got to do with anything?"

He looks at me with great dignity. "Listen, missy, you want the tale, you'll get it. In my own good time."

"Okay," Jake prompts. "You were a tax accountant. I remember that. You worked for most of the big businesses in town."

"Including the Shadow Valley Home for Unwed Mothers." The words seem to burn the old man's tongue, and he actually scrubs at this mouth with the back of his hand.

Foreboding creeps over me. I'm not going to like what's coming.

"What do you know about HUM?" the old man asks, after a long silence.

"We know that the employees have all been rather—unfortunate," Jake says.

Vermeer nods his head and I have a thought. "Your wife?"

He twists the ring hanging loose on his knobby finger. "She was a warning."

Jake doesn't like this. "Oh, come on, Gerry. She was eighty-five. She had a heart attack."

"Yep. And the day before that heart attack I told her…" His voice fades and his gaze turns to the window, where he's staring at nothing. "I signed a confidentiality agreement not to ever disclose to anybody any information about the place. It was easy for me to keep quiet. I didn't actually work up there. What did I know, really? Only lists of things that don't make sense. Expense reports, lists of equipment. Things that don't add up. What does a place like that need with test tubes and chemicals?" He drags the back of his hand across his eyes. "Years I kept it all quiet. Years."

"What made you tell her?"

"Numbers. Numbers didn't add up. There was the census—every girl who went there was pregnant, right? And there were the adoption lists. What happened to the other babies?"

"What do you mean?" Jake has that intensity about him again.

"Too many dead babies," Gerry says at last. "The charge for disposal of the dead ones. Way too high. And there were too many. Plus all those adoptions and so few adoption costs. Tax evasion, I always told myself. Who isn't guilty of a little tax evasion?"

"Until?"

"Until the place closed down. Until the employees started dying off. So I mentioned it to my wife. You need to tell somebody, she said. And the next day she was dead. But then I thought—what else do I have to lose? What do I want with my life now that she is gone? So I told."

"Who? Who did you tell?"

"I don't know. It was a long time ago. I called the FBI. There was a shuffle from one person to another, and then I talked to this nice-seeming lady."

"Her name, Vermeer. Think."

"Flowers. Something to do with flowers."

"First or last?"

"Never got her first. Gardner, maybe? Although I thought at the time it was an odd last name and Gardner is normal."

I flip back through my memory banks. "Iris, maybe?"

He levels a finger at me. "Bingo! I remember thinking of her as purple to remember."

I know this lady. She was part of the paranormal team, but already old when I came on board. Should have been dead a long time ago, not taking calls from concerned citizens.

Vermeer licks dry lips and wrings his hands together. This is hard for him to tell, and hard for me to listen to, because I know what's coming. I wish I didn't, but I do. To quell the itching of nerves in my own hands, I get up and fetch him another drink.

Jake can't help a noise of disgust as the old man smacks his lips over his beverage.

"You think I asked for this?" Vermeer demands, waving the glass. "You think I wanted to be this—thing? I was going to die. That was the plan."

"What happened?" I keep my voice calm, encouraging. Because even though I know the ending of his tale, I need him to tell me. And I need for Jake to hear.

"I planned my death. Best to take myself out before the bad guys came for me, and why would I want to go on living without Lucille? Best make the last night special, I thought. And I couldn't do it at home, with her spirit maybe watching me. So I rented a room in a nice hotel in Spokane. I'm in the bar and this girl comes on to me. She's all big eyes, breasts almost spilling out of her top. Me, I think my days are done, but she touches me and I—well, I find that I'm not quite dead yet. I've been drinking, to make the death easier. Maybe she spiked my drink. The world seems very unreal, all of a sudden, and I'm floating in it. She takes my hand and the next thing I know for sure I'm already half across the bar, following her. We go up to my room and she…" There's a roughness in his throat. He coughs and starts over. "She disrobes and starts touching me. By now there's an alarm in my head somewhere—beautiful young woman like this, old wretch like me—and I think maybe she's a hooker who's going to steal all my money. But I can't move by now, can't run or fight, and next thing I know she's not a beautiful girl at all."

He shudders. "Ever seen one of those things?"

"Looking at one now," I remind him.

"No, I mean really see one? Not when it's pretending to be human? All shrunken leathery skin and fangs and these eyes that glow…"

"Yes, I've seen one. More than one."

"Well, she bites me, and there's pain, but also this pleasure that…" His expression turns crafty. "Pleasure that a lady like you would never understand."

I'm not so sure about that, but I'm not going to enlighten him.

"What happened then?" Jake's mask slips, a pure, clean rage shining through. No chivalrous noises of trying to protect me from this crass behavior, which I appreciate.

"Anyway. It's so intense I actually lose consciousness. And when I wake up—"

"She's gone."

"Yes, she's gone. But at that point I'm thinking, no big deal. For some reason I don't remember that part with the fangs and the biting, only the part where she was taking off her clothes. One last fling. I don't think Lucille will mind, and I want to get on with it, to be with her. So I follow through with my plan. I couldn't abide the thought of hanging and pills seemed too easy. I didn't have a gun and I figured a gunshot in the hotel would cause too much commotion."

"So you slit your wrists."

"My throat, actually."

He tilts back his head and runs his finger straight down his jugular. Now I can see a thin white scar. Unless he only cut skin deep that should have done it, all right.

"And?"

"I went to the mirror to do it and I couldn't see myself. That totally freaked me out at first. I thought I wasn't real, that maybe I was dreaming. But I told myself that if I was dreaming it was no big deal and if I was awake even better, and I just figured out where the vein was and cut. Who needs a mirror?"

"But you didn't die."

"No," he whispered. "I didn't die. There was a lot of blood, but I didn't feel any different. It bled for a bit and then just healed over. Housekeeping came in hours later and found me and all the blood. They called an ambulance. I was raving, trying to tell people I was a vampire, but nobody would listen. I've been crazy old Vermeer ever since."

The perfect way to silence somebody and punish them all at once. Who would listen to an old guy who claimed to be a vampire? And if he wanted to die but was doomed to live undead forever as an old man? Diabolical.

"And the teeth?" Jake is restraining himself with difficulty. I'm not sure whether the anger is directed toward the old vampire or elsewhere, but I make a note that I don't want it ever coming in my direction.

Vermeer waves a hand dismissively and sighs. "Oh, those. Mail-order dentures."

Fair or not fair, I remind myself, he is a vampire. And I'm pretty damn sure he's not been confining himself to his bags of blood.

"So what happened with Dora?"

"I tell you my tale of tragedy and woe and that's all you can think of?"

"What did you do, old man?"

"She was willing. She'd been reading vampire romances and was willing to overlook my inadequacies in the handsome young man department. I bit her, I sucked a little blood. And then I left. Maybe she had a heart attack."

"And Alma?"

"We play. She's doing research for her book."

"Quite a tale," Jake says. "What do you think, Maureen?"

"I think you and I need to have that talk we discussed earlier. Can you arrange it?"

"I can."

"You should also have a look at this." I open the secret door in the back of the closet, but I know that if I go down those stairs one more time I'm not going to make it back up, so I just stand there, holding the door.

He hesitates, not quite trusting me.

This stings for a second, but mostly I'm glad he's being careful. I don't know that I'd go down with him standing at the top holding a secret door, accompanied by a vampire. Even an old and mostly toothless one.

Our eyes meet and I'm about to voice the fear for him when I catch myself. Am I really about to acknowledge that my body won't let me go down and up a flight of stairs?

"Right behind you," I say instead.

He nods and takes the first step. I follow, cursing myself and my pride all the way down. But I really couldn't let him go down alone, not with the Jelly Thing lurking. Even though I have no idea how to kill it when it shows up. By the time we hit the bottom of the stairs all my senses are on high alert, feeling for trouble. I let Jake explore it for himself—the hallway, the rooms, the laboratory with its metal table and outdated equipment. "How did you find this?" he asks, his back to me.

Something raw and primal in his voice keeps me from the lie I try to tell him. "Phil left a few clues."

"So this is why he bought this place?"

We need to talk. Not here. So I shrug, even though he can't see me. "Maybe." The stairs look like a mountain to me and I can't imagine doing the butt-scoot routine while this man watches me. Neither do I want his help, which leaves me at a bit of an impasse.

"This isn't the whole basement," he says, walking to the center wall.

"There's another passage from my room. Leads to the rest of

the basement—water heater, storage. Normal, mundane things."

"So why does it need a secret passage?"

"The wall was put up when they renovated."

"But why not just get rid of this altogether?"

He turns to look at me then, and a cold finger traces its way up my spine. I see it now. Somebody wants to use this space. Maybe somebody is using it now. But for what? That is the million-dollar question.

Jake seems to be considering that question, although he's looking at me. "What happened to your leg?"

This was not the question I was expecting. "Bullet. Shattered the bone—all full of hardware."

"And this happened when?"

I tell him.

"And you're traipsing around like you're twenty-five and bulletproof. Are you insane?"

"Definitely not bulletproof."

"So if I offer you a hand up the stairs, can we do that without you hating me forever? Good God, woman. What are you trying to prove?"

I'm not even going to begin answering that question, but fortunately he doesn't seem to expect a response. "Let's go. We've got work to do." He tucks an arm around my waist and I grab at him to keep my balance. His arm is steady, his hand warm even through my shirt. Amazing how much easier that first step is with a little lift and support, though, and he's so matter-of-fact about the whole thing I find I'm not particularly humiliated by accepting a little help.

When we get to the top he lets me go and before I can head it off I feel a pang of loss and the loneliness of my interrupted nightmare descends. Which is ridiculous, of course, and I shake it off.

Vermeer sits waiting for us and Jake just shakes his head. "So what do we do with him?"

"If we keep the teeth he can't bite anybody."

If he's telling the truth, of course. If he doesn't have other—

gifts. We can't take the chance of him harming one of the residents.

Speaking of which, there's a tap at the door and it cracks open.

Crazy Alice pokes her head in, sees me. A smile begins to form at the corners of her mouth, then stops, an unfolding bud nipped by frost as she sees Vermeer. Her soft bottom lip begins to tremble. "I didn't tell," she says, tears welling. "I swear I didn't tell."

CHAPTER SIXTEEN

Alice won't get in the elevator.

This is the most rational behavior she's shown since I came to the Manor. I don't like elevators either. But I have to take my chances because I'm not going to make it down the stairs. I can't abandon Alice here, terrified as she is. She's beside herself, her body trembling, tears pouring down her face. If she could tell me what she's so scared of, maybe I could fix it. Or maybe I'd be scared too.

In the meantime, if I need to go downstairs, then I need to take the elevator, and she needs to come with me.

"Look." I put both hands on her shoulders. "I'm going to give you something that will keep you safe, okay?"

She sniffles and wipes the back of one hand over her nose. But her sobs calm a little and I take this as a good sign. Unfastening the chain that holds my silver cross, I put it around her neck. "This is my special talisman. It keeps the bad guys away. A vampire like Gerry Vermeer can't come near you when you're wearing this."

One of her hands touches the cross, then clutches it.

Her sobs have stopped, and she nods. "You won't let it get me?"

"I'm not going to let anything hurt you. Now, come on. Let's go get breakfast."

She's still sniffly and reluctant, but with the cross draped around her neck, and me holding one of her hands, she allows me to lead her onto the elevator and off in search of food.

There is no breakfast in the dining room. Not so much as a cup of bad coffee or a container of yogurt to be seen. The room is full of people sitting restlessly, drinking water and dropping silverware and napkins. I push Alice toward her chair and slip into mine.

"My watch must be wrong. When's breakfast?"

Chuck makes absolutely no acknowledgment that he came on to me in the hallway last night. Pulling on the gold chain ostentatiously pinned to his jacket, he draws out a pocket watch, which he consults at length. "Breakfast is generally at nine. It is now 9:47—"

"And you've all just been sitting here for forty-seven minutes?"

"Exactly what I've been saying. It's inexcusable," Julia says in her affected accent. "They should charge less money if they can't even deliver meals on time."

Sheep, I remind myself. Be a shepherd. This very nearly chokes a laugh out of me, which wouldn't be much more helpful than violence with a woman like Julia.

"You all do know that there was a murder here last night, right?"

I can't imagine that gossip of that sort hasn't made its way through the ranks.

"I agree with Julia—there's no excuse for poor service," Ginny says. And then quickly adds, "Although of course it's very sad."

Alice moans, rocking back and forth in her chair.

"I really don't see why death should interrupt the food supply."

Chuck has a point. Food shows up for funerals and wakes. There's no reason why anybody should starve.

I'm thoroughly disgusted with the lot of them, but since the Manor belongs to me, the responsibility to make sure the sheep are fed and safe is now mine. The "safe" part is a little tenuous right now, so the least I can do is make sure they get regular meals.

"Why don't I go see what's wrong with the cook?"

Nobody tries to stop me, or even chimes in with an "Oh, good idea!"

It's not far to Matt's room, and I already know where it is.

I knock on the door. No answer.

By now worry begins to wind its tendrils around my heart. I left him here alone last night, without knowing where the Thing had gone, or who the murderer was.

Well, technically, I didn't. He ended up driving Sophie home, but still.

His door is unlocked. The instant it cracks open a foul odor swells out into the hallway, made up of sweat, alcohol, and dirty sheets. Matt lies naked on his belly in a tangle of bedding, motionless, legs and arms splayed wide. His back is tanned; his naked white buttocks look vulnerable.

"Matt! Wake up!" I'm not much for whispering and I say it with energy and force, but still not so much as the twitch of a finger.

The portraits above the head of the bed all seem to be staring, eyes following me as I step into the room. The clock measures my steps toward the bed, *tick, tick, tick.*

No sign of injury or even struggle. I look for signs of breath but don't see any movement at all. The room looks about the same as it did last night, with the addition of a fifth of MacNaughton on the bedside table, mostly empty.

At last I reach out and put my hand on his bare shoulder. "Matt!"

He is warm to my touch, and surges upward, yelling, "What the hell?"

The force of his sudden rising catches me unprepared. I totter for a minute, fighting vainly for balance, and then topple over backwards like a fallen tree. It takes a minute to get breath back into my lungs, and I lie still, scanning my body mentally for damage. Wonder of wonders, all seems to still be intact. A few new bruises, nothing broken.

It's an interesting vantage point.

"Did you maybe want to put some pants on?"

"Seems you might expect a little nakedness if you barge into a guy's room while he's sleeping."

He is quite a lovely young man, top to bottom. I'm not too old to notice, but I am too old to be much bothered. Not true that once you've seen one you've seen them all, but there does come a point where the naked male body no longer carries the ability to shock and embarrass.

"I thought you were dead." Grunting with pain and effort, I work on levering myself to my feet, remembering the days when getting off the floor was as easy as breathing. Which was easier then, too.

Matt has the grace to look ashamed. He turns his back and pulls on a pair of sweatpants.

"What are you doing here?"

I decline to explain myself. "The natives are getting restless. No breakfast. Personally, I'm just hoping for coffee."

"Oh, shit," he says, clutching his head. "Shit, shit, shit. I'm so fired. Is Betty totally pissed?"

"She will be. The dead are mourned, the living fired. It's a rule."

"God. It really happened, didn't it?"

His face has gone a horrible color and it's a good thing there's a trash can close at hand. When he's done vomiting I throw him a dirty towel, picked up from the mess on his floor. He wipes his face, rakes his fingers through his hair, and looks up at me.

"I was drinking last night."

"Obviously."

"Not until after I took Sophie home. I was completely sober until then."

"Did you kiss her goodnight?"

He stares at me, the picture of misery. "No."

Oh, but he wanted to. It's all there in his face. "She's a little young for you. Did she invite you in, show you around?"

His face hardens, and I'm suddenly very aware of my weakened physical state. I feel small and vulnerable and figure I'd better not push him too hard. Still. There are questions to be asked.

"I'm not a perfect man but I have some decency."

"And you came home when?"

His mouth twists, ever so slightly. His eyes slide sideways and up, as though looking for inspiration in the photos above the bed. "What's with the interrogation?"

I shrug. "Curious."

"Are you law enforcement or what? Seems like it's none of your business."

"The guy who was killed last night," I say, carefully. "His name was Abel. I knew him. And Phil Evers was my friend." I'm watching for a reaction.

He lifts his hands, lets them fall back.

"I'm sorry about your loss," he says finally. "And I'm sorry that I'm probably out of a job. Don't know what I ought to do next."

"I suggest you make the people some breakfast. And me some coffee."

"Look, I need this job. If you have any pull at all…"

"Do I look like I have pull?"

He fumbles around on the counter and comes up with a bottle of ibuprofen, swallowing a handful dry. "Actually, you do."

I shake my head. "New kid on the block. Humble resident of the Manor and not entirely welcome here. You're on your own."

He splashes some water over his face and runs a comb through his hair. "God. Maybe it would be better if I were dead. Now, are you ready to vacate my room?"

Obviously he's not inclined to leave me here alone to snoop, which is disappointing but understandable. And fine. I can always come back later.

• • •

An hour later, and Matt has cleaned himself up and put together a brunch worthy of considerably more preparation. No way should I be hungry again, but I'm ravenous. Lunch, I tell myself. I was up early.

The food is good, but the coffee is better. It burns all the way down to my stomach, a line of heat that means all pain sensors are active and functioning. Life is pain, as the Man in Black told us, and for the first time since I woke up in a hospital bed with tubes sprouting out of every part of my body, I think maybe I'm grateful for it. Planting my elbows on the table, mostly to annoy Ginny and Julia, I inhale the aroma of bacon and pan-fried potatoes. My stomach gurgles its approval.

Betty, who was noticeably not here earlier this morning, is busy reasserting her control of the situation, clattering around with cups and plates and making a racket. A bit ago she was shrilling at

Matt in the kitchen with a volume and pitch that must have sent his hangover into orbit.

Now she stops by my chair. "We can move you into the other room today. It's been all cleaned." She talks loud and very slow, as though I'm deaf and also stupid.

I eat another piece of bacon, perfectly crisp. "I'm not moving."

"You can't stay in the suite—"

"Actually, I can. I plan to."

"But—"

No better time than the present to spring the news. I blot my mouth with a napkin, fold it, and lay it back on the table. Then, speaking clearly so they will all hear me, I tell her.

"As it turns out, I'm the new owner of the Manor. And I've taken a fancy to the suite."

A moment of shock. Everybody stares at me, forks halfway to mouths. And then Betty pats my shoulder. "That's nice, dear. We'll talk about it later. Eat your breakfast."

I've had about enough of Betty and her casual condescension. "You don't like old people, do you?"

"I don't know what you—"

"Just because I'm older—not even officially retirement age, mind you—you assume I must be incompetent, rather than that an old friend might actually have left me something in his will. I suggest you be very careful, if you plan to stay here."

Maybe I shouldn't have said it in public, but she treats them all this way, with a visible distaste for their age and a dismissal of their worth as human beings. Even though my tablemates are not the type of people I'd care to hang out with, they deserve better. With the possible exception of Chuck.

Not hungry anymore, I push back my chair. "All right, then. Official announcement coming soon. News at four."

CHAPTER SEVENTEEN

Around noon, Jake shows up in a rental car.

He's out of uniform, but the jeans and T-shirt make him look more serious rather than more relaxed. But then, maybe that's the subject matter at hand. My heart does a treacherous little backflip at the sight of him.

Once in the car, doors closed, radio on to make us harder to hear in case someone has managed to plant a bug, he gives me a long, assessing look. "You sure this isn't an overreaction?"

"I'm sure."

We're quiet then, for a bit, while he gets us out of town and onto an untraveled road, while I search for the words that will open the secret that has been lodged in my gut for twenty years. It's settled there, grown in. Dislodging it feels like major surgery.

"So, it's bad then," Jake says.

"What do you think about paranormals?"

"I don't know what you're asking."

"Where do they come from? Are they a natural phenomenon? Are they aliens? Demons? Did somebody somewhere mess with the genome and create them?"

"If a thing is going to kill you, does it matter where it came from?"

The answer to which should be simple, but it isn't.

• • •

Twenty-five years old, and I'm full of questions about paranormals. Not surprising, since I'm involved in regular hunts and exterminations and nobody seems to know anything about them. Most of the people in my unit have some sort of special ability. They can see the invisible, or have psychic abilities, or whatever. My only claim to fame is that it takes a lot to scare me.

I ran into a paranormal scenario by accident as a brand-new rookie on a more mainstream FBI unit. Vampires. They didn't scare me much and I was able to keep my head clear while more experienced agents were running for cover. A little creative staking, a couple of dead vampires, and I found myself transferred, willy-nilly, into one of the FBI's secret branches. It's called Paranormal Relations, PR for short, but there's precious little relating and a whole lot of killing.

It doesn't take long before I develop a reputation as the chick who will run in where angels fear to tread, and this leads me to Phil Evers.

He's damn near mythical in the division. Agents hero worship his fearlessness and his brain. As if that's not enough, he's diabolically good-looking, with a reputation as a fabulous, if not constant, lover. He's referred to behind his back as 007. To his face, he's Mr. Evers or Sir.

Phil is looking for a female partner on an undercover case and takes a chance on me, totally based on recommendations. It turns out we have incredible chemistry, both as work partners and in the sack, where we inevitably end up. We work together off and on, and it always ends with a night somewhere.

I'm well aware I am not the only woman in his life, but I'm still head over heels under his spell, daydreaming about the day he'll realize that I am so much more than just a casual lover. So when he invites me into a partnership for a new venture I'm ready to sign up without paying any attention to details of the job.

Paranormal Research Facilitator.

How can you go wrong with a title like that?

Instead of blasting paras into smithereens, we'll be trying to take the critters alive and transport them to a research facility where their structure and origins can be studied. Maybe we can learn to contain them, or at least find better ways to kill them. Maybe I'll finally learn what they are and where they come from.

It all sounds good and noble with a healthy dose of exotic adventure thrown in. Not to mention more time with Phil.

Phil refers to the whole thing as Project Paranormal, and it's tucked away in an underground cave in Nevada, a hundred miles from anywhere. We meet in Vegas, not in a casino hotel but in a little dive off the strip, where he presents me with a stack of confidentiality agreements.

I'm ready to dive in and start signing my life away, but Phil puts his hand on top of the stack and looks me directly in the eye. "This is serious business, Maureen. You read every word. And you think hard before you sign."

His intensity makes me uneasy, and the content of the papers doesn't help. They make it clear I must never speak of the lab or the project to anybody. Not to my mother or my grandmother or my priest, not even my dog. No mention of pain of death, but I read it between the lines.

Since I don't talk to my mother, my grandmother is dead, and I lack both priest and dog, I figure there's not too much to lose.

I look up at Phil, who is sitting across the room, watching me. "You signed this shit?"

He nods. His face has gone very still.

"Have you seen the place? I'm not asking you to tell me about it or talk about it, I was just..."

His lack of response unnerves me and I trail off into silence.

Still he doesn't speak, and I sign. This is the opportunity of a lifetime and I'm not about to quibble over the terms. As I lay down the pen, my hands are just a little bit slippery with sweat, my pulse a shade faster than usual. Without a word I hand over the stack and he slips it into his briefcase and gestures toward the door.

As I open it, and the desert heat blasts into my face, I hear his voice behind me saying, "No. No, I haven't seen it yet."

• • •

A cold breeze blows in through the window of the rental car, pulling me back from the heat of the desert. The man sitting behind the wheel has that same still, waiting look on his face that Phil wore all those years ago.

"So you committed to silence and you haven't talked about this in what—thirty years?"

"Thirty-three."

"I need a smoke. You got one?"

"I've corrupted you."

But I pull out the smokes and we step out of the car into the cold sunlight of a fall afternoon and lean on the hood.

"You're going to tell me about the lab now, right?"

"Can't argue with fate."

Still, I can't help looking around to make sure nobody is around to listen. Jake had the good sense to stop in a place where cell towers will be useless, where even a satellite feed would have some trouble in the shade of the sheer cliff that backs us. The only possible approach is up the road that winds away below us, visible for miles.

It still feels terribly dangerous to talk.

• • •

If the paperwork hasn't already scared me out of any schoolgirl fantasy notions about the lab, the security finishes the trick. The place is invisible from above—any airplane or helicopter flying over is going to see nothing but unbroken desert. Not even barbed wire or guard stations. They aren't needed.

A driver picks us up in a black Suburban with heavily tinted windows and drives us for miles on unmarked roads. When we finally roll to a stop I see nothing but desert stretching away in all directions, and when the driver tips his hat and drives away, leaving a trail of dust behind him, I think maybe they've decided to dispose of us and have left us here to die.

Phil stands with his hands in his pockets, stoic and unconcerned, and about half a minute later a man walks right out of the earth, or so it seems. He is all business and looks military—khakis, crew cut, and dog tag. When he's satisfied himself as to our credentials, including fingerprints on a handheld electronic scanner, he motions for us to follow him around a small hillock.

On the other side I now see the door built right into the side of the hill, shored up with stone. He types in a password, performs a retinal scan, and then manually turns a wheel. "Some of the paras can shapeshift," he explains. "We employ multiple levels of security at every entry point."

As soon as the door is open, revealing a dimly lit tunnel, I see he means this. There are marines stationed on either side of the door, weapons at the ready. One of them has a rifle. The other one is carrying something that is a complicated array of tubes and pressure valves. I'm dying to ask what it is and what it does, but we're hurried on down the tunnel to the next passage.

This looks like plexiglass. A low-level hum alerts me to something electrical. There's also a visible cage of laser beams.

"Quite the gauntlet," Phil says.

"Yes, sir. Can't take any chances of escapees or intruders."

More fingerprints. Computerized passwords. Retinal scans.

"Okay. You'll have exactly twenty seconds to get through each level before it reactivates. We have no manual control to delay that. Understand?"

I don't like this. "What happens if we don't make it? I mean, say I twist an ankle or something?"

"Don't," the marine says. "Ready?"

The lasers shut off.

"Go."

Without so much as looking at me, Phil strides forward. Not a male protective instinct in his body, which is fine by me. I follow. The buzz behind me as the lasers turn back on raises the hairs on the back of my neck but we clear the area with plenty of time to spare.

The plexiglass lifts.

We walk through.

Next is a heavy steel door. Another marine stands at this

checkpoint, and he also asks for our credentials. Then he pushes a button and the door slides upwards. There are sharp metal teeth all along the bottom. If that comes crashing down on my head there will be no visiting the lab. Or anything else. Ever.

It's also a longer distance this time.

"Go."

We go. Side by side. Phil doesn't run or look like he's even breaking a sweat. I stride along beside him, ticking off the seconds in my head. We make it through with five seconds to spare. Behind us the metal door clangs shut.

One more door, this one just an ordinary laboratory security door that opens to a fingerprint and retinal scan from each of us. On the other side of it we are greeted by a pleasant-looking, middle-aged woman. Her blonde hair is pulled back into a neat twist, her glasses perched on her nose. She's wearing a lab coat and carries a clipboard. Just like any ordinary scientist in any ordinary lab.

She holds out a hand, first to Phil and then to me. I don't like the way she looks at him, but then every woman looks at him that way.

"I'm Dr. Sorenson," she says, in a low and carefully modulated voice. "Welcome to Project Paranormal."

Something about the way she says it alerts me that she is more than a research assistant assigned to show the new blood around. Her voice caresses the name of the lab, and she's old enough to be senior research staff. I wonder what she's done to be relegated to tour duty, but she seems to be enjoying herself, so maybe it's not punishment at all.

"Follow me, please, and stay close."

She leads us a short distance down the passage and then into a large room full of plexiglass cages.

"This is our main collection area, where the paranormals are studied without interference. They are fed at regular hours and allowed to sleep according to their schedule. As you can see, we have all the common varieties here, as well as some rare species."

It is quite a collection indeed, and we are given time to walk between the cages, as though at a zoo viewing the exhibits. I'm already familiar with some of the specimens. The common vampire, for instance, and a number of more exotic strains. Werewolves, werecats, and other shifters, including a freakish toadman with huge goggling eyes. There are a few creatures that look like the demons in medieval paintings—horns and reptilian skin and misshapen phalluses too big to ever safely enter a woman.

Each is contained in a cage just big enough to allow for small movements.

"If we don't allow for sufficient movement they become ill," our guide says. "Too much, and they become dangerous."

Phil stops to look at a female of the common werewolf. She's in her human form, crouched at the edge of her cage, knees pulled up to her chest, arms wrapped around them. Her hair is a matted, tangled mess, her face dirty. There are deep, inflamed grooves carved into her cheeks and forearms, and her eyes are flat and disinterested.

"Are there many staff casualties?" I recognize the dangerous undercurrent in Phil's tone, but Dr. Sorenson seems to miss it.

"Staff? Oh, no. We're very careful. There hasn't been a staff incident in almost a year. But the creatures do commit acts of self-destruction. We learn from our errors and have developed what seems to be the optimum space for each species."

"I take it we haven't found the magic formula for this one."

"Ah, number fifty-four. She's responded well to experimental treatment, with the exception of her turning on herself. She's been in human form for three months. If she doesn't shift at the next full moon we'll consider her a success and she'll be euthanized so we can do a detailed study of her brain and nervous system. Now, let's move on. We haven't much time."

I've had enough contact with weres to not be fond of the creatures. In wolf form they will kill without compunction or remorse, and I have no problem with taking one down, if it's a clear case of kill or be killed. But this scenario turns my stomach. The wolf girl looks far too human and is wretched and suffering. My big mouth is just about to get me in trouble when Phil gives me the very slightest nudge of an elbow and I shut it.

Dr. Sorenson leads us from room to room. Each area is reserved for a different kind of research designed to answer questions I hadn't thought of asking. Can paranormals grow back limbs if they are removed? What are the effects of starvation? What substances repel them, burn them, kill them?

The sheer magnitude of the project overwhelms me, and we are followed by a constant cacophony of creatures in pain. Squeals, roars, growls, hisses, and in some cases, human voices.

Phil's face is expressionless and I work to keep mine that way as well, but in reality I feel queasy and want to go anywhere other than here.

The final room Dr. Sorenson takes us to does nothing to make me feel better.

It looks for all the world like a nursery, if all the babies in a nursery were kept naked in plexiglass boxes instead of cribs. No fuzzy blankets, no mobiles, nothing cozy or warm to be seen. All are crying, save one, who has a hopeless, resigned sort of look on her face, and another that is clearly dead.

"Feeding time," our guide says, and pushes another button. Tubes descend, each with a nipple on the end, and are inserted into the open, wailing mouths. The cries change to little grunts of satisfaction as the little ones begin to suckle, all except for the dead baby and the one little girl who turns her face away, disinterested, as the milk pours over her cheek and pools on the plexiglass beside her.

I'm not much of a baby person. That feeling my few girlfriends talk about getting when they hold a baby has been nothing more than a mild curiosity for me. What I'm feeling now still isn't strictly maternal. It's rage. I don't want to pick up and cuddle these babies; I want to start shooting all of the people who put and keep them here.

"They may look human," Dr. Sorenson says, as if reading my thoughts. "But they are truly not. Watch this." She pushes another button, and the feeding tube for the baby who is ignoring the milk fills with crimson. A shudder goes through the tiny body, her limbs contract, and she turns her head and eagerly attaches to the nipple this time, suckling down what I assume to be fresh, hot blood.

"See?"

I'm no longer able to keep my mouth shut. "Will you be cutting off body parts at this age? Or maybe putting quicksilver in the formula?"

"I don't really think—"

"Will you observe the decomposition process or does somebody cart off the dead babies at some point?"

"A cleanup crew comes in every other day. I don't appreciate your tone—"

Phil puts a hand on her shoulder and leans in, lowering his voice a little to that "just for your ears" timbre that makes women's knees go weak. But the vowels are tighter, the consonants more clipped, than his usual speech. "The cribs aren't labeled as to species; is there a reason for that?"

She relaxes under the onslaught of a dose of Phil's renowned charm. "We're not sure what they are going to be. We are observing emerging traits. So far, the evidence leads toward shifters, as all of them will drink milk. Except, of course, for our bloodthirsty little lady on the right."

On the words she moves forward, placing her hands against the glass and leaning her forehead against it, for all the world like she's gazing in at a cuddly baby. "She's my favorite of them all. So feisty. So interesting."

The smile Phil gives her is tight and a little robotic, although he leaves his hand on her shoulder in a gesture halfway between professional interest and something a little more.

"This is quite fascinating, but I'm more interested in the breeding program. Most of us never have the opportunity to see pregnant paranormals. Is it possible to see the brooding and delivery cells?"

Her face takes on a visible tinge of rose, her pupils dilate, her face softens.

Phil has her practically purring. "I'd love to show you, but we have no pregnancies at this time, at least nothing visible. They don't breed well in captivity."

So where, then, do all these babies come from? It's on the

tip of my tongue to ask, but Phil shoots me a barely perceptible signal—nothing more than a cool, impersonal glance, but it throws cold water on the flames of my anger and gets my brain back to thinking straight.

I shut up, and do my best to behave.

Still, the nursery concludes our tour. Whether it's due to my behavior or whether this was always the plan is never known, but our guide, after a curt nod to me and a lingering two-handed handshake for Phil, passes us off to a marine who leads us out of the facility and to the maze of traps that will allow us to escape out into the big wide world above.

Apparently the papers I signed before coming here are not sufficient, because I'm ushered into a small room apart from Phil and presented with another entire stack. There is nothing in this room but a folding table and a folding chair. The floor is concrete. The walls are reinforced steel. And the door locks from the outside. No windows, no light switches, no ceiling panels. And, of course, no bathroom, no water, no food.

They leave me there longer than is necessary to go through the papers. Long enough to make me wonder if they are going to let me out, or if I will die here like the baby para in the nursery. I've been around long enough to recognize the psychology of this and the power play involved, as well as the implicit threat. Every paper I sign swears that I will never speak of this. If I choose to be part of the research team, and if I am deemed worthy, I will be able to speak only to my teammates, and only under certain approved conditions.

The very last paper asks the million-dollar question: "Do you still wish to be considered for the Paranormal Research Team?"

I can't see a camera, but I know damned well there has to be one. So I make a show of thinking about this question when I've already formed an answer. I put the pen down and pick it back up, then tap it on the table instead of signing. I fidget in my chair, shuffle my feet, reread the paper. At last, with a furrowed forehead, I write my answer and sign my name.

Maybe an hour later, a marine comes to let me out.

"Hey, it's about time," I tell him. I really need a bathroom and a drink by now, but no way in hell am I going to ask. He offers no information other than "This way, ma'am."

When I'm finally released, two marines, not one, conduct me down yet another hallway. Fear transmutes into anger, as it always does for me, and I'm eyeing both of their gun belts and wondering how the alternative weapons work and if I could possibly get my hands on one when I find myself back at the place where we came in. Without a word, the marines salute and leave me there.

No operator is in sight, and after waiting a few minutes I'm almost ready to try the retinal scan/fingerprint thing and see if I can bust out of here on my own, when footsteps sound in the hallway and Phil joins me.

Reassured by his presence, I'm able to navigate the retinal scanner and maintain my calm, but as soon as we're through the door and back in the desert I'm forced to have him turn his back while I pick a spot of sand and empty my bladder. The Suburban shows up shortly thereafter.

All the long ride back to the hotel neither one of us says a word. Phil reaches for my hand and holds it, linking us together, but it's becoming clear to me how this is going to end. When we are standing on the pavement out front of the hotel and the car has driven off into the dark, he cups my chin in his hand and kisses me, a long, sweet kiss that starts the tears flowing silently down my cheeks.

"I assume you said no."

I nod, and manage to find my voice. "You?"

"The same."

"It's so…" And now my voice does break and I give up on looking for words.

"We can't see each other again," he says. "Or talk. Or write. You understand why this is so?"

I nod.

Phil smiles then. "You're quite the woman, Maureen Keslyn. It's been refreshingly real." And then he just walks away, out of my life and into the darkness, never to be seen or heard from again.

Until now. When it turns out that while I've been busy pretending the lab visit never happened, he's sacrificed his life to do something about it.

• • •

Jake looks like he's going to throw up. "So those babies—they were at least paranormals, right, besides how they looked?"

"I wish I could say that's true. But I've seen paranormal babies since then, of several varieties. Vamps, werewolves. None of them looked remotely human. They come into the ability to shift around puberty."

"Shit," he says. That's all, but the expression on his face speaks volumes.

"All these years, I thought Phil had just run away from the problem like I did. Buried it. Pretended it didn't really happen, tried to believe the little ones were born to paranormals. That still felt horribly, terribly wrong, but at least I could live with it. After I'd been around for awhile and seen a lot of stuff—like the little paras—I couldn't believe any longer, but I didn't know how to fix it. One word from me and I figured I'd be dead—"

"Like all the employees from the Home."

"Yes. And like Phil. And Abel."

"So you think the FBI came after them? Because they knew something?"

"That's what I think."

"But Abel has to have been killed by a paranormal."

"He was stabbed first."

I let him absorb the full impact of this and what we are up against. "Why now?" he says finally. "I get the why here part, but the rest doesn't click."

"That's what I've been trying to figure. Unless they've been watching Phil all along, waiting for him to make a move. But I can't believe it took him this long to find Shadow Valley—"

"So why make his move now? Good question."

"There's one more research factoid I've been able to dig up, by the way."

"Do I want to know?"

"Too late, for that, isn't it?" I light up another smoke. My life is looking increasingly short, the more I think about it. Might as well enjoy what remains. "Project Paranormal closed on April 15, 1982."

"Same time frame they decommissioned Shadow Valley."

"Precisely."

"Something happened, and that something is related to what is happening now. If only there were an algebraic equation for that," he says after a thoughtful silence. "Well, we figure out what we can. Vermeer might know more than he thinks he does. And there's another angle to pursue."

"Which is?"

"Some of those dead employees had kids. And those kids would have been old enough to listen behind doors and maybe get some info they aren't supposed to have. Of course, we might be putting them in danger."

"They're already in danger."

He just looks at me.

"Jake, if we can find them, so can they. Trust me on that. But maybe, small town and knowing everybody, we have an edge."

Not a man to linger, Jake. He's already in the car and I slide in just a shade behind him, slowed down by the cursed leg and the way my belly hurts every time I bend or stretch. Jake doesn't offer a hand, he's too smart for that, but there is just the right amount of sympathy in his voice.

"Critter really messed you up, huh?"

"Just drive," I tell him, but the truth is I'm warmed by his company and grateful to not be in this mess alone.

CHAPTER EIGHTEEN

The minute we drive out of the dead zone, Jake's cell starts chiming alert messages. Before he gets to the end of the first voicemail, he tromps on the gas. No siren in this rig but he drives as if there were, taking the corners at a speed just below death-defying. When we pull into the parking lot of the Manor there's a sheriff car on site, red and blues flashing. The death van is parked at an angle as close to the Manor as it can get without driving on the grass. Sophie is manhandling a stretcher out of the back and spins around at Jake's voice, green eyes sparking fire.

"What are you doing here?" he asks.

"I came for Alma."

"I'm not sure we want you to take her."

"It's protocol. Staff called about an hour ago."

"Which staff?"

Sophie shrugs bony shoulders. "Betty. Said to come immediately, so I did."

"Leave the stretcher here," Jake says. "And come with us."

"But she'll need—"

"You can come with us, or I cuff you and you wait in the car. Your choice."

Even I feel the lash in his voice. On the surface she doesn't flinch, but I can feel something in her go cold and shut down. "You've been listening to the gossips." Her voice sounds, finally, like a lost teenager. "You think I kill people."

"I make up my own mind about things. I need you where I can see you."

He's right. Despite my unexpected rush of sympathy, he's right.

I gesture for her to follow him and bring up the rear.

Betty is waiting just inside the door. Her legs are braced, her hands at her hips like a gunfighter. I don't see any weapons but this doesn't make her feel less of a threat.

"Chris is already here. You're not needed."

"I'm sure Deputy Harris has done a swell job. I want a look at the body. You'd better come along and tell us what happened." Jake walks around her without further comment.

For a minute I think she's going to refuse. Her fingers twitch. Her eyes narrow. Something in my face makes her think twice and she turns and falls in behind Sophie.

Alma's room is on the ground floor, not far from the main lobby. Close enough that if a person were to scream, the staff—meaning Betty—ought to hear.

"How did you happen to find her? Why did you go to her room?"

"I already explained this to—"

"Do me a favor and tell it again."

"She didn't come for lunch. Nobody worried when she wasn't there for breakfast, but Alma isn't one to miss lunch."

This room is different from Dora's. Not so tidy, and no frou-frou to be seen. There's a laptop on a desk, a printer, a stack of manuscript pages. One small bookshelf overflowing with paperbacks. A general clutter of books and paper on every surface.

Matt stands in the hallway, looking like a melancholy young god with those tangled curls and soulful eyes, and his effect on Sophie is visible.

A young deputy guards the doorway, boyish face tight with worry. "Sir," he says, his face full of relief when he sees Jake. "I thought it best not to disturb the scene, in case."

"Good thinking, Chris. So calling for Sophie was not your idea."

"No, sir."

"This is ridiculous," Betty says, trying to push past him into the room. "Sophronia already told you I called, and I don't understand your problem with that. Alma died, as old people do."

"So you didn't call 911."

"Why on earth would I do that? I called the funeral home. It's protocol. Always has been."

"Except when we're talking murder instead of natural causes." I make a move to enter the room. The deputy blocks me, and I want to pat him on the head for doing a good job. Since he's got a good twelve inches on me and would be offended by this, I settle for a killing stare.

"It's all right," Jake says. "Let her in."

Betty makes a move to follow and he blocks her with an outstretched arm. "Not you."

Alma lies flat on her back, just as Dora did. Eyes wide open and staring at the ceiling, face frozen. An expression of terror. The blankets are drawn up to her chin. I wait for Jake to snap a series of photos with a camera borrowed from the young deputy.

Normally, I'd expect an ME or at least the coroner to give the body a going over, or wait to do it myself until the crime scene is cleared and the body is in the morgue. But given the propensity in this town to cremate people at a moment's notice, I'm not prepared to wait.

I do give Jake a questioning look. He nods.

Stripping back the blankets, I'm somewhat appalled to see that Alma is a naked sleeper, folds of flesh and fat free and abundant. Sadness touches me then, that a woman who is obviously a sensual free spirit should have lived trapped in this body. Together, one on each side, Jake and I give her a once-over, running our hands over limbs, lifting skin folds to look for any wounds lying beneath.

When we get to the neck, it appears at first glance to be smooth and unmarked. I shine my penlight over the skin, though, and find several sets of scars. Old. And one fresh wound. No blood. Her skin is too pale, and even when I press my fingers against the wound there is no oozing.

"What is that?" Jake asks, but he knows.

Vampire teeth are sharp and leave clean punctures. This is ragged; the skin is torn and there are loose flaps. But the placement is directly over the jugular.

"Who called you?" I turn to the young deputy.

"Anonymous caller, male. But the call came from this facility."

That narrows down the options. Chuck, Gerry Vermeer, Matt, or any one of the ten male residents who live here.

"Wasn't me," Matt says. "I didn't know until you showed up that anything was wrong."

Old people just die. Their hearts stop. Small vessels rupture in their brains. But something else has happened here. Jake moves around the room, looking, not touching. When he gets to the manuscript he bends to read, then puts on a pair of gloves and moves the pages, scanning.

Sophie watches everything, her face in shadows. I half expect her to grow fangs and come across the bed after me. But then she turns things upside down. Stepping forward without permission, she lays her hand on Alma's forehead, and her face crumples in a look of pain.

"Can she tell you anything? Like who attacked her and how she died?"

"I keep telling you—the dead don't talk. I read souls. And hers is...hers is missing. Like Abel's." Her eyes are dark. "You have to stop this," she says. Not to the deputy or to Jake. To me. "It's an abomination. Nothing good can ever come of soul stealing."

Jake comes to stand at my shoulder. "Tell me about this soul stealing business."

He's blowing my cover wide open, but apparently it's already blown. Sophie has figured out I know something about paranormals. Matt and the deputy now know too.

No point going on pretending, so I answer honestly.

"There are paranormals who can steal a soul. But I don't know any that also bleed a body dry like this."

"I got here as soon as I could." Charlene has materialized in the doorway, dressed in a neat skirt and tight sweater, hair and makeup perfect. "This one goes with me, I assume. You'll want an autopsy, Jake, yes?"

Her voice purrs. She looks up at him from under long lashes, cocks a hip almost imperceptibly.

I catch myself wishing that I had the power to kill with a glance. Me and Sophie could be quite a team.

"What's the protocol here?" I ask, keeping my voice curious. "When does the coroner get called in, versus the undertaker?"

Jake has his poker face on. Betty blinks. "If they are obviously dead I can declare it. No coroner needed. And then I call the funeral home."

"So you didn't call Charlene?"

The moment of doubt is dispelled by Charlene's easy laugh. "I was listening to the scanner. Heard dispatch say there was a death at the Manor. Under the circumstances, I figured I'd be wanted and didn't wait for you to call."

She takes possession of the body at this point, and Jake lets her. I see the way he's watching her, though, and I let her be. She leans over the body, touches a hand, actually takes out a stethoscope and listens for a pulse, even though rigor has already set in and there's clearly no blood in the body. Bending over to listen for a heart that has long stopped beating does give her the opportunity to display some cleavage. It's a missed opportunity; her target is distracted by other things.

He's left me to watch Charlene and is focused on the rest of the crowd. "So, let me see if I've got this all straight. You" —he points a finger at Betty— "were here working and noticed Alma didn't come for lunch. Which Matt was busy cooking and serving. Yes?"

"I suppose." Betty's eyes glitter with malice.

"You suppose? You don't know?"

"All right. Yes. Matt was serving lunch. But that doesn't mean he couldn't have done this during the night."

"Matt?"

"You already know about my night. There was the incident with…the death. I took Sophronia home."

"And then?"

"Then I came back here and got shitfaced on MacNaughton. Maybe if I hadn't been hung over I'd have noticed Alma didn't show up for breakfast."

"Where were you last night?" Jake whirls on Betty.

"You dare to suspect me of something? All the long hours I put in here for next-to-nothing pay—"

"Just answer my questions."

The tension in this room is beginning to frazzle my nerves. All of these people could be dangerous, I'm thinking, with the exception of the young deputy. He's got a choirboy face and the green-gilled look of a man seeing his first-ever dead body.

"Fine." Betty almost spits her answers. "I left here yesterday evening at six. Then I went to church. Left there at nine thirty p.m. and went home to bed."

"Anybody at home that can verify that?"

"My dog."

Jake has a notebook out now and is making notes. "Soph— what time did she call you?"

"About one p.m."

He looks at his watch. It's two thirty now. The timeline fits, but there are so many variables. Any one of these four could have killed her, except that they didn't. It's time to share that with Jake; he's done a good job of putting the fear of God into everybody.

"Give me your knife," I say to him.

"What are you going to do?"

"I'll show you. Just give it to me." If I tell him, he'll say no, and I need to do this here and now, in front of all of them. A long silence and I'm thinking I'll have to pull my own out of my ankle holster, and I'd really rather not try to bend that far when he puts it in my hand.

Quickly, before any of them can stop me, I grab one of Alma's hands and make a quick slice into the vein at the wrist.

Sophie gasps.

"What the hell?" Jake barks, and then he sees.

No blood, no serous fluid. Not so much as a pink ooze. The vein is full of a clear jelly. I wipe the knife on the bedsheet and then hand it back to him. He stares at it, and then at me.

Sophie, standing with one hand on Alma's forehead, shudders visibly and bends down to gaze into the blank, open eyes. It must be a trick of the light that Alma appears to be returning the look. "Evil," Sophie whispers after a long moment. "Evil, evil, evil." She bends over further to pull a sheet up over the exposed body, and the action serves to bare the strip of back between her low-slung jeans and short T-shirt. That tattoo again, of the dog-headed man.

Now I recognize it, wondering how I missed it before. Anubis, the Egyptian god of the dead.

"Where were you last night, Sophronia?" She couldn't possibly have done this and yet there is something about her I need to keep poking at.

"Home. Alone with the dead."

"How long did Matt stay?"

"He didn't. Walked me to the door like a gentleman, insisted I lock it. And then he drove away—I watched through the window."

"I don't suppose there's anybody who can attest to that, your father being away on a trip and all."

Jake's hand makes a small movement but he doesn't intervene. He's got a soft spot for the girl and he knows it, but he's cop enough to know I'm right to pursue this.

Her green eyes have a light behind them that reminds me of a coming storm. Lurid and dangerous. "If you're suggesting—"

"I've suggested nothing. I'm merely asking you the same question that's been asked of everybody in this room."

"Except her." Sophie's gaze lashes out at Charlene, standing next to Jake now and looking cute and fluffy and untouchable.

"Right. Except her. What about it, Charlene? Where were you last night?"

Her pretty face creases into a frown. "I'm not even going to dignify that with a response." She edges a little closer to Jake, so that she's brushing against him, close enough for him to smell her hair and her perfume. Her lower lip trembles just a little; she looks young and vulnerable.

Men. I think he's going to fall for it, but then he says, "I think it's a fair question, Char."

Her blue eyes fly open wide. "Jake, these are geriatric people. They die. Are you going to launch a full-scale investigation every time somebody has a heart attack or just quietly goes to sleep and stays that way? We had three, four deaths up here last year and we didn't do autopsies."

We all stare at her. There's no way she can have missed my theatrics with the knife. She's the medical person, after all. She sags, all at once, her body posture going limp, all of the perkiness gone out of her. She dissolves into tears. "This is all so horrible. And it makes no sense."

Jake's face doesn't soften and he isn't moved to put a comforting arm around her shoulders. "You are a professional, Charlene. I expect you can handle it."

She flashes him a quick, cunning look I won't forget. Sophie, on the other hand, has begun to look visibly ill. Her breath is too shallow and her jaw has gone slack. Matt's there behind her, though. He twists her long hair into a tail and lifts it up in one hand, placing the other on the back of her neck. "Deep breath," he advises, and she manages one, and then another. Matt steers her over to the sink, turns on the water for her, and she's able to splash some over her face and regain some level of composure. Matt stays at her shoulder, as protector or bodyguard or both, and we're back to an impasse.

"So what do we do with the body, then?"

"Alma," Sophie says, her fire dampened but far from out. "She's still Alma."

I feel that way about Phil and I know what she means. "All right. Where do we keep Alma safe while we pursue this investigation?"

Jake runs a hand through his hair, thinking. "Well, the funeral home is out of the question."

"But—"

He lifts a hand to silence Sophie and she subsides. "Surely you can see this. Whether you had something to do with it or didn't, there's no security there to prevent meddling with the body."

"Hospital morgue," Charlene says.

"Same problem. No real security. I'll get a deputy to ride down to Spokane with the body in an ambulance. We'll get it into forensics."

There are all sorts of problems with this idea, but I know he's aware of them and I can't think of anything better. So I let my mind drift into a whole new territory. It's no longer safe to live at the Manor. I'm going to have to send everybody home.

• • •

I've asked everybody to assemble in the parlor. Which, despite everything, makes me laugh. *Parlor* implies some level of luxury and state, and also makes me think of the old Clue game. Only this time it isn't Colonel Mustard with the candlestick, and this is not a parlor. More of a games room, with bingo tables and shuffleboard and a magnetic dart board on one wall. No way are they going to let a bunch of old, half-blind geezers loose with a real set of pointy darts.

I catch myself on that thought, realizing that the "they" in question is really now me, and I can institute as many pointy darts as I wish.

Matt follows me with a rolling tray holding coffee and pastries.

When we enter the place goes quiet. A group of men playing shuffleboard abandon their game unfinished and hobble over to their seats. Nobody makes a move to come and get coffee. Obviously they've all heard what happened by now, and are appropriately uneasy. Which will only help me accomplish what I'm here to do.

At a nod from me, Matt starts pouring cups and passing them out.

"Thanks for all coming down on such short notice," I tell them, mentally counting heads.

"We've never had a house meeting," Virginia says, after a short silence. "It's rather a nice idea, I think." She glances over at Gerry Vermeer, who has been encouraged to attend with a little help from both me and Matt. He sits off to the side, not bothering to talk to anybody. Virginia flutters her lashes at the old coot, but he looks stony-faced straight ahead, and doesn't deign to give her so much as a smile.

"Always lovely to be surrounded by the ladies." Chuck lifts his cup, first to Virginia and then to Julia, whose lip trembles, her eyes big with tears.

"Are we really going to just pretend Alma didn't die?" A voice cuts into the atmosphere like a knife through cheese. "That Dora didn't die?" It's one of the men from table three. He's tall, thin, with a visible tremor, but he has an intelligent face. Dan Haskins, former engineer.

"No, we're not. That's why I've brought you all here." I keep my voice low, pitched to carry to all of those hearing aids.

"Zebras," Alice says. She's the other outcast, sitting directly opposite from Vermeer, hands twisting in her lap.

Chuck makes a snorting sound in his nose, half laughter, half disgust, while Virginia murmurs, "Lord have mercy." A ripple of giggles runs through the ranks and I'm reminded again that most of them are just high school idiots in old, wrinkled bodies.

Alice twists her hands in her lap, tighter, clenches her jaw, and then stands up and sweeps her gaze over all of them. Her hair is disheveled, but she is clean and neatly dressed and looks a little more mad scientist than demented old bat. "Zebras live right next to the lions. All the time. The herd doesn't run off even though the lions are there. And when a lion takes one of the herd, they just go back to normal like nothing happened."

At that, eyes go to coffee cups, the laughter goes silent.

"Thank you, Alice." I stand at the center of the room. Matt has stopped passing out coffee and is also watching the room. I can feel him. There's an intensity there, an energy signature, that doesn't waft off of anybody else. I'm pretty sure he has some sort of paranormal gift, although he hasn't fessed up to it yet. It surprises me a little that he's hanging out by Alice and not Vermeer, who would seem to bear the most watching. But then, she is the weakest of the herd, the most likely target for one of the lions.

Dan from table three hasn't touched his coffee. "I noticed the police and the coroner both made an appearance when Alma died.

Is there information you could share about that?"

Virginia hugs her coffee mug to her chest, as though it will protect her from the evil in the world.

Murmurs run through the room. "Sheriff and the coroner?"

"Yes, and that little soul-sucking brat that belongs to the undertaker."

"Not just the sheriff—a deputy too."

"Doesn't mean anything." Chuck is dismissive of the whole thing. He's slurped down a whole mug already and holds out his empty to Matt. "Could I get a refill here?"

Matt doesn't move, and after a minute Chuck gets up and makes his own way to the coffee pot, hobbling with a little extra emphasis to make a point. I wait for him to pour his cup, stir three packets of sugar and some cream into it, and make his way back to his chair before I drop my little bomb.

"I'm closing the Manor."

Silence before the explosion, lasting about twenty seconds.

"Whatever for?"

"You can't do that!"

"I've got no place to go!"

I hold up a hand for silence. They all ignore it, the clamor rising into something that will rapidly become hysteria.

"Zebras," I say, at last, cutting through the noise. They turn their heads to look at me, as though I'm the lion in the herd, ears pricked, nostrils flared. If they do opt for flight I figure it will be the slowest stampede in history, but then the lion in question isn't exactly speedy. This whole analogy spawns unholy laughter that nearly chokes me when I try to stifle it.

"We need to be smarter than the zebras," I say, when I'm able to speak again. "Four deaths within the last few days—"

"Old people do die," Julia interrupts. She can say this with equanimity, as she's young yet—forty-four—even though her disease is likely to take her long before these tough old codgers succumb.

"They do. But there have been some...extraordinary circumstances surrounding these deaths. And Abel was young."

The zebras fall quiet, giving these words time to settle in.

Vermeer's hand twitches in his lap, but he is otherwise impassive.

"You really think we're in danger?" Dan from table three finally asks. "Are you thinking serial killer? Can't we just get some security?"

"What if the killer is a staff member?" a frail old woman asks from the back corner. She looks like the lady who played the organ in church all the Sundays of my childhood.

Here's the problem. You can't explain to a group of old, traditionally minded people that there are more things in heaven and earth than they've ever dreamed of. Still, I have to try. Signaling for attention, I wait until they hush enough that I can be heard. "We're not entirely sure that the killer is human."

A sea of faces looks at me blankly, and then at each other. Some hands go to ears to adjust hearing aids. A few shake their heads, expressions clearly indicating that they think I've lost it.

"You can't shut it out," Alice intones into the silence. "Lock the doors, bar the windows, but it still gets in. Seeps through the cracks, finds you when you're sleeping." She smiles at everybody with childlike innocence. A shiver runs down my spine as I remember her words on my first day in this place. *Run. This is a house of death.*

"Somebody hush her. She gives me the creeps." Julia has wrapped her arms around her body as though she's taken a chill.

Fear travels across about half the faces in the room. And then Chuck booms out a big belly laugh. "It's like that movie—with Elvis and JFK in a nursing home haunted by a mummy."

Virginia takes it up. "Oh, right—who was in that again? I can't remember…"

Matt shrugs his shoulders and lifts his eyebrows, the corner of his lips quirking with amusement. As for me, I'm thinking I'd rather go head to head with the Jelly Thing than try to get this crowd to see some sense. No point arguing, just stick to the facts.

Once again I signal for their attention. "Law enforcement is looking into the deaths. Until we figure out just what is going on, I'm closing the Manor. You will all—"

"You can't just kick us out." Chuck again. "We've got

nowhere to go."

A murmur of agreement to this. Now they look frightened.

"I hate to admit it, but he does have a point." Mr. Table Three is beginning to annoy me. "You'll need to give us an eviction notice to legally make us go anywhere. And some of us have nowhere to be."

"This is for your safety. I'm not trying to throw anybody out in the street. I want to save your lives."

About half of them shrug, nearly simultaneously, and I feel like I'm facing a cast of rebellious teenagers in wrinkled skin and dentures. "Look, I don't believe you have nowhere to go. If you can afford to live here, then you've all got money—"

They all exchange a look, and I feel it coming before I even know what it is. "Not so," Table Three says. "The kids have control of my finances."

"In my case it's my parents. I'd rather be murdered in my bed than go live with them." The vehemence in Julia's tone rattles me, and looking back, I see all of their faces reflecting the fire of her words.

"You can always call the children," Virginia says, her voice full of a quiet dignity I hadn't expected. "And maybe they'll come get us. Or not. I, for one, won't go with them. You'll have to get a court order."

I look from one face to the other. "Chuck?"

His face is flushed and fallen, shoulders slumped, all the brash good humor stripped away. Virginia answers for him. "Chuck's kids are the worst. He's lucky they let him come here—send him home and he'll get stuck in some nasty-ass nursing home on the bad side of town."

"There is no bad side of town in Shadow Valley—"

"I come from Chicago. Land of opportunities."

"Well, I'm terribly sorry, but you'll have to go to nursing homes temporarily, then. Medicare should cover—"

"Medicare doesn't cover beeswax. You'll just have to find a way to keep us safe." Virginia actually stands up to say this, delivering her line with movie star intensity. "Hire some security or something."

I'm not quite beaten. "Listen carefully. I can't guarantee protection or safety for any of you. I'll do what I can. But I want it clearly understood that I've asked each and every one of you to move out for your own safety. Here it is in writing."

As Matt passes out the pages I prepared earlier, I contemplate the little group. I underestimated them all, taking them at surface value, never realizing the quiet tragedy playing out behind the money and the privileged manner. They are all as dispossessed as I am. Which gives them license to be obnoxious.

I still don't like most of them much, but I'm going to do my damnedest to make sure none of them comes to harm.

CHAPTER NINETEEN

In the end, over half of the residents of the Manor opt to leave. I'm left with ten who sign a release. This includes everybody from my table, even Chuck. I spend the rest of the afternoon making arrangements and talking to the residents' children, who purport to be concerned but mostly are looking for a reason to sue, and by dinner time I'm exhausted.

Just about the time I finally peel my shoes off my aching feet, planning a good hot soak in the tub and then bed, the phone rings.

I damn near don't answer, but the caller ID tells me it's Jake, and I know he wouldn't call if he didn't have news, and whatever news he has is going to mean a little more action for my weary bones.

"I'm coming to get you," he says when I pick up. "Be there in about five."

"Can't it wait?"

But he's already hung up and there's nothing for it but to put my shoes back on. He's at my door before I can make it downstairs.

"You're looking a little worse for wear," he dares to tell me, bending over to pet the cat, who saunters over to investigate.

"This better be good."

"Oh, it's good."

He hands me a single piece of paper, a copy of a birth certificate.

Elizabeth Jean Cameron, born March 22, 1974, in Shadow Valley, Washington. Parents: Michael and Grace Cameron.

My brain is weary and I stare at it for a long moment before its significance sinks in.

"Betty."

He nods. "Father, Michael Cameron, was a physician and her

mother was a nurse. Both of them worked at the Home."

"And both of them are dead."

Betty is already suspicious in my mind for a lot of reasons, and not just because I don't like her. She has access. She hates old people. Add in motive and she's a hot potato.

"Still mad at me?" Jake asks, with an easy smile.

"You're forgiven. If you can drum me up some decent coffee on the way out of town."

Betty lives way up Willow Creek Road, well out of the bounds of what I think of as civilization. We lose cell phone signal about five minutes after leaving town, but this time Jake is driving a patrol car and we do have radio contact. If another disaster happens at least dispatch can reach us.

Which is a good thing, because the isolation up here is breathtaking. Forty minutes by the clock after we turn off the main highway, and we don't pass another car.

"What sort of person chooses to live out here?" I ask.

It's getting dark outside, and the trees beside the road are so thick I can't see through them to the houses I assume lie beyond. The road must be pretty near impassable in winter. Or during spring thaw, or heavy summer rains, for that matter. I'm guessing that electricity is erratic and if you called 911 it would be hit or miss whether anybody got to you at all, let alone in time.

"Those who want to be left alone. Lot of old vets who prefer to be alone with their PTSD and a bottle of booze—that way they don't hurt anybody when the triggers hit. Pot farmers. We had a serial killer out here a few years back."

"Not your average family-friendly neighborhood."

"Not so much. Although there is also an entire colony of hippies out here somewhere. Rumor has it they're pretty friendly."

I shoot him a look and he grins at me. "Real hippie commune. Started in the sixties and never gave it up. Guys have braided beards down to their chests, women wear tie-dye. Kids who have never been to school and don't know what an Xbox is. They come into town for groceries now and again."

"And Betty lives out here why?"

He shakes his head. "Betty is a bit of a mystery. She works, she attends her church, she goes home."

"She hates old people."

"I think she hates everybody."

The endless trees are beginning to give me the shivers. Lots of paranormals prefer forest, everything from the shifters to walkers and Sasquatch. They could kill all over the place out here and nobody would ever know.

"Why do you think she's working at the Manor?"

"This is the question."

Or one of them anyway.

At length we turn off the traveled road, such as it is, onto a dirt and gravel track, bouncing wildly over ruts and potholes, around a sharp curve, up a steep hill, and there in a little clearing is a manufactured home—a little shabby and faded, but the yard is perfectly groomed and free of clutter. An enclosed lean-to has been built onto the side of the house. A stack of firewood is neatly piled in a roofed shed across the yard, which also contains a wheelbarrow and a chopping block with an axe.

"Dog," Callahan points out needlessly, as a woolly beast emerges from behind the woodpile, barking its head off. It's a big dog, yapping like a puppy and as effective as a full-on air raid siren at announcing our presence. So much for any snooping we might have done unobserved.

The front door opens. For an instant Betty is framed against the darkness of the interior behind her; then she steps outside and closes the door.

Not a word does she say, not to shush the obnoxious dog, nor to ask what we're doing here. She just waits, hands folded in front of her as though in prayer. She might be a martyr waiting for the inquisition, except there's nothing of humility or resignation in her face, much as she tries to compose it into serenity.

I'm a little uneasy about the dog, which looks like he might have some pit bull in him. He does nothing more than bound around us like a planet around a double sun, his high-pitched bark piercing my ear drums. Jake's hand rests on the pepper spray at his tool belt.

Can't remember the last time I've allowed myself to take refuge in the strength of some other person, and the fact that I do scares me more than the dog.

At the bottom of the steps, we pause. The dog ceases its antics and presses up against my legs to be petted. An odor of wet wool and sour blankets wafts up out of his fur, and his weight against my bad leg threatens to throw me off-balance. Still, the silence is blessed and I rub his ears. If he has fleas I'll find a way to give them back to his mistress in spades.

In the meantime the silence has grown into its own small universe, enclosing us all, the three humans and the dog. I notice that Betty's fingernails are rust colored, as though she's been painting and hasn't had time to give them a good scrub. Above her head, a hand-painted sign reads, As for me and my house, we will serve the Lord.

"You could tell me why you're here."

"We could," Jake agrees, pleasantly. "Or you could invite us in and answer a few questions. I'm sure you've got nothing to hide and we'd be much more comfortable inside."

"I'm comfortable here." She stands a little straighter, flinging her braid back behind her shoulder.

"Unfortunately, I'm not." Jake bends his right knee a little, taking his weight on the left. This one micro-movement manages to make him look decrepit and frail. Even his voice sounds weak. "I've hit that age where arthritis sets in. I'd be ever so grateful if we could sit for a minute."

Illustrating his point, the dog pushes a little too hard and I start to go over with a little hiss of pain. Jake grabs my arm and holds me on my feet. We must look quite the picture, and my pride objects. A warning pressure on my arm reminds me that at the moment my damaged state might work to my advantage. I try to look pitiful.

Betty's face shows no softening. Her lips pull into a tight, flat line. "Unto the least of these," she mutters, opening the door and holding it for us as we hobble up the steps.

The house is dark despite the bright daylight outside. All of the windows are covered in heavy, dark brown draperies. The walls are taupe, the carpeted floor a colorless beige. Cross-stitched homilies hang side by side with dead animal heads on all four walls, the incongruity threatening to pop something loose in my brain. A prim couch and chairs, so pristine I wonder if she keeps them under plastic most of the time, are wedged in between an assortment of taxidermied animals.

The air feels as heavy as an old wool blanket, and smells of damp fur and chemicals, with an added tang of blood and an underlying taint of decomposing flesh. An antlered deer head looms above me, low enough that I could reach up and touch his muzzle, while Jake actually has to duck as he enters the room.

The moose head on the opposing wall looks like it wants to lock horns with the deer. A bearskin rug is draped over the back of the couch, head still attached. The mouth is wide open, the teeth yellowish and sharp. Fake eyes stare at me, glittering.

"So, sit, if you need to." Betty will accommodate our weakness, but politeness isn't on the menu. Jake takes the couch. It looks like the bear is gunning for him, up behind his shoulder.

For me there's the armchair and a coyote.

It looks startled. I hope it was dead before she skinned it but I wouldn't put anything past her. I find myself carefully inspecting the lampshades to make sure she hasn't done some Hitleresque thing with humans.

A rack on the wall holds a selection of guns—an AR with a scope and two shotguns, one double barreled, one single. There's a wood stove at center space, not currently lit. A magnetic strip attached to the wall holds an array of knives, some that look like they belong in the kitchen, others that are clearly for hunting, flaying, and other procedures.

Betty stays in the kitchen, behind a large island that takes up most of the space. Her hands rest on the limp body of what looks like a spaniel. One floppy ear hangs down over the edge of the counter. A skinning knife is laid out and ready and she picks it up and holds it, telegraphing the signal that she would like to get to work if we would get on with it.

"You neighbor's dog, then?" It's a wild gamble, but I figure since she already has one outside who doesn't seem in danger of the knife, maybe she doesn't carve up her own.

I wish I hadn't said anything, because my question seems to give her permission and she sets to work with the skinning.

"As a matter of fact, yes."

"So is it dinner, then, or what?"

Looking up from her task just long enough to glare at me in disgust, she goes back to her work. "It's taxidermy. Not fresh enough for dinner. Although I do find it interesting that we think some animals fit to eat and some not. Nothing wrong with dog if it's cooked right."

"Tell that to Buster."

"His name is Rex. And he's much more useful as he is. When it gets so he can't work, then we'll see. I didn't kill this dog, by the by, so if you're looking to throw charges at me on animal cruelty, you can look again."

I really don't want to look at all. Her hands are very deft and sure, and despite her protestations of old meat, the flesh appears quite fresh and bloody to me.

"Are all of these your handiwork?" Jake asks. He manages to sound engaging and curious, and I remind myself that a lot of people like taxidermy.

"Most. The moose was my father's. His work is in museums, for the most part, but when he did that one he had developed Parkinson's. His hands shook. It's defective."

Her tone is accusing, as if the old man had inflicted Parkinson's on himself somehow.

"How long since he died?"

"You've had your chance to rest. I've answered nothing but inane questions so far. Tell me why you're here, or get out."

"We want to talk about your father."

She stiffens, her hands going still. "I told you, he's dead."

"He was a doctor, wasn't he?" Jake's voice is still light and easy. "Worked up at the Manor back when it was the Home for Unwed Mothers."

"What does that have to do with anything?" She's clutching that knife in her right hand and no longer skinning the dog. I find my own hand gravitating to my revolver. I'd like to be on my feet, but the chair is softer than it looks. I've sunken down, and I'm not entirely sure how I'm going to get up without pulling the hell out of everything.

"Probably nothing," he says. "But he died under unusual circumstances. I guess we're looking for any connection to what happened to Alma."

"She was a worker of evil, her and those twisted books of hers. Don't you dare compare her to my father."

"Now, now," Jake says. "Let us speak kindly of the dead. She was an old woman—"

"The old are the worst! They have entire lifetimes in which to accumulate evil! Years in which the devil wears them down and finds ways of access to the soul!" Betty vibrates with zeal and passion, her face alive with unveiled hate as she points an accusing finger first at Jake and then at me. "Don't think I'm not watching!"

"I doubt she'd done anything in her life vile enough to deserve that death. Where were you that night?"

"If you are insinuating —"

"I'm not insinuating anything. Yet. Two murders up at the Manor last night. Are you sure you were here at home?" Jake's not showing any sign of a limp now, his voice firm and authoritative.

"I worked, I went to church, I came home. Just like I said. How dare you call me a liar?"

"Curious, you working at the Manor with the evil old." I've worked my way to the edge of the chair and am pretty sure I can get up fast if I need to.

"They need watching," Betty says. "You need watching."

"It's pretty clear you didn't want me at the Manor. Maybe you're the one that needs watching." And I am watching. Her eyes. Her hands. The changing tension in her body.

"Anything you'd care to tell us about the closet in Maureen's room? Maybe your daddy mentioned something about where it leads and what—"

She lunges.

He's going for his gun but she's too close. I'm already moving, using momentum and my shoulder to knock her sideways against the island. Jake grabs the wrist of her knife hand and squeezes.

She cries out but struggles and kicks.

He slams her wrist on the edge of the island, once. Twice.

The knife falls onto the floor with a clatter, splattering blood.

I'm behind her with the revolver in her ribs and she stops struggling.

"You're evil too, Sheriff. What did you and your kind do when my father was killed? Looked the other way. And now you've grown old. Flesh decaying off your bones. Muscles wither, your organs failing little by little. The old never know when to die."

"Enough body function left to arrest you, as it turns out."

I keep the gun on her while he cuffs her. "You have the right to remain silent—"

"Oh, shut up, you old hypocrite—"

Jake can handle her now that she's weaponless. Listening to her tirade and his voice cutting over and through as he cuffs and Mirandizes her, I look through the rest of the living area. Death everywhere, all aligned with the dainty little cross-stitched Bible texts. "All witches and soothsayers shall be stoned," next to a stuffed raccoon. "Man is born to evil as the sparks fly upward."

A bookcase holds a few thick tomes that appear to be Bible commentaries of some sort, and a collection of large jars filled with clear liquid. They aren't canning jars, and I lean closer to look. Definitely glass, but they look old as dirt, and they come in all different shapes and sizes. The liquid varies from clear to amber to various pale tints of greens and blues and pinks. All together, they make a surprising and beautiful collection.

"Are you coming?" Jake calls from the kitchen, and I follow them out, glad enough to leave the house of death behind.

"What about the dog?" I pull the locked door closed behind us as Jake frog-marches his prisoner out to the car. My hands feel sullied. For an instant I've felt her hatred for my flesh. Vile, evil flesh. We should die, the both of us, and not afflict our oozing, decaying bodies on the young.

"Standard protocol is to notify the shelter. They'll come pick him up."

The dog, who ran outside during the altercation rather than rushing to his mistress's defense, sits beside me, tongue hanging out of his mouth in a pink festoon as he pants. When I put my hand on his head, tentative, he leans it against me with a little whimper.

"Can I take him?"

Jake stares at me over the top of the car. "I'm having difficulty seeing Rex here interacting with the likes of Virginia Slater."

"Precisely."

This thought gives me some joy. No more confining the critters to my room. I'll make them free to roam the Manor and interact. Anybody who doesn't like it can leave.

The dog is happy enough to jump into the back of the car beside his mistress, slathering her face with dog kisses. Hands behind her back, all she can do is shove at him with her shoulder and turn her face toward the window. "Get him away from me. He's disgusting."

I find myself smiling. The sun is warm on my face and I crack the window, partly to let in the freshness of the spring air, partly to let out the smell of unwashed dog. My leg aches viciously, but my skin feels the pleasure of the breeze.

• • •

It's late when I get back to the Manor.

We took Betty straight to the jail on charges of assault of an officer. Chris, the young deputy from this morning, looking about as tired as I feel despite his younger years and supposedly nondecaying flesh, comes out where I'm waiting and says Jake asked him to drive me home. Which he does, quietly and efficiently, and with no more talk than common courtesy dictates.

He's not happy about the dog in his car, and I don't blame him. The creature stinks and has absolutely no manners. Once inside the Manor, he dashes up and down the hall while I'm waiting for the elevator. Maybe I'll laugh at his antics in the morning. Right now, all I want in the world is bed and a space of oblivion. I just know this critter is going to attack the cat and that will require negotiating.

I'll put the cat in the closet, I'm thinking, as I unlock the door and squeeze in, holding onto the dog's collar and anticipating disaster.

As it turns out, the cat and the dog are not my biggest problem.

Sophie sits in the chair, the cat draped across her lap, fiddling with the salt sprayer. "You seem extraordinarily fond of animals," she says. The cat opens one eye and then closes it again. The dog walks over calmly and lies down at Sophie's feet with a little huff, resting his nose on his paws.

She wrinkles up her nose. "He needs a bath."

"You can feel perfectly free to do that. Tomorrow. Do you care to tell me what you're doing here?"

"What's this?"

"Don't turn the handle, you'll make a mess. It sprays salt."

"What for?"

"There are paranormals who don't react well to salt. What are you doing in my room?"

"Betty."

"What about Betty?"

She doesn't answer me, just gives me a long stare that runs a chill down my spine. Her hand strokes the cat the whole time, and his eyes are open now and staring at me too, both pairs of green eyes catching a glitter from the hall light.

"I think Betty is a lot like me." She leans forward.

The cat arches his back, fur standing on end, ears back. The dog points his muzzle toward the ceiling and howls.

I yawn and switch on the light. Enough with the theatrics

already. I'm tired. I want my bed. She's young and still feels the need to play games, but I don't have that problem.

"You're not scared?" she asks, and there is a wistful hope behind the words that I can't quite ignore.

"Of you? No. I'm exhausted, though, and would really like to go to bed. So I'd like to skip the drama and get around to what you came to tell me."

She considers this for a minute, and then nods. "I think I know what Betty is. It's not good, what she can do."

"And what is that?"

"Remember when I said your friend didn't have a soul? That it was missing?"

"I'm not likely to forget. Can I sit in that chair for a minute to take off my shoes? You're welcome to the sofa."

She moves. The animals leap up beside her and although I'm cringing about the filthiness of the new arrival on the furniture, I let it be.

My body is sore beyond measure, and I can't quite bite back a groan as I sink into the chair and lean my head back, too tired for the moment to tackle the challenge made up by shoes.

"I've just been down the stairs in your closet."

I'd been too tired to notice, but the circle around the closet door has been disturbed, all right. It needs to be fixed, but that would require getting up again. With an effort, I keep the irritation out of my voice. "Making yourself at home, I see. What does that have to do with Betty?"

"There are souls down there. All kinds of them. Some are children. Some are—I don't know what they are."

"And you think Betty has to do with that."

"Do you think I'm a soul stealer?"

So that's what's bothering her. I hide my face and buy myself some time by bending, very carefully, to untie my laces.

"What do you think?"

"I don't—I don't hurt them. I help them cross. It feels right, what I do."

But there's a hesitation in her voice, as if she's never questioned this before but is suddenly unsure. Cursing the fate that has left me as the only teacher for a powerful and half-lost girl when I am so damn tired, I just breathe for a minute, thinking about what to say.

"From what I see, you are comfort and guide to the deserving, and conductor to the others. What you do—what you are—follows the natural order of things. A soul stealer, on the other hand, destroys the very essence of a life. You think that's what Betty is?"

"She walks around covered in residue. It feels wrong. And I'm only guessing, really, but I have a sense that they're not destroyed, like you just said. Dora and Alma and, and, Abel, your friend. I can sense them, sort of, somewhere. Not ghosts. Just—trapped. Only I can't find them. They're not downstairs."

Tears track down her cheeks. She cries like a child, without self-consciousness. Her mouth turns down at the corners, and she draws in quavering breaths.

Somebody ought to pat her and hug her and tell her everything will be all right. Only things are far from all right and I'm not much of one for caresses. "Look," I say finally. "Betty's in jail. So she can't hurt anybody for a while."

The shock of this freezes her in mid-sob and sets her to coughing. Which is good for her and shakes her back to her senses. "But how will we find out what she's up to, or what she's done, if she's locked up?"

"We'll go to her house and have a look around. You and me." I see the light coming up in her face and hold out both hands in a warding gesture. "Tomorrow. Now, go home. Okay? Get some rest. You've done what you can today, you'll do what you can tomorrow."

She nods, scrubbing at her face with her hands and sniffling. Betty's mutt licks the tears off her face.

"Can I take him with me, for company? I'll bathe him."

"You go right on ahead. Lock the door on your way out!"

I've got a hell of a lot to think about, but not more than a minute after the door closes behind her I tumble into bed, still fully dressed, and fall into the deep, deep sleep of exhaustion.

CHAPTER TWENTY

Things don't look any better in the morning.

For a brief moment I think my legs are paralyzed until I realize there's about twenty pounds of cat weighing them down. My body feels like it's been beaten with a cudgel and my room smells like dog. It's raining, but there is fresh snow on the mountains. They look remote and cold.

A long, hot shower eases stiff muscles enough to let me get dressed. Today I'm taking no chances, so I buckle on my holster, shrugging into a loose flannel shirt to cover it. I'm not going anywhere unarmed, not even downstairs for coffee. After a brief consideration, I fasten the flashlight onto my belt as well.

Only then do I head downstairs for my caffeine fix, which I am in desperate need of by now. Thank God, Matt has a pot on in the kitchen. He takes one look at me and pours a cup, waiting until I've downed at least half before he says a word. What he does say, a line of worry marring his beautiful forehead, wakes me up more effectively than the entire pot could have done.

"Alice hasn't come down for breakfast. I was just going up to check."

I know he's thinking what I'm thinking.

"Feed the zebras. I'll go see."

But he follows me, anyway. I'm not crazy about having him behind me, and my fingers itch for the comfort of the revolver in my hand, even though I can feel its familiar weight in the holster. I'm also really wishing I had Phil's weapons stash.

The distance to Alice's room seems to stretch into miles and my body won't move fast enough to get me there. No answer when we knock at the door, and Matt kicks it open with all the finesse of a movie star in the rescue scene.

As it turns out, no rescue is needed, at least not of the hero variety.

Alice stands in front of her mirror, half dressed, lips and chin smeared with lipstick. She doesn't show any surprise at our sudden and loud arrival, doesn't turn around.

"Not right," she says to her reflection, as though we're not even there.

"Oh, shit," Matt says. He looks sad, and older than I'd thought.

"Go finish with breakfast," I tell him.

He hesitates and I think he's going to refuse. But this time he nods and walks away.

"Let me help you," I say to Alice. "We'll fix it."

I wet a washcloth at the sink and wash away the lipstick, along with the accumulated dried food and other goop on her face. Once she's squeaky clean I comb her hair, dig through the piles of clothes on the floor for something less stained than the rest, making a note to hire somebody to take care of her laundry and her room.

She whispers then, harsh and a little too loud. "I didn't tell."

"You didn't tell what?"

But she shakes her head and continues muttering, "I didn't tell, I didn't tell, I didn't tell."

I wonder if she's on medication, and look around for pill bottles.

A jumble of clothes and books spills from drawers and closet, covering the floor. The bed is a tangle of sheets and blankets. But there is one organized and pristine space in this room: a shelf of books, all hefty tomes of math and science.

Alice comes to stand beside me. Her hands have stilled. Tears flow silent down her cheeks. "Gone," she says. "All gone."

I know a little of how she feels. Everything that I value is slipping away from me, little by little, except my brain. Lord have mercy, please let me keep my brain.

"Let's go find breakfast," I say at last. "Here, get dressed."

With her hair combed and her face clean, she looks less wild and I can see glimmers of the self she must have once been.

"I didn't tell," she whispers one last time. Her fingers, dry and cool, close around mine and she follows me out of the room in search of breakfast. Trusting, I think. Somehow, I need to find a way to keep my promise that she'll be safe.

• • •

Sophie is waiting for me out front of the funeral parlor, Betty's dog sitting obediently beside her. He looks like a different animal, washed and brushed and trimmed.

"Looks like you've got yourself a dog," I tell her as she opens the door and orders him into the back with a couple of words.

"I can keep him?"

"Absolutely." There's no way I'm letting the dog go back to Betty, even after she gets out. And it's good to be able to gift somebody something I didn't want in the first place. Karma without sacrifice. Except that I don't believe in karma, and if I did I'm pretty sure it would know when I'm being a hypocrite.

"I've never had a dog." Sophie has left off the makeup this morning. She looks a little less freakish without the heavy black kohl lining her eyes, but somehow more dangerous. I can feel her staring at me while I drive.

"What?"

"I'm trying to figure out what you are."

"Human."

"What else?"

"Nothing else." I'm not going to tell her about my FBI connections, especially since I don't exactly have any now. With Abel gone, this badge I'm carrying around is more liability than protection.

"Then how come you know all this shit?"

"Think of me as a bounty hunter. Now. Let's go over some safety rules."

I talk to her about fingerprints and how to search without leaving traces. She seems to be listening.

Betty's door is unlocked. This rural community business is starting to grow on me. No nosy neighbors to call the police. No security systems.

The dog seems happy to be home. He runs around the yard in insane dashes, as fast as he can for about a hundred yards, sliding to a stop, then skidding around to run in the other direction. When the door opens he careens past me, knocking me sideways and almost on my ass as he skids on the linoleum and thunders off down the hall. Sophie could maybe get him under control but at the moment she's more of a problem than he is. Already she's walking through the house with unwiped, muddy shoes.

A stench of rotting flesh hits us both at once.

Sophie crosses the kitchen to the island, where the little dog is now buzzing with flies and giving up a mighty stink. She makes an inarticulate, strangled noise and lifts one of the floppy ears.

I'm not much happier than she is. The house feels alive with a quivering, gelatinous energy that adheres to my skin. When I move a hand to brush it away there is nothing physically there, but I still feel it, crawling over my body.

Sophie moves like a sleepwalker, out of the kitchen to the middle of the living room and stands there, eyes closed, a listening expression on her face. The dog comes back to press against my knees, panting, and I'm actually grateful for the dog smell and the living warmth of him.

"You feel it?" Sophie asks.

I sure as hell feel something. "This place is haunted, isn't it? How many are there?" I can handle ghosts. I don't like them, but I can deal with them. For the most part they are harmless, unable to do more than make my flesh crawl on my bones. The particularly angry ones, though, have enough energy to do some damage.

She shakes her head. "No ghosts. At least—I can't see any."

"And you usually can, right?"

A frown creases her forehead. "I always can. Something's wrong."

"Well, let me know if you figure it out. I'm going to look for some stuff, okay?"

"What stuff?" Now her eyes do come open and I wish she'd close them again. They are literally shining with a green flare that isn't reflected from any source I can detect. I wish they wouldn't.

"I'll know it when I find it."

I click my tongue for the dog to come with me, but he whimpers and cowers between my feet. I damn near trip over him because he sidles along with me. In my peripheral vision something by the fireplace seems to move, but when I look all is still. The moose and the deer are staring at me from their places on the wall. They give me the creeps.

What makes a woman spend all of her spare time skinning animals? And if she's really a soul sucker, as Sophie believes, then how does she do that? Witchcraft is the only way I know for a human to steal souls. It's not an easy spell to work, and all the Biblical texts around this house would seem to indicate that Betty would be against the practice of the occult. Particularly the darker arts.

On one level or another she's not what she says she is and I'm looking for anything that will keep her locked up. Maybe she's not fully human, but I can't present that to a judge.

The bathroom is clean and painfully neat, with the one exception of a decorative jar containing what looks like a fetal pig with two heads. No cosmetics. Generic two-in-one shampoo and conditioner. A hairbrush. Toothpaste and toothbrush.

What I want is information, and there are simply too many hiding places in Betty's house. Any one of these stuffed critters could contain contraband. Fortunately it's a small house, and I'm starting in the obvious places, more or less.

I rule out the living room. Betty doesn't strike me as mastermind enough to think of hiding things in the open. She'll have stashed what is important to her somewhere more conventional. An underwear drawer, maybe. Or a filing cabinet.

The bedroom then, is my place to start.

At the door, the dog whimpers and flees in the other direction, tail between his legs.

On the surface, nothing appears threatening. Betty's furniture consists of an antique six-drawer dresser, a bed, a wardrobe, and—bingo—a filing cabinet. I check the wardrobe first. It's full of precisely folded sheets, towels, a stack of lace doilies, neatly separated skeins of cross-stitch thread.

On the top shelf is a row of canning jars holding what looks like chemicals and a big plastic jug labeled "embalming fluid" with a felt marker. A plastic basket beside them contains rolls and rolls of white bandages. These could be used for making the framework for her taxidermy projects, but they could also be used for making mummies, which are bad news, no matter how you look at them.

A crash of glass from the other room, followed by a wild howling that would make a wolf run for cover with his tail between his legs, turns my knees to jelly.

"Sophie?"

An almost inhuman wail of rage and pain answers me, and with my heart in my throat I run in her direction.

She looks okay, apart from the expression of horror on her face. She's holding a decorative jar in her hands, and another lies shattered at her feet, the pieces of glass half submerged in a pool of amber liquid. I don't think she even sees me.

"So many," she says.

The jars are lined up on the bookshelf where I spotted them earlier, a cheap plywood build-it-yourself deal that probably came from Walmart. The colors of the liquids travel the whole spectrum in shades of blues and greens and reds and combinations. A presentiment of what is stored here makes every hair on my body stand on end.

"Sophie!" I raise my voice to try to draw her back to a place where I can reason with her. "Let's make a plan. I don't think—"

Crash!

The jar in her hands hits the floor. For a flicker of an instant I see a dim shape bloom out of the rose-colored liquid, female and human, but then it's gone. Sophie has another jar in her hands. This one's a vivid crimson. Auras, I'm thinking. What does the red color mean? I have a bad feeling about this, very bad.

Crash!

A flicker of something I can't quite follow and then the moose head is moving. The ears rotate in my direction; the neck turns. I'm no longer imagining that the eyes are looking directly at me, and they're not soft and lazy cow-chewing-cud eyes, either. That bull moose is pissed, and I can't say I blame him.

Two more jars, and other heads activate, writhing and twisting, trying to get free from the wall where they are attached.

With a mournful howl the dog makes a run for the door and vanishes out into the sunlight.

"Sophronia! Stop this. You're going to get us killed!"

If she can hear me at all she's past caring. An invisible wind swirls her hair out into a cloud. She seems taller, more goddess than human.

A smart woman would follow that dog out the door, get in the car, and drive as fast as the road conditions allow.

Instead, I clump unevenly down the hall, pushing my bum leg at the thought of the coyote, the bear skin, all of the stuffed animals in this house that are not nailed to walls. If that bear is as unhappy as the moose, we're in trouble.

No animals that I can see in Betty's room, and I slam the door behind me to shut out what's in the rest of the house, only to find myself trading gazes with a large crow sitting on a shelf. He's dusty, and I'm pretty sure he's been on that shelf for years, but at the moment he's thoroughly animated.

The crow makes a demonic squawking sound and launches at me. Grabbing a pillow from Betty's bed, I hold it in front of my face as a shield and get on with my search. I'm not going to have much time.

I search the dresser drawers with one hand, holding the pillow over my head with the other to keep that damn crow from shredding my scalp. Nothing here but clothes. Utilitarian underwear, heavy wool socks, the shapeless skirts and sweaters she likes to wear.

A thud jars the door, hard enough to make it jump, followed by a low growl that judders my innards. Another couple of hits like that and whatever is on the other side is coming through. There's no good place to hide. If worst comes to worst I can go out the window, although I doubt my ability to get through it at any speed, and I know my leg isn't going to take kindly to the drop.

Meanwhile, the crow continues its mission, tearing the pillow to shreds with claws and beak, sending white and grey feathers drifting everywhere. Maybe it takes some offense on behalf of its kindred, because it redoubles its efforts, clutching my shoulder with its talons and beating at my head with its wings while pecking at my neck.

Another thud rocks the door, this time with a splintering sound. I've got seconds to search this room before I'm under attack by something a whole lot bigger than a crow, and the bird is getting in my way.

I draw my revolver. The angle is awkward for the shot, but I take it anyway. I'm going to be deaf for a week, but the claws release my shoulder and a cloud of black feathers fills the air, drifting down to join the innards of the pillow. The crow looks like a broken toy—the inner taxidermy framework of wood and bandages visible where the bullet has torn apart the skin. It's still moving, though, flopping about with its broken wing and trying to get upright.

I don't think it can reassemble itself—I hope not—but this answers one question. A bullet isn't going to kill whatever is on the other side of the door, and probably won't even slow it down much. What's needed here is a full-scale exorcism—that or burning down the house. Neither of which I have the wherewithal to do. With the crow out of the way at least I can use both hands, and I tackle the filing cabinet, no longer taking time to be neat, dumping files on the floor.

Damn it, I need more time.

Betty has labeled the files in tiny handwriting and I have to squint and bend close to see. Somewhere in here, I'm convinced, will be something linking her to HUM, or maybe some information about her parents. Forgoing reading the labels, I start flicking through the files, just eyeballing them for anything that looks of interest.

Bills, receipts, tax records. All possibly of interest but not what

I'm looking for.

My period of grace is over. With a loud crash the door slams open and smacks into the wall. The bearskin fills the doorway, mouth open in a snarl. Like my friend the crow, his eyes glow green. Unlike the crow, he's an animated skin with teeth and claws. No stuffing to spill, no framework to break apart. He moves like a stingray, rippling his skin where he needs to for leverage.

Behind him, fully equipped with a body, is a large mountain lion, ears laid back, crouched to pounce.

The bear weaves his head back and forth, those claws raking gashes into the floor.

I fire a shot into the bear's open mouth, and another at the cougar. Both shots hit, traveling right through their heads and slamming into the wall on the far side of the hallway. No brain there to splatter, and the outraged spirits are not amused.

They are both going to launch at me at once, and I'll never make the window.

The wardrobe beside me is still open and gives me an idea. Grabbing the first bottle my groping fingers find, and muttering a silent prayer that it holds what I think it does and not another animal spirit, I fling it at the bear, striking him right between the eyes. The glass shatters. He lets out a roar of rage and pain. Some of the liquid also strikes the cougar. Wherever it hits, it eats away at fur and flesh. The bear rubs at his face with a paw but the cougar inches forward, tail lashing from side to side.

Backing away, I see one chance to save my own skin.

Just one.

Aiming with as much care as I can manage, I take a shot at the bottle of formaldehyde. A flood of foul-smelling liquid bursts out of the bottle and onto the floor. The cougar snorts, but he's not about to run. Half of the bear's face is melted away, but he's not about to run either.

This whole situation is starting to piss me off. It's not that far to the window, and not far at all to the ground. A year ago I wouldn't have thought twice about a dive from where I'm standing, but somehow I've been transformed into this fragile flesh-bound bundle of muscles and nerves that can't quite manage this maneuver and is worried about the pain that will follow.

At this point, it's pain versus death.

I pull the matches out of my pocket, strike one, and toss it at the puddle on the floor. Fire blazes up with a whoosh between me and the raging predators. Grabbing as many file folders as I can carry, I run for the window, break the glass with the butt of my revolver, and leap. The ground hits hard and fast, but I've curled up in as much of a ball as I can manage, rolling when I hit the ground. The jolt runs through my leg and jars my teeth together. A flare of pain stabs through my side, straight through my belly and back into my spine, sharp enough that I wonder, briefly, if I've fallen on a knife.

But all of the pain fades to a brutal ache and I'm capable of movement. Which is good, because I'm pretty sure that mess of chemicals is going to explode. I launch myself into gear, still clutching the file folders, hobbling as fast as my body will take me toward a giant glacial deposit of stone about fifty feet away.

A blast of heat and sound picks me up and carries me where I wanted to go, or almost, tearing the files out of my hands and dropping me hard on top of the rock. I can hear nothing now but the flames, the heat intense on my back. It takes a minute to manage a breath.

I can't move. Something warm and wet touches my cheek once, and then again, accompanied by a panting sound and a smell of animal.

Cold terror floods through me. They've managed to follow somehow, despite the flames.

After everything that's happened to me in my long life and all the paranormals I've faced, I'm going to be eaten by a reanimated museum piece. The thing doesn't seem interested in using its teeth though, and keeps slurping at my face and the back of my neck as though bent on licking me to death.

"We might want to go before the fire department gets here."

For a minute I think it's the animal talking, before I'm able to connect Sophie's voice with her body. The beast barks, and I realize it's just the dog. My head obeys the signal from my brain and I get my eyes open to see the two of them blurring in and out of focus. The hairy face of the dog, the otherworldly face of the girl.

Breath is flowing pretty regularly into my lungs now, and despite the way my head is pounding, I'm able to lift it, and then push myself up into a four-limbed crouch. Relief floods through me. Death doesn't scare me too much, but the thought of life as a petrified not-quite-vegetable is terrifying.

The dog licks my face again with great glee and bounds all around, barking and whining.

Despite the way the world persists in spinning and the quaking of the rock beneath my feet, I manage to get to my feet, partly as self-defense. Sophie is no help whatsoever, just stands there watching, so I ignore her. I could use a hand but I certainly am not going to ask for one.

My revolver is in the holster where it belongs. The papers are scattered from here to kingdom come. Bending over feels like every muscle in my body has been pulverized with a rock.

We need to get out of here before any authorities show up. Flashing my consultant's badge isn't going to get me off the hook for illegal entry and especially not for arson. Nobody is going to believe the reason why I've firebombed Betty's house. Except for Betty, maybe. At last I'm forced to humble myself.

"You could help," I say drily, as the dog grabs a mouthful of paper and gambols off.

"What are we looking for?"

"I'll know it when I see it. If I see it."

"You mean you don't have it?"

"I don't know if I have it."

She shoves her hair back behind her ears and glares at me. "Maybe you should have thought of that before you torched the place."

"Maybe I wouldn't have torched the place if you hadn't let loose a bunch of crazed dead animals."

"They wouldn't have hurt you."

At that I stand up straight, both hands pressed to my now throbbing lower back. I just stare at her, then I show her my right arm, the skin shredded and bloody.

"From your fall?" she asks.

"No, from the freaking reanimated crow. If the bear and the cougar had caught up with me there would be no me left to be having this conversation."

Watching her face, I let the anger slip away. "You didn't notice any of it."

She shakes her head. "I was somewhere else, I guess. I don't know how to help the animals. I was focused on the humans."

"How many?"

"Maureen, we have to go. That's a long-ass driveway. We don't want to be passing the fire truck."

She's evading, for some reason, but I'll catch her later. I let her pick up most of the files and carry all of them. Fortunately, the Jag is parked on the side of the house away from the explosion and is untouched.

As it turns out, no fire truck is forthcoming. This is, after all, the middle of nowhere and nobody will even call until the smoke is noticed. And the nearest fire truck is probably half an hour away. I'm a little uneasy about leaving something burning unattended like that.

"We should call," Sophie says, looking over her shoulder.

"We can't."

"Why not?"

"Do you have an explanation for why we were stealing things from Betty and burned her house down? Something they'll believe, and that won't get us locked up," I hasten to add.

"No, but we can't just leave it. Forest fires happen."

"It's wet. How bad could it be?"

I prefer not to think about the implications of that and just focus on driving.

Sophie doesn't even look tired. More a little supercharged, like her hair is going to ignite in some sort of spontaneous combustion.

I can feel the energy sparking off of her, in fact. For a few minutes she watches the trees go by, apparently thinking things over, and then she turns to the files in her lap.

"Ohhh, now here's something interesting."

"What did you find?"

"Betty's birth certificate."

"Seen it."

"She was adopted."

"Wait—what?" I slam on the brakes and we skid to a halt. "Let me look at that."

"Thought you said you'd seen it. And you can't just stop in the middle of the road—"

"Nobody behind us. Let me see."

She hands over a file. A birth certificate—the handwritten format, not the official printed document, written for Baby Girl Cunningham, born at Shadow Valley Home for Unwed Mothers to a Gail Cunningham. And a set of adoption papers, signed by Betty's adoptive parents and, purportedly, by one Gail Cunningham.

I check the rearview and shift back into gear. "Well, that puts a different spin on things."

"Tell me."

I figure she deserves to know. It might put her in danger, but I suspect she may be in danger anyway. "I believe the Home was used for paranormal research. Babies born there may not have been—human—in the strictest sense."

"So Betty's a soul sucker?"

"My guess is that if she was the true deal she wouldn't be putting them in jars. She'd be swallowing them whole. So she's half human, half paranormal."

"Maureen?"

"Hmmm?" Her fingers are fidgeting with the file folders. Nervous habits aren't usual for her, and I pay attention.

"About my parents…"

The words and the thought seed just float in the car between us for a bit. When she glances up, her face is luminous. "Do you think maybe that asshole isn't my real father?"

"You could ask him. If he wasn't missing."

She turns back to the files. "Top of the agenda whenever he comes back." Something in the tone of her voice makes me suspect that she knows more than she's saying.

A minute later: "Do you think I'm human?"

I can't tell from her voice whether she's hopeful or torn apart by the idea. "Shadow Valley closed before you were born," I say slowly. "And you're not like any para I've ever met. Some humans have paranormal gifts. Clairvoyance, telepathy, that sort of thing. Some can talk to ghosts. And there are a few who help souls cross over."

"You've met these people?"

"I've worked with one. You want to meet her?"

Her hair has fallen over her face, so I can't see her expression. I'm thinking it's been a lonely life for her so far, what with the absent mother and the asshole father. Kids at school aren't going to have taken well to her spookiness, especially combined with the fact that she lives above the funeral parlor.

She's still looking through files. I feel her go still. Hear her stop breathing. And then she asks, in a strange voice, "Maureen, where are we going?"

"To talk to Jake. Let him know what we found out about Betty."

"I don't think that's such a good idea."

"Why ever not? We need his help."

"You can't talk to him. Or I mean, you'll have to, but you can't..." She sighs. "Look, this is a list of employees that worked at HUM. Right here, it says Jacob Callahan. Employment dates 1963 to—well, he didn't work there very long. But he still worked there."

CHAPTER TWENTY-ONE

So we don't go to Jake. We go looking for information elsewhere.

Charlene's house is brand spanking new.

And big, for a single woman. It sticks out like a sore thumb in the primarily older construction of this small town. In my opinion it's cheap and tacky, although I'm sure she paid plenty for it. In other communities I've seen whole neighborhoods of houses like this spring up, all identical to each other with the exception of paint color and landscaping.

They're modern, though. And new. With all the extras and amenities built in.

I park the Jag in the empty driveway. "Stay in the car," I tell Sophie. "I'll only be a minute."

I check my revolver and loosen the knife in my ankle sheath.

Sophie sucks in a little breath of surprise. "What exactly are you planning to do?"

"Talk."

"So why the heavy artillery?"

I don't answer, just get out of the car and walk toward the house. Sophie trails behind me, ignoring my instructions. "She's probably at work."

I knock on the door, polite and civilized.

No answer. No sound from inside. I knock again.

"Neighbor across the street watching out her window," Sophie warns.

"And I'm just knocking politely on the door. Nothing for her to see."

"Yeah, but, you do look a little...worse for wear."

I hadn't thought about that. My jeans are filthy from rolling in the dirt, and I catch a whiff of singed hair at odd intervals when the wind blows over my head. Based on the throbbing of my cheekbone, I'm also probably bruised. Still. I shrug. "This is Shadow Valley. Can't imagine anybody will care."

Still no answer. Maybe she's sleeping. A nap, or if she was up all night in the line of coroner duty she could be catching up. The blinds are all drawn too tight to peek. And if the neighbors really are watching we can't just walk in.

"Are you going to shoot her?" Sophie asks in a too-loud whisper.

"Why ever would I do that?"

I step off the porch and try the gate in the high wooden fence that screens the backyard. It's not even locked.

"Because she was sleeping with Phil."

Of course she was. Exactly the type of distraction Phil would fall for. Put that together with the speed of the cremation and my instant dislike of the woman and Charlene becomes a hot suspect. Not enough evidence to get a warrant, of course, but I don't need one.

The back door is unlocked. Even in a small town locking the door isn't something a coroner would be likely to overlook. I put a finger to my lips and motion Sophie to move around to the side of the house. When she's out of sight I nudge the door open with my foot. No volley of shots. No alarm. No dog throwing a tizzy. Revolver drawn and ready, I push the door open wider and peer into the house.

Nobody in the living room.

Taking my time, gun at the ready, I search the house. Kitchen and bathroom empty. Fancy dog dishes and one of those automatic water fountains in the corner. Downstairs bedroom, which looks like a guest room so pristine I doubt it's ever been used, empty.

Which means stairs.

Sophie gets bored waiting and comes bouncing in.

"Sophie! Get back here. You don't—"

"She's not home."

"I haven't cleared the upstairs. You don't—"

But she passes me and runs up to the second floor, taking the steps two at a time. I feel like a tortoise with two bad legs.

"Hey, Maureen, you gotta see this."

My finger itches on the trigger and for just a hairsbreadth it's not Charlene I want to shoot. When I hit the top of the stairs I ignore Sophie and clear all the rooms properly.

All of them are empty.

The bed in the master suite is frilly but neatly made. The sheets and the quilt are pink. No particular fragrance drifts up to meet my nose. A few short, wiry hairs at the foot of the bed indicate that her dog sleeps with her.

Sophie points out the empty closet and dresser drawers. No cosmetics in the bathroom. No shoes in the closet.

"It's the study you really need to see."

She's right. A paper shredder is full to the gills. There's a safe in the wall, open and empty.

Her email has been cleared, as has her browsing history. Sophie watches over my shoulder as I scan her DNS cache for recent visits. Key Bank comes up. And Alaska Air. It would take some serious hacking to figure out exactly what she did on those sites, but it's already pretty clear. It would be nice if I could call Jake about now and get him to find out which flight she took and which direction her money was moving, but that is not an option.

"You think she's, like, a hit woman or something?" Sophie asks.

"I'm not putting anything past her at this point. How well did you know her?"

"She's afraid of dead people and doesn't believe they have souls. We didn't exactly hang out."

"Maybe she's just running scared. Might have thought she was next."

Everything here is circumstantial evidence. Even if she did suddenly pull up stakes and abandon her house and her job, it doesn't mean she killed Phil.

I'm damned sure she knew something, though, and now she's slipped through my fingers and taken her information with her.

CHAPTER TWENTY-TWO

About five steps from the bottom of the stairs, my cell phone starts vibrating. Both hands are full of Charlene's computer, which I'm hauling back to the Manor for further investigation. The phone is in my pocket, of course, so I can't see who's calling and since precious few people have this number I'm pretty sure I'm going to want to answer.

If I put the computer down I'll never be able to pick it up again and I'll have to ask Sophie for help. The thought of this is intolerable, so I just keep up my slow crawl down the stairs. By the time I reach the bottom the phone has stopped and I just keep moving, through the house and out the door and into the car. Once I've stowed the computer in the trunk I can finally get to the phone.

It's Jake. I know what I have to do, but my feelings have gotten in the way again. For some reason I'd thought this shit would get easier as I've gotten older, but it seems to be the opposite. I hold the phone in my hand, remembering the way he helped me up the stairs, the clean soap smell of him, how it feels when he looks at me the way he does, after the years of Ed's indifference.

Sophie sets the paper shredder down beside the computer. She's unnaturally quiet and avoids eye contact.

"It's not theft," I hear myself telling her. "Charlene's not coming back."

"You need to talk to my father."

The disconnect of this remark on top of everything else in my brain leaves me totally disoriented.

"I thought you didn't know where your father was."

"I lied."

This I don't disapprove of, in theory. Lies can be very useful and I use them myself. I just take exception to being lied to.

"I can find him," she says, "And I'll take you there, but if somebody is going to kill him, it's going to be me."

My brain takes a couple of double hops and a skip and jump to try to catch up to her. "What is it that makes him need killing?"

"He's an asshole."

"And? If we killed all the assholes we'd endanger the population."

She rolls her eyes and does a perfect teen girl head fling, complete with the hair flick over the shoulder. "I can't believe you're missing this. He's been the undertaker here for, like, forever. He didn't exactly work for the Home but—"

"Where is he?"

The phone rings again and this time I answer.

"Kinda busy here."

"We need to talk." Jake's voice makes my heart flutter like I'm some lovesick teenager.

My free hand automatically checks the revolver, my reminder that emotions have to remain outside this equation.

"Funeral parlor," Sophie says.

I take a breath and bring my mind to focus. Phil taught me this, giving me word problems to solve while he shouted in one ear, or fired weapons, or ran his hands over my body and tried to seduce me.

One thing at a time. I can handle this.

"Your house, in an hour," I say to Jake, shifting the car into gear. "Give me the address."

I'm marginally surprised that he gives it to me, just like that, but then I remember how small this town is and what an easy thing it would be to find it on my own. "I'll be there."

I manage to keep the car to the speed limit even though every cell in my body is screaming to go faster.

At the funeral parlor, knowing Sophie's father is there somewhere, I'm on full alert. He's an unknown quantity and I have no idea whether he's a victim in this mess, or a perpetrator.

190

Sophie takes me through the sales room, full of coffins on display. One of them is closed. It's a shining affair of polished hardwood, embossed with gold. Glass panels laid into the surface reflect our faces as we walk by, Sophie's pale and intense, mine bruised and blood-spattered and smeared with black.

For a minute I think Sophie's father is hiding inside the coffin, but she leads me past it, out of the showroom and down a hallway. In the middle of what is basically a storeroom, Sophie kicks aside a throw rug and kneels to pull up on the handle of a trap door.

She shrugs in response to my questioning gaze. "He's a survivalist. Said he always wanted a bomb shelter during the Cold War and didn't have one. Believes the government now is more dangerous and so he turned the old root cellar into a shelter. When Phil Evers bought the Manor, dad got all freaked out and moved in. He's going to kill me for showing you this."

"If you don't kill him first."

She doesn't answer, just turns and makes her way down a ladder. No way am I going down that ladder, not with my leg. Not with an unknown asshole at the bottom, waiting for me.

Voices come up from below. His, raised and hard. "Sophronia, if I've warned you once—"

"We're past that," she says. "You need to come up."

"What for?"

"Somebody you need to talk to."

"You showed somebody my hideout? What's wrong with you? You're my daughter, for chrissake."

"Am I?"

Silence, and then her voice again. "Up. Now. Don't even think about trying to hit me."

A head emerges from the opening, and stops to take measure of me. A lot of women would consider him handsome. He's got thick, dark hair gone silver at the temples and well-formed features. But his mouth is cruel and all the lines in his face are those of an angry man.

"Shit." He wants to go back, like a turtle into a shell, I can see that. But he's got Sophie below him, and I think he knows she's as dangerous as I am.

"Come on up. We're just going to talk." I give him a friendly grin, knowing full well how it's going to look on my bruised face, and wave my revolver at him.

He grimaces, but complies. He's built completely unlike his daughter, a tank of a man, all muscle, with meaty hands that look more conducive to fighting than readying the dead for burial.

"What do you want?"

"It's about the Manor."

"Always knew the government was involved with that place," he says. "Surprised it took you so long to find me."

"I'm not the government."

He gives me another look, a little more appraising. The way he opens and closes his fists makes me want to take a step back, be sure I'm out of reach. That would be my undoing and I hold my ground. Never let them see your fear.

"If you're not the government, then what do you want with me?"

"You've been working in this town for years. What I want is information about strange deaths. Injuries that don't fit the facts."

He laughs. It's a harsh, unpleasant sound, and I don't miss the way Sophie's muscles tighten.

"This business is full of that sort of thing. People die in all sorts of odd ways, lady. I'm not the ME. Not my job to ask questions."

"Nothing so strange it made your blood run cold? No weird shit from, say, the Home for the Unwed?"

His face goes solid, jaw set in a stubborn line. "Get her out of here, Sophronia. I've got nothing to say."

"She's not working for them, Lysander. There's a dangerous thing on the loose. And if it comes for you…" She draws a finger across her throat and lets her head fall to the side, tongue sticking out between her teeth.

His gaze shifts from her, back to me. "I guess I can believe that. You're too old to be FBI."

"Thank you, ever so much. Now, if you could tell me anything of interest from the—"

"I didn't work at the Home, just so you understand. They never called me over a dead baby."

"No, I don't suppose they would have. I expect we'll find some buried out back somewhere."

He's not as good at controlling his face as he'd like to think he is; his eyes are shifty and his right hand pulls at his ear. I hope he doesn't play poker much.

"The mothers, though," I say slowly. "They'd be taking too big of a risk burying mothers out back. Somebody might find out."

"Women die in childbirth. More back then than now, but it still happens." His voice is defensive, and I think maybe he's got the rudiments of a conscience after all, even if he hasn't bothered to listen to it much.

"How many?"

"What?"

I take a step closer. "How many women from the Home did you bury?"

"Nine, ten maybe."

"Seems a pretty high death rate in the age of modern medicine."

He shrugs. "High-risk population. Single women. Drug addicts, runaways. Some of them had no prenatal care before they came here."

"That's the party line. Now tell me what you know."

I must look like I mean business with the gun, because his hands are halfway up now.

"Tell her," Sophie says.

"I only—once I got curious and had a look. Not my job, you understand. That's up to the ME. But this one girl—well, she was so young. Not more than sixteen, I reckon. Blonde hair, pretty thing. Lot of blood on her and I—well, I cut into her belly to see what was what."

He swallows hard. A man like this isn't likely to be squeamish. I just wait, giving him time. He needs to talk about this, I can see it in his face.

"Her innards were shredded. The wall of her uterus looked like…if I didn't know better I'd say it looked like it had been chewed by an animal. They told me her baby died, but I don't know. I've always wondered."

I feel my own blood running a little cold.

Sophie's face is a study. She's only a child, I remember with a pang. Shouldn't be involved in this at all. Tears flow silently down her cheeks.

"And Sophronia?" I ask him, letting my voice carry all of my outrage.

"What about her?"

"Is she yours? How did she come to you?" The girl needs to know, or the questions are going to twist her. She's carrying enough power already that the idea of her turning to the dark is terrifying.

"I was there when she was born," he says. "She belongs to her mother, sure and certain. Who her father might be I can't say. Thought it was me at the time but then she up and—"

"Don't."

"Soph—"

"Don't try to tell that story about how she ran off with another man. I remember the way you beat her. And don't tell me stories about how she was clumsy and ran into doors, because I heard your fists on her flesh and I heard her screaming. I remember that she loved me. I don't know what happened to her. Maybe I don't want to know. But if you try one more time to say she just ran off with another man, I'm going to let myself believe you killed her and cremated her, and I'm going to do the same to you. You hear me, Lysander?"

Her eyes are glowing again, her hair moving a little in a breeze I can't feel.

Apparently Lysander isn't stupid. "I hear." He holds his body perfectly still, barely breathing, and doesn't argue.

"Are you done with him, Maureen?"

"I'm done."

194

"Get back in your rat hole," she says. "Don't come out anytime soon."

"I'm still your father—"

"You just as much as said you're not. Not. Another. Word."

Hands still up and at half-mast, he makes his way to the top of his ladder. For just a heartbeat he pauses and my finger tightens on the trigger, but he thinks better of it and descends.

"You okay here?" I ask.

"Nothing new." Sophie's voice is weary, though, and there's a hurt in it that ought not to be there. "Was your father an asshole, Maureen?"

My father. He died when I was fifteen, and I haven't given him so much as a thought in years. He was so invisible in my life I don't even know whether he was an asshole or not. He just—wasn't.

"Not so much," I tell her. "But my mother was."

She smiles a bit at that. "You said you'd tell me later what I am."

"Yep. But this isn't later. I need to go talk to Jake."

"Do you think he—did this?"

"He had access and opportunity to everything and everybody. The ability to cover things up. He lied to me about what he knows. Confiscated Phil's weapons. If he's got motive…"

My voice drifts off into a silence neither of us wants to break.

Sophie's face hardens into something that sends a slither of cold up my spine. "If he killed those poor women, and Abel. If he was working with Betty—shooting's too good for him."

"He's looked out for you, it seems. Done good things."

"Cover," she says. "A few good deeds doesn't wash out evil."

I find I don't want to talk about this.

"I'll see you later."

Just like that, she's just a teenager again, looking for a thrill ride. "Are you kidding? I'm going with you."

"No, you're not. You will stay here. Right here. Don't go to the Manor, don't go to Jake's. For the love of all things holy do not go back to Betty's and try to talk down the unhappy animals."

"Be careful," is all she says, which amuses me a little.

Way too late for careful, as far as I'm concerned.

CHAPTER TWENTY-THREE

Still, Sophie's words are in my head when I knock on the door at Jake's. A little caution wouldn't go amiss. The revolver is in my hand. I'm past worrying about whether he's going to arrest me; I'm much more worried he's called me here to add me to the ever-growing list of the dead.

My revolver isn't much use against all of Phil's weapons, but my head is cool and clear and I'm ready to do whatever needs doing.

Until Jake opens the door for me and it all goes to hell in a handbasket.

He's not in uniform, just a well-worn pair of Levi's and T-shirt. No tool belt, no visible gun. This doesn't make him look softer at all. He might be sixty-five, but he's kept himself in shape. For an instant there's a sensory blur of male muscle mingled with the scent of clean soap and shaving cream.

My head clears, and I'm hyperaware that he's a good foot taller than me, and a whole lot stronger.

I can see past him into the house. The door opens into the kitchen. A small table, two chairs. Spotless. A little stark. Not so much as a visible crumb on the counters and everything shines. His service weapon sits on the table, in plain sight and near to hand.

He doesn't go for it when he sees my gun, only says, quietly, "You won't be needing that." I hold his gaze without answering, and after a long moment he steps aside to let me in, closing the door behind me.

The sound of it, wood against wood, highlights the risk I'm taking. I cross the floor and eject the cartridge from his SIG. He watches, without a word, his face giving nothing away, other than fatigue. There are shadows beneath his eyes. He hasn't shaved, and the grey stubble on his chin softens him a little.

"You look like a man who didn't sleep," I say, watching him, the revolver deadly and ready in my hand, even as my heart betrays me and my hands want to smooth the lines of weariness out of his face.

"And you look like you've been wrestling a wildcat."

"It was a reanimated crow. The wildcat was coming for me, but I took him out."

He lights up with something darker than laughter, fiercer than joy, and there's an uncharacteristic roughness in his voice. "From any lesser woman, I'd take that as sarcasm."

"I've been to Betty's house."

"Ah," he says, and the light fades. He looks old, in that moment, defeated. I don't like this look on him, at all, but I'm not here to consider his happiness and I let the silence stretch and carry him forward. "Betty is one of the things I need to talk to you about. Been awake all night wrestling with my conscience."

He crosses the kitchen away from me, leaving the door clear, to lean against the counter, careful to keep both hands in sight. No sudden movements, no display of power.

I'm not sure what to say to any of this, so I just wait. He called me here; he's the one with something to say.

"I lied to you."

"I know."

"Somehow that doesn't surprise me."

We stand there in a silence neither one of us wants to break. Outside a crow caws and another answers from a distance. A car drives by. A burst of static comes off a police scanner set up at the corner of the counter, right next to a phone.

"Maybe you should just spit it out," I say, finally.

"I'm thinking you already know Betty isn't precisely normal."

"You think?"

He ignores my sarcasm. "If I asked what exactly happened at her house, would you tell me?"

"Sophie found a collection of bottles that she says were

trapping souls. Animal and human. Evidence indicates the animals were not happy about their captivity."

"Sophronia is another thing," he says. Again the silence. His eyes shift to that cool, predatory intensity I saw when we first met. He moves, as though to adjust his position a little, to ease his back, and just like that, quick and cool and efficient, he's got the drop on me and I'm looking down a barrel that is up close and personal. "Time to tell me what you're really doing here."

My body goes cold, then floods with heat. Apparently I'm not the only one who can wear a small-of-the-back holster and get away with it.

"Put down your gun, Maureen. It's over."

"Not going to happen. And this is far from over."

"Tell me how you did it," he says, his voice still level and deadly cold. "How you killed Phil and Abel. How you connected with Betty and that ridiculous vampire so you could all work together. What your true involvement with the Paranormal Research Lab is, and I don't mean that tall tale you spun for me the other day."

"What?" I heard him okay; I just need a minute to let the puzzle reassemble itself into a whole new picture, one in which I am, apparently, cast as the villain.

"I'm not stupid. You're FBI, and you came for me. I get that. I've been expecting it for nearly forty years. What I don't understand is why Phil? Why Abel?"

"I think Charlene killed Phil. She's on a flight to somewhere."

"You are a piece of work," he says. "If you're wondering why I didn't shoot you straight up, I thought at first you might be legit, here to stop the bloodshed rather than continue it."

"If you'd bother to check, you'll discover I was in the hospital like I told you."

"Hospital has internet and computers and phones. Doesn't mean you couldn't have put this together from there."

"Except that I didn't."

"I should have known it was the government all along," he says. "When Vermeer told us he'd gone to the FBI, and what happened next, I started putting the pieces together. And then you told me about that research lab. Why you told me, I don't know. But I aim to figure it out."

"Abel and Phil recruited me for this. I didn't even know what I was walking into."

"So you say. You realize I've only got your word for any of it."

"You think I somehow plotted to take out two very sharp FBI-trained investigators—"

"They knew you. Thought you weren't a threat."

He believes it, I realize, and my heart sings a little, despite the weapon trained on me. Despite everything. He believes I'm capable of a plot of this magnitude. He's trying to stop it. In this context, the lies he told me make perfect sense. Protecting Betty. Protecting himself. My problem now is that a good man believes me to be a threat to humankind and has the ability to kill me.

Which is no small dilemma. Whether it's a good man or a twisted one pulling the trigger, I'll still be equally dead.

"What's my motive supposed to be?"

"That's where I'm stuck. Revenge? Although why that would make you attack the innocents at the Manor is beyond me."

"Jake." I keep my voice low and steady. "I see where you're getting this. But you're dead wrong. You've got no evidence, only an interesting theory."

"I've been up all night thinking, and it's the only one that makes any sense."

"I've had every opportunity to kill you, if that's what I had in mind."

"True. That's a thing that doesn't fit. Just because I don't see it yet, though, doesn't mean I'm wrong."

"What's interesting here is that I came to talk to you about your part in killing everybody. Quite a challenge to get my mind around the idea that I did it."

"You—what?"

"Means, opportunity, and oh, let's see, motive."

Confusion takes him for only a minute, and then he says,

carefully, "Betty had records?"

"Betty had records."

He's quiet. Thinking. Watching.

I'm the one who finally takes the risk. "Look, neither of us is big on trust. You think I did it. I think you did it. If we're logical for a minute, that right there indicates maybe we're both wrong. Let's put the guns down. Both of us. Equal distance between us."

"That gives me an advantage."

"I know."

He waits so long I think he's going to refuse, but at last he nods. "Count of three."

I let him count it down, and we both slide our weapons to the center of the floor. I'm cheating, of course. I still have my knife. But he probably has one, too.

"About Betty," he says, then. "I thought I was protecting her."

"I'm listening." The silence stretches again, before he goes on.

"Do you want to sit?"

I do, in fact, want to sit. The damned leg aches, my face hurts, my whole body feels like I've been run over by a train, but sitting makes me vulnerable and I can't risk it. So I just shake my head no.

"I don't suppose you have another smoke on you?"

I don't even bother to respond to this. He adjusts his position a little, leaning back against the counter. "All right. Here's the whole sordid tale. I was young and stupid, a brand-new recruit to the sheriff's department and short on money. I'd met a girl and—well, that's another story. But I needed—thought I needed—wheels, a decent apartment, money to take her to dinner and buy her shiny things. And I got offered a job to make some freight runs for the Home. I figured, why not? They were offering good money, way better than I was going to make moonlighting anywhere else, for sure.

"I should have known better, right? But it was a home for unwed mothers, supposedly run by a church group. I told myself there couldn't be anything wrong with what I was doing. When I'd show up at HUM the truck would be all loaded and waiting for me.

I'd drive all night, sleep a couple of hours, and drive through the next day. There was a meeting point—a pretty much empty stretch of road off the highway. When I'd get there, another truck would be waiting.

"The other driver was a guy I knew as Slim. Nice enough, seemed like. We'd smoke a cigarette, talk about nothing, and then switch rigs and head back in opposite directions."

"And you weren't remotely curious about what cargo you were carrying."

"I was paid to not be curious."

"Oh come on. I've known you for about three days and I know better than that."

"I wondered what was in the truck. And as we went on I began to get uneasy. You'd think there'd be a lot of babies coming out of a place like the Home. There were a couple of adoptions in the community, Betty being one of them, but nothing in proportion to the number of girls staying at the Manor at any given time. And there were no babies there. I got called in to help with handyman projects a few times. No children. No babies crying. Just quiet, pale girls with bellies, who wouldn't look at me and didn't talk. It was all wrong.

"So yeah. One night I pulled the truck over in a quiet place and looked. They'd prepared for that. When I rolled open the door, there was a locked panel. Solid, not mesh. So I couldn't see what was behind it. I was about to shrug off my curiosity and get on with the trip when I heard a baby crying.

"You have to believe me—all of my suspicions never ran to babies. Drugs, I thought. There's a lot of pot grown in this area and that made sense. Back then I smoked a little myself, didn't really see the harm in it. Guns, maybe, which was something a little more serious—but then I'd fall back on the fact that the Home was run by church ladies, for God's sake. Guns just didn't fit the bill.

"Anyway. I heard a baby cry and it nearly dropped me. I figured they were transporting them en masse for adoption or operating a child slavery ring or some such. At that point I hadn't—I didn't—"

"The idea of something paranormal never entered your head."

"Right. So there I was, twenty-one years old and transporting babies in the back of a truck, like cattle. I didn't know what to do. I was standing there trying to think what action I could take that wouldn't get me killed, and then another baby started up. It triggered something, some deep primal thing that made me crazy. I got out a tire iron and hacked and pried my way through the door.

"They were stacked in boxes, Maureen. Clear, plexiglass boxes. No blankets. No diapers. There were lights in the truck—grow lights, as though they were plants or something—that kept the temperature warm enough they wouldn't be cold. But even so. I panicked. I couldn't finish the trip, I couldn't take them back, I had no blankets, no food for them, and I couldn't hold and comfort them all.

"So I came up with this harebrained scheme. I turned off my route into the nearest town. It was the middle of the night. The Walmart was open, so I went in and bought a pack of diapers, some blankets, and some formula. I wrapped up one of the babies, diapered it, gave it a bottle, and took it to the hospital. The ER was locked, you had to ring a buzzer. So I left the baby right in front of the door, rang, and ran for it.

"Kept driving for the next little town and repeated the whole performance.

"Would have done it for all of them, only—"

"They found you." I feel like I'm going to be sick.

But Jake goes on, oblivious.

"Must have had a tracker on the truck. They intercepted me just after the third stop. By then I wasn't at all sure I was doing the right thing. That third baby had teeth. Bit the nipple off the bottle and its eyes were red. They took me off to a hospital somewhere, pumped me full of drugs, and told me these stories about how they were the good guys, ridding the world of evil. That part's all a blur. The only thing I remember with any certainty was making the decision to make them believe I was reprogrammed before they managed to do it for real.

"So I came back here to work, with the understanding that I would watch out for paranormal activity and report it. Sometimes I did. Sometimes I didn't. Every time somebody who used to work at the Home wound up dead, I received an anonymous note to let me know. I figured they were coming for me next, so I tried to make them believe I was on board with their program while I tried to protect people here."

I harden my heart. Just because I understand his actions, it doesn't make them right. "And now people are dead," I say. "A lot of people."

He flinches like I've slapped him. "Too late, too slow. Over and over and over I failed to protect people, one way or another. I was—watching Betty. Didn't want to believe what she was, I guess. I remember when she was just this cute little girl, and I was glad she'd found a home."

"How long will she stay locked up?"

"Don't know for sure. We don't have enough to hold her more than a couple of months."

"She went for you with a knife! Isn't that a federal offense?"

"An attorney will get her out on bail."

He's right. We can't make a case against her for soul stealing, or we'll find our way to the looney bin.

"She needs to be killed." I don't soften it with euphemisms. I'm not thinking about removing her, stopping her, or changing her program. I'm thinking full-on annihilation and watching to see what he'll do with that.

"I've been thinking about how to do that," he says, slowly. "But you were first on my agenda."

"And here we are again. Now what?"

I watch his gaze travel to our weapons lying side by side on the kitchen floor.

A burst of static on the scanner startles us both. The dispatcher clears her throat. "All available units—we've got a call from up at the Manor. Elderly woman reports vampire activity, says she is in immediate danger."

Jake hesitates. He's listening, but he's got a long way to go before he gets to trust.

Another voice comes on the scanner. I recognize it as belonging to the deputy who responded to Abel's murder. "Chris here. On my way."

"Take some garlic with you." There is laughter in the dispatcher's voice. "Caller's name is Alice. Reports she is in the basement, attempting to avoid a vampire attack."

It turns out Jake is adept at creative swearing. I appreciate his fluency, but choose to save my breath.

"What are you doing?" Jake's voice is a whiplash but there's no more time to play.

"Retrieving my weapon. Look, there's a thing in that basement way more dangerous than Gerry Vermeer. And I promised Alice I wouldn't let her get hurt."

I holster my revolver and hold out his backup pistol. We've talked. This is the decision point, and either we're working together or…

Well, I don't like the or, but there it is.

"You should stay clear of this," he says, after a long moment, taking the pistol from me and shoving it into his holster.

"A little late for that."

"Story of my life," he says, brushing past me to pick up his service SIG from the table and slamming the cartridge into it.

CHAPTER TWENTY-FOUR

Jake makes good use of his siren, blowing through red lights on Main Street in a way that makes me wish I'd been a cop myself so I'd get to drive like this. We skid into the Manor parking lot in a cloud of dust. A patrol car is already pulled up outside the front door.

"Shit," Jake says. "Kid's a rookie. Wouldn't take much to eat him alive."

Matt's beat-up Subaru is parked in its usual spot. I take a breath of relief to see that the funeral van isn't here and Sophie is well away.

Jake doesn't wait for me or make concessions to my slower pace. He's all cop now, gun in his hand, striding up to the Manor, clearing the doors before entry. Apparently he trusts me enough not to watch his back.

I've got my revolver out, following his lead as fast as my limp will let me. No sign of anybody in the lobby or the office. Halfway to the elevator we pass the little sitting room. Julia and Ginny are engaged in a heated game of Scrabble. One of the other residents sits by the window with a book open in her lap, chin nodding on her chest. Four are clustered around the blaring television.

I don't see Chuck.

"Clear the building," Jake barks, his voice pitched loud enough for deaf ears.

Ginny's mouth gapes open. There is lipstick on her teeth. Even now, there's an inner part of me that takes secret delight in this. All of them just stare at us, dazed, deer in the headlights.

Ginny's nose wrinkles and turns up just a little. "It's cold outside. What are we supposed to do out there?"

"Not get eaten." I'm out of patience with the lot of them. I point my finger at her. "Zebra. Lion. Grrrrrr. Is that clear enough for you? Now get the hell out of the building!"

For another second they stare at me, but then the lights go on and there's the slowest stampede in history, walkers and canes tangled up as the lot of them creak to their feet and make a shuffle for freedom.

Hopefully the action stays in the basement and the herd will all be okay without anybody watching over them. Jake is already moving down the hall. He's going to take the stairs, I realize. Up to Vermeer's room, then down into the old lab. I'm just going to slow him down, and I punch the elevator button with considerably more force than is required.

He hesitates, looking back over his shoulder.

"I'll be right behind you." He nods, and hits the staircase, two steps at a time, while I stand there, wasting precious seconds, waiting for the elevator. It will be faster in the end, I tell myself, but when it finally shows up it seems to crawl upward, and I'm convinced it's going to stall halfway up and leave me trapped, unable to do anything.

The infernal thing stops at last, and when the doors open it's even nearly level with the floor. Jake most likely went in the right direction, but I take my time in the hallway, one doorway at a time.

Vermeer's door is ajar and I flatten myself to the wall and peer into the room before taking a better look. He's nowhere to be seen. The wheelchair sits abandoned at the top of the stairs.

Sure enough, the secret passage door gapes open.

My brain runs down a hundred different rabbit trails at once, none of them leading to a happy place. Jake will take care of Alice, I try to tell myself, but his gun is only going to be good against humans. That invisible bloodsucker down there won't care if he has a gun, and neither will the old vampire, for that matter. I want Phil's weapons, all the weapons, but Jake screwed up on that one and they're all locked away somewhere.

Except for the salt sprayer.

I don't think this will be of much use in current circumstances, but then again it is Phil's salt sprayer, as of yet untested and untried. I go back.

Everything in my room looks as it should. The salt sprayer is on the closet shelf, right where it should be, and the cat is curled up in the corner. He blinks up at me with big, lazy eyes, then tucks his nose into his paws and goes back to sleep.

I take the time to check my weapons. Revolver, loaded and ready. Extra ammo in my pocket. Knife in its ankle sheath. Salt sprayer. Flashlight. It's all I've got to work with, and I make my way back across the hall and begin the long descent down the secret stairs in Vermeer's closet.

No sign of Jake or the young deputy. I proceed down the tunnel on high alert. Something on the floor reflects the light with a silver glimmer. My cross. The one I gave to Alice.

My stomach turns over and I pick up the pace, pushing past the pain in my leg to break into an awkward jog.

And then Alice screams. One long, wordless, bloodcurdling wail, rising in both volume and pitch into a shriek, which breaks off sharply.

The following silence echoes in my head.

Gritting my teeth, I manage an extra burst of speed. Suppressing the impulse to burst into the lab with my gun blazing, I slow my pace, even as I realize how loudly my footsteps resonate. Anybody remotely alert is going to know I'm coming. There will be no element of surprise.

So I take a few breaths outside the open door, peering in to see what I'm up against.

Alice stands in the middle of the room, untouched, unthreatened by anything I can see. The young deputy, face damp with perspiration, has his pistol in hand but is just standing there.

I can't see Jake. Betty, clad in an orange jumpsuit with "Stevens County Jail" stamped on the back, stands with her back to me. She holds an open jar in her hands.

Alice screams again, and I burst into the room, revolver out and aimed at Betty.

"Drop that jar!"

The words aren't even out of my mouth before I see my mistake.

Jake is strapped down to one of the stainless steel tables. When he sees me he begins to thrash against the bonds, trying to shout something, but his mouth is duct taped and all I hear is inarticulate noise. Matt lies on the table next to him, eyes closed, not moving. His face is dead white. Vermeer stands beside him. He's still old and bald and twisted with arthritis but looks anything but frail. Blood drips from his chin.

Betty turns toward me, and her eyes flash red as the human veneer falls away. My finger tightens on the trigger, but before I can complete the shot I hear a crack and a sizzle. All of my muscles contract at once and my legs go out from beneath me. There's a blaze of pain as I hit the floor and I lie there, dazed and paralyzed, my cheek pressed against cold, gritty concrete. I taste blood where my teeth and tongue connected from the jolt.

I hate Tasers. There's not much worse than complete consciousness combined with an inability to move or act. I've dropped both of my weapons and I can't retrieve them. All I can do is breathe as the sweet-faced young deputy leans over me. He gives me another jolt, the current knotting all of my muscles and then leaving them about as useful as a rag doll.

He grins and says, "Thank you for volunteering to be part of our research program. Let me show you to your table."

CHAPTER TWENTY-FIVE

Deputy Chris deposits me on the table next to Jake, smacking the back of my head down hard so that it rings like a bell, both outside and in, and I see a flash of stars. Before I get enough muscle control back to make it hard for him he's got me fastened down at both wrists and ankles, the straps digging into my flesh.

Just as I'm starting to get my mind around the idea that this apparent choirboy is a sadistic bastard and possibly the mastermind behind a complex operation, Alice bends over to pick up both my revolver and the salt sprayer. With great difficulty I'm able to begin shaping the words "Be careful," but then I notice something is off.

She's no longer screaming, for one thing, and doesn't look frightened. She picks up the revolver like she knows a thing or two about guns and tucks it into the back of her sweatpants. As for the salt sprayer, she turns it over and over in her hands.

Something about the expression on her face generates a germ of thought in one corner of my brain that tries to connect with another fragment in a distant memory.

"Interesting," she says. "If I had to guess, I'd say Phil Evers built this contraption. Which means it's not meant for growing plants. What does it do?"

Genuine curiosity shapes her voice as she examines the little hose, the crank, all the while taking great care not to trigger it.

The world rocks a little as the sense of familiarity grows. I've met this woman before, in a time before she was crazy Alice. I need to remember, it's important, but the connection continues to elude me.

Movement is returning to my muscles, for all the good it does me. The deputy has done a stellar job of fastening me down to the table. I can wiggle my toes and clench my fists but the only weapons I've got access to are my brain and my tongue.

I'm not at all confident that either will suffice, but taking a wild guess, I dive into uncharted waters. "Pity you killed Phil, he might have been able to tell you what it is."

"I didn't kill Phil." She's discarded the glasses and the effect of her clear gaze is disconcerting. "Oh, come now. You're a reasonably intelligent woman. Do you think I would have wasted him in such a fashion?"

"I have no idea what to think."

"No? I'm disappointed. I thought you were smarter." She whistles between her teeth, and sets the salt sprayer down on the empty exam table to my right. "Vermeer, come. I've got a fresh one for you."

The old vampire appears at my side in response to the command. He's short, so his old buzzard face is right up front and personal. Fresh blood has made his vampire nature stronger. He still looks mostly human, maybe because he lived so many years before they turned him, but his eyes are nearly black, with only a rim of blue remaining. Either he had an extra set of dentures or he grew some teeth of his own, and the fangs protrude over his bottom lip and give the effect of an elderly walrus in a bad mood.

"Is this your research project?" I ask Alice, who is looking down at me from the other side.

Her gaze brushes over Vermeer with disdain. "My projects are elegant and complex. He's here because I thought he might be useful."

"I wasn't talking about Mr. Vermeer specifically. I meant this whole thing—the lab, bringing us all together like this."

She smiles. "Ah, I hoped you would remember."

So I have met her somewhere before, if only I could figure out where. Her eyes, no longer half hidden by thick lenses heavily smudged, are hazel with flecks of green and blue. A thin, barely visible scar bisects her chin. Allow for the ravages of time, firm up the wrinkles, and I do remember.

I also realize that the trouble we're in is even darker and deeper than I thought. Which is saying something.

Alice pats my shoulder. "Don't feel bad that you missed it. It has been a long time."

"So this is what? Revenge? Because we didn't want to work on your little project?"

"I prefer to think of just rewards, meted out as they are deserved. You and Phil ruined years of important research with your games."

"What games? All I did was decline to be on the team."

"We were unable to find other operatives of sufficient caliber. Phil's refusal generated inquiries. Officials wanted to know why an operative like him would decline to participate. Our methods and purposes all came under the microscope. You could have helped with the greatest research project on Earth, and instead you closed my lab."

Alice might not be as crazy as I thought she was, but she's got a different kind of madness. At the moment my greatest hope is that if I keep talking long enough she'll drop dead from a heart attack. And she's got the deputy, and Betty, and apparently Vermeer as lackeys. I've got a horrible suspicion that the Jelly Thing is lurking and also under her control.

Vermeer has been standing by, waiting on her signal, but he won't wait long. Saliva collects at the corners of his dry lips, his nostrils flare as he leans over and breathes in. Fear will feed him, I know, not as much as blood, but it's something vampires thrive on.

"What about the guys? What did they ever do to you?"

Matt hasn't moved, as far as I can tell. I can't see if he's breathing. Jake has stopped thrashing, but he's alive. I turn my head and find him looking at me. His eyes have that shark look, and I take courage from his calm.

My hands work methodically against the straps. They are leather, which means, theoretically, that they can be stretched. Maybe I can get enough wiggle room to get a hand free if I can keep Alice distracted. But the leather is old and brittle and the deputy has pulled the buckles good and tight. I try collapsing my thumb joint to make my hand go small. A bit of a slip and an instant of hope, but not nearly enough.

Alice smacks Jake across the jaw with my purloined revolver, jolting his head sideways. "This one disrupted the supply of research babies between here and my lab. I've been waiting to get my hands on him."

I take advantage of her shifted attention to pull harder at my restraints. My left wrist bumps against something cold and hard still attached to my hip.

The flashlight.

I remember how it hung on the wall of the shed right by the salt sprayer. Maybe it's more than it appeared. If I can somehow get a hand free I'll have one chance. One. A very tiny seed of a chance. Even a flashlight makes a nice hard weight to slam over Alice's head.

Vermeer's left hand comes down on my shoulder. He lowers his head, mouth half open, a string of saliva drooling down toward my face.

Nothing sparkly about this vampire. Fear loses out to a mixture of disgust and pity. I don't want those flabby old lips, so unnaturally red, anywhere near my body, and the drool about to touch my face is revolting. At the same time, I grieve for the fate of an old man who tried to do the right thing.

On a hunch, I whisper a name.

The old man freezes.

The saliva does not.

It hits my cheek in a cold, gelatinous streak I can't wipe away.

"Lucille," I whisper, and then again, louder, "Remember Lucille."

The thin rim of blue in his iris shifts toward human.

"She's waiting for you, Gerald Vermeer. Don't let her down."

"No soul," he says. "I can't cross."

I try to hold him with my eyes, my voice. "You still have a soul or we wouldn't be having this chat. I'll find a way to help you. I swear it."

A sharp retort, the sound of two solid objects meeting with

force, whips my head around in the other direction.

Sophie stands behind Betty, holding a fire extinguisher in upraised hands. Betty's face has gone slack. The jar slips from her fingers and crashes onto the floor, shattering. Betty follows, crumpling into a heap, a pool of blood spreading out from the back of her head.

"Run!" I shout at Sophie. "Get the hell out of here!"

She obeys about as well as she has so far, which means she darts further into the room, ducking under an empty table for shelter.

Alice's face contracts in anger. "Christopher, catch her; don't kill her. First, close that door and lock it."

"On it," the deputy says. I see movement in my peripheral vision. With a little difficulty I'm able to turn my head enough to see him, Taser in one hand, the other outstretched like he's herding cows or something, stalking toward Sophie's hiding place. Alice, watching him, shakes her head and purses up her lips. "Vermeer—go help him."

"No." Vermeer's voice sounds oddly muffled, as though somebody has a stranglehold on his throat, although nobody is touching him. "Won't harm the Guide. Can't make me."

"You'll do as I tell you." Alice's voice lashes out, harsh and strident. She swings at him with the revolver. Misses. Vermeer scuttles off out of her reach. It's the first sign to me that she's not in total control, and I immediately start thinking about how I can use that.

I hear a scuffling sound and when I look, Sophie is no longer under the exam table. She's nowhere within my limited field of vision, and apparently the deputy can't see her either. He blinks, then turns in a full circle, scanning the room.

Alice pinches the bridge of her nose between thumb and forefinger. Takes a deep breath. "Surely a well-armed officer of the law can locate and secure one young girl."

"I'm looking, I'm looking. I blinked and—"

"Don't blink. For heaven's sake."

Something in the tone of this exchange, the familiarity with which they speak to each other, together with the edge of her frustration, presents me with an idea. They are related, somehow. He's too young to be her son, though.

"Your grandson must be quite a disappointment." It's a guess and a gamble, but I've got nothing better to do.

"He's a good boy nevertheless. Loyal."

Pay dirt. If nothing else, a means of distraction to keep her eyes off Sophie, so I keep talking.

"I can see that. I assume he's the means of securing Jake. And I'm guessing he got Betty out of jail. How is Betty, anyway? Still breathing?"

As soon as the words are out of my mouth I know mentioning Betty is a tactical error.

Alice's smile chills me from the inside out. "She can't be killed so easily. Would you like to see what she can do?" She turns aside and changes her voice to command. "Betty. Come here."

Betty doesn't look like she should be going anywhere. But at the command, a finger twitches, then a whole hand. She pushes herself up into sitting. Blood clots her hair and streaks her face. When she moves, her coordination is not quite right, so that she looks a bit like a robot in need of a tune-up. Her eyes are crimson and have no pupils.

By rights she shouldn't be able to see, but she gets to her feet and comes toward me, one slow, disjointed step at a time.

Alice watches her, beaming with pride. "Betty is one of my successes. We implanted cells from a soul sucker into a pregnant woman, right here in this lab. Her powers weren't visible at birth, and I thought she was a failure, so I allowed one of my doctors to adopt her. She has lived in this town as human all these years—"

"Sucking souls all the time." I make myself as dismissive and bored as I can manage, given the circumstances. "I already know about Betty. I've been to her house and freed all those souls." I deliberately leave Sophie out of this. It's best if they don't know what she is.

"You'll pay for that." Betty's voice has changed. A little more guttural, a little too slow, as though her batteries are winding down.

"Your house burned down, too, with all the taxidermy projects. That was sort of an accident."

She leans over me, breathing in with her mouth half open, as though she can smell my soul and is hungry for it. Those red eyes are disconcerting, but a lot of paranormals have that feature and it doesn't bother me as much as her breath, which reeks of garlic.

"I don't believe you can actually suck the souls of the living. You're not strong enough. My guess is they need to be half dead, or dying, before you can take them. And I'm neither, so back off."

Betty snarls, and there is nothing remotely human in the sound. She leans closer, her mouth only inches from mine.

"Betty, stop. I have other plans for Maureen," Alice says, coldly.

"You promised me souls."

"Take the beautiful young man." She means Matt. I'd thought he might be dead and I'm torn between relief and fear.

Betty's face lights up, then falls. "My jar is broken," she says.

"Oh, for crying out loud. There's another in the cupboard." Alice's voice takes on that exorbitantly patient tone people get when they're frustrated. "Christopher, stop playing hide-and-seek and fetch that, will you?"

"What self respecting soul sucker needs a jar?" I ask, hoping to draw Betty away from Matt and back to me. "Any reasonably intelligent human with a good spell book can pull that off."

"Maybe I don't need a jar." She leans over Matt, breathing him in like perfume. He stirs as if he senses her there, wrists tugging a little at the restraints. Blood drips off of Betty's face onto his, and his eyes fly open.

"Betty!" Alice orders, "Wait!"

Matt's arms and legs jerk at the restraints, frantic, desperate. "No, no." His head shakes side to side. "Not my soul."

He knows what she is. My heart goes cold in my chest.

"Maureen," Matt cries out, his voice taut with desperation. "I didn't—"

Betty silences him, attaching her lips to his in a ghoulish mockery of a kiss. His limbs set up a renewed thrashing against his bonds, his body arcing upward, every muscle clenched in an attempt to get free.

There's not a thing I can do to stop it.

A loud crash echoes through the room. The deputy slumps with his head and upper body out of sight inside an open cupboard. Sophie stands behind him, face and hair spattered with his blood, the fire extinguisher in her hands dripping with gore.

Vermeer sidles toward the fallen, sniffing audibly like a hound dog on the trail.

Alice lets out a wordless cry of grief and rage.

"What have you done?" She rushes for the far side of the lab as fast as her body will take her, even as her grandson's body collapses.

Sophie is oblivious. Long black hair swirls around her in an invisible breeze. Her eyes glow with an unearthly green light and she seems to float across the room toward Betty. "Release him. You can't have his soul." Her voice is a command, reverberating through every cell of my body.

Betty breaks off her suction hold on Matt, but keeps her hands on him. "He is mine. I have taken him." She seems to have grown; the clothes she wears are now tight against her body.

"You can't contain his soul," Sophie says. "It dribbles from your lips. Even now it expands, it grows."

That invisible wind encompasses all three of them now. Long hair swirling, skirts blowing, the two lock gazes over the body of Matt lying limp and still at the center of the whirlwind.

Betty's hand goes to her mouth, as though to press something back.

"It leaks through your fingers," Sophie says, leaning toward her. "You cannot hold it. Without a jar to contain the souls you call, you are nothing. I freed them, and sent them all across. They are waiting for you there. Are you ready to join them?"

Betty shakes her head, still holding her mouth closed with her hand. Her face works as though she is going to vomit, and now her body is distorting, first here, then there, as though something invisible within her is struggling for space.

The room charges with supernatural energy.

"You will never contain it," Sophie goes on. "No matter how hard you try. All I have to do is call it to me."

Betty shakes her head, no, but the expression on her face now is one of torment.

"Come!" Sophie commands.

A sound like air escaping from a balloon fills the air. Betty deflates back to her ordinary size and crumples to the ground. Sophie, holding her breath, bends over Matt, parts his lips, and presses hers gently against them.

One long, slow, exhale from her.

Placing a hand on his forehead she whispers something in his ear. He gasps, his chest rising convulsively. And then he blinks, focusing on her with a look somewhere between disbelief and awe. Once more she bends and presses her lips to his, this time in what is undeniably a kiss.

"Stop moongazing and get him loose!" I bark at her. She comes back to her senses and starts unbuckling his wrist restraints.

Alice is still kneeling at the far side of the lab, her hands on her grandson's chest. I can see from her face that he's not breathing, nor should he be. Half of his head is caved in, and her hands are slick with his blood.

Matt sits up and starts to work on his ankles.

Sophie turns back to Betty, who cowers on the floor at her feet.

"It is time for you to cross."

"Send my maker instead. She's the guilty one."

"But I'm talking to you."

"I was made this way! It's not my fault."

"You had choices. If the vampire can choose, so can you."

"Have mercy. I will do better."

"Too late."

A cold wind flows over me. And then it feels like all of the air has been sucked from the room and I can't draw a breath. The lights flicker and come back on.

When everything clears, Betty lies dead at Sophie's feet.

Matt is free and upright. I'm not sure if this is a good thing, but he starts to work on releasing Jake's restraints so I shift my attention back to Alice.

"You'll pay for this. You'll all pay." Her grip on my revolver is awkward, but that doesn't make her not dangerous. In a relatively small place like this it's very possible she could hit one of us by accident, or that a ricocheting bullet will catch us even if she misses and hits the wall.

Matt is edging toward her. Assuming that he means to disarm her, not help her, I aim to attract her attention. "Are you going to shoot us now? That would seem to be so easy. Such a waste."

I don't dare look away to see what Sophie and Matt are up to, lest she follow my gaze, but I feel cool hands on my left wrist and hear Jake stirring beside me.

"Shooting is too good for the lot of you." Her shirt is soaked with her grandson's blood and there is a smear on her cheek.

"You're rapidly running out of minions."

"You think?" She smiles, and that is the most frightening thing I've seen all day.

"Oh, shit," Sophie says. Her hands stop moving with my wrist restraint only half undone. I follow her gaze across the lab to the far corner. The blood is disappearing off Alice's face, and then her hands, and then the floor.

I start tugging against the restraints, and Sophie resumes the task of unbuckling the unyielding leather. "Get out of here," I whisper.

"Not leaving you," she replies, as my wrist comes free. I wiggle my fingers and rotate my wrist. It's stiff and painful; my fingers are half numb, but functional. I start working on the other restraints.

"Please get out of here," I say again. Sophie shakes her head, stubborn as a mule.

Alice laughs. "I don't really need you restrained. It's just more fun that way. Medusa! Dinner!"

Silence.

A skiff of a breeze.

"It's coming," Sophie says, frozen with terror. "It's—I don't know what it is."

But I do. The last page of Phil's book. The blank page, with the invisible thing that he's not yet found a way to kill.

"Nobody move!" Alice orders. She aims the gun at Matt, who ducks behind a table, and then Sophie, who does likewise. Jake is still trapped, working at his ankle straps.

There comes a slither of cold against my skin.

My flesh puckers in goose bumps. My heart skips a beat.

"Here you go, baby," Alice croons. I have just enough time to think that she looks a bit like a deranged Sunday school teacher before she reaches down and draws the knife from my ankle holster. Without the smallest hesitation she runs it vertically along my wrist, just above the restraint.

Blood wells up in a smooth red line.

Slimy cold nibbles at the edges of the wound, and the blood disappears. My hand and forearm turn white as all the blood is sucked away. I can feel the cold filling my arm, moving up past my elbow, toward my chest.

Alice leans over me, observing.

"Fascinating, isn't it? We combined cells from several different creatures. She retains enough humanity to do as I tell her. Intelligence enough to understand that I will reward her with meals, or punish her when she is willful."

The cold moves up into my shoulder, as though I am being pumped full of something both liquid and solid. Something sentient. And hungry.

It finds its way into my bloodstream and I feel the spread, every frantic beat of my heart pushing it out into arteries and veins. The cold fills my head and pushes into my chest, reaching for my heart.

A few more seconds is all I have.

I rage against my fate. I'll never have the chance to avenge the deaths of the innocent. But there's nothing I can do to defend myself, to fight back. The thing is in my lungs now, I can't draw another breath. My vision is gone, the black is closing in, and there's a buzzing hum in my ears worthy of a hive full of bees.

A pulse.

A shiver.

And the cold retreats. My body sucks in air. My heart hammers so hard it shakes my body. Again the advance, the sensation of my lungs turning to jelly. The quiver of revulsion. The retreat.

Little by little the alien sensation recedes. Out of my chest and back to my belly, growing there like some twisted child and then retreating, down my arm and out through the wound in my wrist. It feels like quicksilver on my skin, an amorphous mass, half liquid, half solid. I bend my elbow and squeeze my hand into a fist, trying to peel it off of me.

My fingers sink into invisible jelly and through it, and I feel it coalesce again around them, gathering itself, still flowing out of my body, out of my blood.

As suddenly as it began, it's over.

I feel the rush of warm blood returning to my body, watch the color return to my skin. The knife wound begins to bleed.

Alice's mouth drops open. She stares, blankly. "But that's not...I don't understand."

My brain is running in overdrive now, trying to understand. What drives the creature back from me? Silver, maybe. There are fragments of it in my body, left behind from the bullet that killed the giant slug.

Jake is working on his last ankle restraint but he's not going to have time. His lip is bleeding. I open my mouth to cry a warning but it's too late. The blood on his chin vanishes. His eyes bulge, his hand comes up to touch his face. He tries to speak, but makes a choking sound instead.

Although my life didn't exactly flash before my eyes just now, a few things did. Mostly Phil and his weapons, the way he seems to have thought this whole thing through in advance. He wasn't ghost hunting, he was tracking this thing.

"Sophie!" My voice is weak and I take a deep breath and try to make it louder. "The salt sprayer!"

Sophie uses the tables for shelter, keeping to a crouch, but when she pauses to grab the salt sprayer Alice aims and pulls the trigger.

There's a sharp retort, her hands recoil.

Sophie ducks, the sprayer safely in her hands. But Vermeer goes down with a hiss of pain.

"Spray Jake. Aim for the head."

Sophie stays down low to screen herself from Alice and the gun, and starts turning that handle. What shoots out is more than salt. A fine, silvery dust clings to Jake's bloodless face. It coats his skin, his hair.

He staggers, about to go down.

Sophie darts to a closer place, the handle rattling as she turns it with all her strength, spraying his face, his neck, his chest. A strange, glittering shape appears, the silver dust making visible what we couldn't formerly see. The creature looks like a giant amoeba, engulfing Jake's face, covering his chest. It writhes and undulates, jelly quivering away from the tiny silver fragments that have invaded it. At last it begins to withdraw down his chest and his torso.

Jake gasps.

The line of refill is visible, color moving from the bottom of his chin, up his jawline, the skin of his face flushing dark red as the blood returns. He gulps in air like a drowning man, but it's not over yet.

The creature sprouts legs and modulates into a form that is almost human, turning an eyeless head toward Sophie. She backs away, still cranking the handle, but the sprayer is empty. My limbs feel like lead and my heart is pounding like a jackhammer, but I manage to sit up and work the straps loose on my left leg. If I slide off the table I know I'm just going to collapse on the floor, so I stay where I am.

Matt has used Alice's moment of shock to charge her and has her gun arm in both hands, pointed upward. He's younger, stronger. He takes the gun from her hands and secures her.

The Medusa wavers in and out of its human shape, flowing across the room toward Sophie, who drops the useless weapon and runs flat-out with the creature pursuing. My world shifts into slow motion as adrenaline floods me with rebellion. Nobody else is going to die for this creature.

Jake half walks, half crawls across the lab toward the dead deputy.

I fumble with the flashlight. The carabiner I've used to attach the thing to my belt is beyond me, and I can't get it free.

Sophie screams as the Medusa reaches out a misshapen tendril to touch her. On reflex, I point the object in my hands at the thing that is threatening her and push the button.

The flashlight beam focuses into a narrow circle of light that turns violet when it strikes the Medusa. The jelly recoils in concentric circles away from the contact point. With a weird hissing sound, Medusa deflates into an amorphous puddle.

It starts moving again, this time toward Alice, me tracking it as best I can with the flashlight still attached to my hip.

The creature wraps gelatinous arms around Alice's waist.

"Medusa! Let me go!" She slaps at it, tries to shove it away, but it clings.

Matt steps back, both hands shaking, but keeps the gun trained on her.

I hit the Medusa again with the flashlight beam, this time moving it in a pattern that turns a wide swath of the jelly violet, then black.

The creature thins and spreads, engulfing Alice's body in its own, writhing and twisting away from my beam and making a shrill whistling sound like a tea kettle.

Alice begins to scream, high and quavering, still trying to peel the thing off of her, but her hands just sink into the jelly.

The Medusa reaches her face and covers her mouth.

The screams stop. There is a gurgling sound, followed by silence. Flesh melts like wax in the heat, and is absorbed into the Medusa jelly, leaving only bones.

Bones that the creature uses to create and hold a human structure of Alice proportions.

A moment of shocked silence, and then all hell breaks loose.

Matt starts shooting, firing again and again. Jake gets his hands on the deputy's gun and joins him. I keep the flashlight moving.

This time, the Medusa holds its human shape. Ragged holes appear where the bullets strike, and a thick, scarlet jelly dribbles out of them. The flashlight beam drills burnt spots as I keep it sweeping back and forth over her body.

The creature howls in pain and rage. Its head swivels, seeking an exit. It tries to flow but is not so fluid as it was, and trips over its own feet. Another wailing cry, and then it masters an awkward sort of walk and lurches toward the door.

Matt is out of ammo, but Jake is still shooting.

The Medusa fumbles at the door but can't manage the lock.

It stands there, its body quivering as the bullets strike and the narrow beam of light burns.

And then the thing just vaporizes. Starting from the head and moving downward, the jelly disappears until nothing is left but a pile of bones and a heap of silver dust.

CHAPTER TWENTY-SIX

Silence fills the lab, but my ears are still ringing.

Sophie kneels down on the floor beside Gerald Vermeer and eases the old vampire's head into her lap. His face is a nasty color, somewhere between purple and grey, both hands pressed over a wound about an inch below his heart. He's gasping for breath. In my head I know this is merely habit; he has no need of oxygen and it's not the chest wound that will kill him.

Alice shot him with my gun, and the first round loaded was silver. I've seen a vampire die from silver poisoning, a long and painful death. Never thought I'd feel guilt over a dead vampire.

"I have a soul," Gerry mutters, so quietly I can barely hear him.

"I can help you," Sophie says. "We can send your soul across."

"Please." Years of pain are in the one word.

Sophie looks like a frail, exhausted child at the moment. What happens if she pushes too hard, travels too far? She should rest now, recharge her psychic batteries, but the look on her face tells me she won't until her work is done.

"What do you need?" I lower myself down to the ground. Despite taking care and going slow, my legs collapse beneath me.

Jake makes an odd noise in his throat and heads in my direction but I don't want help. Not now. I've had my fill of feeling weak and helpless.

My limbs work, after a fashion, and I drag myself over to Sophie and the vampire.

Her glowing eyes meet mine, the essence of what she is burning bright inside the slender human shell.

"I'm going to call his soul. When I say, you're going to stake him."

I stare at her in disbelief. "He's an ally now, not an enemy."

"He's both," Sophie says. "Don't you see?"

And suddenly I do see. They haven't turned him, they've divided him. Part vampire, part human. And if the human part dies first, then nothing will be left but vampire. Not only will his soul be lost forever, he will become a real danger to a group of wounded and exhausted humans.

What we do is risky.

Timing will be everything.

I tense as Matt comes up behind me.

"Here." He presents my knife to me handle first. "You'll need this." Our eyes lock, me trying to figure out what game he's playing. Sophie's voice, sharp with urgency, pulls me back to Vermeer.

"Hurry, Maureen, we don't have time."

Baring the old man's chest, I count the ribs and rest the tip of the blade in the fourth intercostal space, right above his heart.

"Stay with me, Gerry. Lucille is waiting for you." Sophie's voice is soft, but the words are a command.

Gerry smiles. The black in his eyes recedes, leaving only blue.

"Come to me," she says.

He sighs. His eyelids close as if he's drifting into sleep. Sophie looks up at me and nods. "Now."

The blade is sharp and it doesn't take much to pierce the skin. A little more to press through flesh. I'm quick, but his lids snap open before I can drive the blade home. Nothing human in his face now. His body ripples, changes. Gnarled hands grip mine with superhuman strength. I lean all my weight into the thrust and the knife slides in, up to the hilt. His hands tighten on my wrists, so hard I gasp with pain before he goes limp.

I rock back away from him, breathing hard. In death, his body looks small and old and frail.

"Peace," Sophie says, passing a hand over his face to close his eyes.

But there is no peace. Not yet.

"Give me your gun," I say to Jake. His eyebrows go up in a

question mark, but he hands it over.

Trust. It's a strange sort of thing, and warms my heart. But this is no time to go soft.

If I had the option, I'd prefer to be on my feet and not doing this from beside the dead man, but I know I'm not going to be able to get up. Thank God my hands aren't shaking. Yet. I aim directly at Matt. He's still holding my revolver, but I counted the shots and I know it's empty.

"Time to declare yourself. Who are you, really, and who are you working for?"

Sophie looks from Matt to me, her eyes all questions, but she holds her tongue.

"How did you know?" he says.

I don't answer, and after a moment he sighs, and answers.

"My name is Matthew John Pennington." He waits quietly, a trained response that confirms all of my suspicions.

I adjust my aim. My right hand is slippery with blood, which is still gushing faster than it ought to from the gash in my arm. My body has broken out in a cold sweat. I don't like the way the bees are still buzzing in my head.

"Step it up, Matt. No time for games."

If he hadn't helped me right now, if he hadn't tried to defend us against Alice, he'd already be dead.

He holds my gaze. "What gave me away?"

"I'm the one asking questions. Did you help Charlene kill Phil, or just pay her to do it?"

"She was paid. Phil was so sharp I don't think anybody else could have got to him unless we brought in a full-on team to blast him out, and they wanted this quiet. Charlene was his weakness, and she was easily bought."

"So, what, you went to watch?"

"No, I went to talk. Killing an old man didn't sit right with me and I wanted to—I don't know. Verify something. But I got there too late."

"How was it done?" Jake asks. His face has hardened into

professional mode and he shifts his position, his right hand moving unconsciously to his empty holster.

"Insulin. He had a numb spot on his back from a pinched nerve. She shot him up while…" Matt pauses and has the grace to redden a little. "While he was distracted."

"Classy. Did she stick around to watch him die?" My finger twitches on the trigger. Phil deserved a better death, the bang he wanted rather than confusion and weakness and a slow slide into unconsciousness and death. He would have had time to know something was wrong, to get out of bed and wander into the study, growing weaker and more incapable of logical thought as his blood sugar dropped lower and lower.

A state that easily could have been reversed by a hefty dose of sugar.

Guilt squeezes my lungs in my chest, makes it hard to breathe. If I'd gone to him right away, instead of feeling hard done by in that restaurant, maybe I could have saved him. Maybe I would have also caught him in bed with Charlene, but that's another issue and one I don't choose to dwell on.

"Who killed Abel?" Jake is asking, and I force a breath and bring my mind back to the now.

Matt's eyes go dark. "God help me, I did."

Sophie makes a small sound that reminds me of how young she is, but her disillusionment rapidly transforms into righteous rage.

"You did that? I saved your pitiful soul just now. After you did *that* to another human being? Working with Alice and Betty? It's despicable—"

"No!" Matt cries, then. "What I did was unforgivable, but I swear I didn't know Betty was lurking around with that jar, and I certainly didn't know that…thing was anywhere near." He shudders. The emotion rolls off of him in waves and it seems real enough, but I'm not buying. Acting of this caliber is hard to manage, but possible. I've pulled it off myself.

"What about all those former Home employees who were murdered—what did you have to do with that? When did you hook

up with Alice? How did you know where Abel was going to be?"
Jake fires the questions hard and fast.

Matt looks blank. "What Home employees?"

Jake is no longer cool and professional. This is personal. His
town. His failure. He starts naming names. "Harold Keller. Marilyn
Fraser. Janet Marsh. Betty's parents, Doctor Michael Cameron and
Grace Cameron—"

"Stop," Matt says. "Please, stop."

"You killed all those people?" Sophie's eyes are beginning to
glow again, and I start thinking maybe I won't need to shoot him
after all. But then he takes everything I've figured out and turns it
upside down.

"I killed Abel. I'm guilty of that, and you all can do whatever
you want with me. Arrest me, shoot me, take my soul back if you
think you have to. But you need to know that I…they told me…"

He swallows, hard, looking so miserable that an unwilling
sympathy softens me. I'll still shoot him, but I might feel a little bad
about it.

"They told me a group of scientists had been secretly running an
experimental lab where they researched paranormal-human hybrids.
The lab was closed down because the most dangerous of all of their
hybrids had escaped and was traveling the countryside, killing people
as it went. They showed me pictures of the bodies—all drained of
blood like Abel and the rest. I researched that independently; found
out it was true that the lab was shut down, only the reason was top
secret and I couldn't access it. They told me that a man named Phil
Evers was in charge of the program, and that he was reopening
operations here, at the Manor. That the reason he bought the Manor
was to have access to the lab. So I got hired on as the cook—I do
have experience, and references, it's what I did before getting into
the FBI. Small town and all, and Phil hired me. He might have had
suspicions. I think he did."

Matt has had plenty of opportunities to take me out. To take
Sophie out, too, if that's what he was after. "How come you didn't
kill me?"

He laughs, but there is no humor in it. If anything it sounds more like a sob. "When you showed up I didn't know what to do with you. And then when Abel…" He stops again, his face working.

"Abel was my first kill, and I botched it. My hands were shaking and it wasn't a killing strike. Before that Medusa thing showed up, he looked at me and said, "Watch your back. You've got it all wrong." And then—that thing, and Betty with the jar…I believed I was acting for the greater good. That Phil and Abel were monsters who needed killing…"

His voice breaks. Sophie goes to him, despite me, despite everything, and slips an arm around his waist. He lifts a hand as if to touch her hair, and then lets it fall back. But he stands up a little straighter, and says with quiet dignity, "If you kill me now, I understand. But I'd like a chance to put it right."

"You can't." The words come out of my mouth flat, bald, and clumsy. "Phil was a good man who sacrificed years of his life to pursuing these monstrosities and their maker. He's dead. And Abel was another good man, trying to do the right thing. You can't bring them back."

"You think I don't see that? I know what I've done. I have to live with it, always and forever. Dying would be easier, I think."

I'm breathing hard now, too, that tightness in my throat threatening to choke me, while the buzzing in my head gets louder and blackness edges my vision.

Guilt rests heavy on my own shoulders. I walked away from that lab all those years ago and managed to forget about it, about Phil, while all the time he'd been keeping tabs on Alice and her creatures, trying to shut them down. I was willing to believe he'd let it go because that was easier.

So maybe it's my own damn fault that I've got nobody and nothing left. No job, no contacts, no life to go back to or move on to. My body is failing me and even if I was in my prime I couldn't go back to the FBI. Not now, not after knowing what they've done.

I try to cut him off but my tongue is numb. The buzzing in my head has increased to the point where I can no longer make out his words. I try to say something, and then the gun slips from my fingers and I'm falling into the dark.

• • •

I wake up fighting.

My foot connects with something soft that wheezes on contact. My right hand flails against empty air. My left is held fast and I can't get it free.

When I get my eyes open I see Jake doubled up with both arms folded across his belly and his face all blotchy and red, making whooping noises as if he's having trouble breathing. Matt and Sophie both are anchoring down my right arm and Matt holds a suture needle.

"Maureen, settle down already," Sophie says. "We're just putting some stitches in to stop the bleeding."

My heart slows from a full-on gallop to something just faster than normal and I stop struggling, even though I'm not at all happy about Matt being in such close proximity to me with a sharp object.

"One more stitch," he says. "I was hoping you'd stay out until I was done; I don't have lidocaine. Hold still."

The needle pierces flesh and I suck in a breath and bite my lip. My foot twitches and Jake watches it, wary, ready this time to get out of the way.

"We don't have time for this," I say, as soon as the pain eases and I have breath enough to speak. "We don't have a cleanup team. We need a story."

"Betty did it," Jake says. "She was unstable and hated old people."

Sophie nods. "Yeah. She was holding Alice hostage. She shot Vermeer when the deputy came down to investigate."

"How did she get out of jail?"

"Deputy was her secret lover. They were in collusion. He got her out of jail and—"

"And instead of running away together they started torturing old people?"

"No," Matt said. "He was hiding her in the basement until he could perfect a plan to get her away. Alice came down and found them. They killed her to keep her quiet, not knowing she'd already called 911. Same with Vermeer."

"And then I came down," Sophie says, "and when Chris came after me I clobbered him in self defense."

"Which explains why it's the back of his head that's bloody. And we are missing a body if we go with that tale."

"All right," Matt says, tying off a neat suture and cutting the thread. "Here's your arm back, Maureen. How about this. I killed the deputy. A little jail time will get me out of your hair so you can decide what to do with me."

He's done a neat and professional-looking job on my arm, presuming the suture wasn't dipped in some sort of arcane poison first and he's not trying to kill me. "You can't go to jail." I work myself into a sitting position, relieved that the room doesn't spin and my head is no longer full of bees. "You didn't finish the job and whoever hired you will be looking for you. Easier to get at you there than anywhere else. Here's what we're going to do."

It's easy, really. We have all the time in the world to manipulate the crime scene, getting rid of fingerprints and disposing of evidence. Jake has years of credibility in this town, and nobody is inclined to question his word.

The story we agree upon is this.

Deputy Christopher Harris, for reasons unknown, transported Manor employee Elizabeth (Betty) Cameron, an inmate in the county jail, when he responded to a 911 call at Shadow Valley Manor. Cameron was being held on charges of assaulting an officer. The call was placed by Manor resident Alice Sorenson. When Sheriff Jake Callahan also responded he found a scene of carnage with no survivors. Betty Cameron and Deputy Harris were both found DOA, having sustained traumatic blows to the head, later determined to be the cause of death. Gerald Vermeer, resident of the Manor, was also DOA, and had been shot and then stabbed. The presumed perpetrator was witnessed fleeing the building, taking Alice

Sorenson with him as hostage. Both eyewitnesses, Manor employee Matthew Pennington and Sophronia Alexander, report that the perpetrator was a middle-aged white male wearing a Lakers ball cap. He is of average height and weight, carrying some sort of iron pipe with which it is believed the bludgeoning took place. His motives are unclear, but he should be considered armed and dangerous. He was driving a white Taurus sedan, license plates unknown.

This story is put out by Jake in an official statement and airs on the local news. A nationwide APB goes out on the unknown assailant, and also on his kidnapped victim.

Nobody questions any of this, and the crime scene is considered cleared within the course of a week. As soon as Vermeer's body is released by the ME we cremate him, just to make sure there's no coming back. For once, Sophie has no problem with this, since the part we are consigning to ash is purely vampire and his soul has already crossed. She puts him into the chamber herself while the rest of us stand witness—partly out of respect for the old man, partly out of doubt that he'll stay dead.

I keep Matt on at the Manor. His former employers will be reluctant to draw any more attention to this scene, and he's safer here than he'll be anywhere else. Besides, I like to keep my enemies where I can see them. He also serves as bait, because sooner or later the FBI is coming for him, and when they do I'll be ready.

Every time I look at him he reminds me of Phil, and of Abel, and of my own share of guilt in their deaths and all of the others inflicted by the Medusa. Sometimes this means I want him dead, but then I remember he's really a victim in all of this.

Besides, he makes damn fine coffee.

As for the zebras, they stay true to nature, gratefully believing every comforting lie we tell them. I claim to have fallen down the stairs as an excuse for my bruises and the stitches in my arm. Ginny offers to lend me makeup to disguise the damage, which from her is deeply giving. Chuck makes a comment about how elevators never hurt anyone and old people should avoid stairs. He's wrong about this, of course, but I let him believe. One by one the other residents trickle back, and before I know it I've got my hands full with menus and paperwork and schedules.

So far, nobody has come looking for Matt, which is disappointing. But I'm sure they'll turn up sooner or later.

Jake invites me out for dinner or a movie about once a week, and I always say no. I'm not capable of a normal relationship. He's best on his own and so am I.

Life settles into peace, quiet, and a comfortable routine.

Which is worse than a death sentence. My life scrolls out in front of me in an unending desert of time that makes me rethink my plan to live to be old.

One Sunday morning I'm doing paperwork when I hear footsteps approaching the office. These are not the shuffling footsteps of a resident, and I look up in a quick burst of hope and adrenaline while one hand goes to the revolver I keep in an open drawer.

But it's just Sophie, flanked by Jake and Matt. The three of them together is something new, though, and they have the look of collusion about them.

"Time to hire somebody to manage the Manor," Jake says.

"I've been looking. People in this town are strangely nervous about working here."

"Try harder." He places a file folder on my desk. When I open it, the photograph of a corpse stares up at me. She's young, not more than sixteen, laid out on an autopsy table. Nearly every inch of her naked skin is covered in tattoos.

"What the hell is this?"

"It's a blog called *Underground Weird*," Sophie says. "This guy who works in some big city morgue runs it—all kinds of weird shit."

"And I'm looking at this because…?"

Jake reaches down and moves the picture to the side. "Read the next page."

What follows is a brief notation of the autopsy results. No evidence of physical trauma. No evidence of disease. All normal results with the single exception that there was no blood anywhere in the body, even in the chambers of the heart. A strange, jellylike substance coated the inner surface of her arteries.

"Medusa is dead," I hear my voice saying. "We killed her."

"Maybe not," Sophie says.

"Whether it's the Medusa or some other thing, it needs to be stopped." Jake's voice is thick with suppressed emotion.

Matt steps up to the desk, always keeping his hands where I can see them. His eyes are dark and brooding. Sophie stands on the other side of Jake and something twists inside me at the sight of both of their faces. They are too young to carry this weight.

"I'm going after that thing," Matt says, with an intensity that dissipates my boredom like sun on fog. "I know you can't trust me, and I'm not asking you to. Just being clear about what I plan to do."

Jake's face is set, his grey eyes piercing. He nods, imperceptibly, and I know he's not going to let this rest.

"We need you, Maureen," Sophie says. "You're the one who knows all about this stuff."

I don't trust a one of them.

Jake lied to me, pure and simple. Matt killed people I love, and that's not a thing I can forgive and forget, no matter what his justification. As for Sophie, I'm not quite sure yet what she is or what she is capable of. I doubt that she knows, herself.

Which makes them pretty much perfect, since I don't trust anybody. At least this is all out in the open. Besides, what else am I going to do? Sit here and die by inches while wallowing in guilt?

"Well, hell," I say, after letting them all wait a good long minute. "If Matt's leaving, who would make me coffee? I'm in. Just as soon as I can find somebody to run this bloody Manor."

ACKNOWLEDGMENTS

This book would never have been written were it not for my friend Linda Grimes, who sparked a weird little streak of dark magic when she dared me to write a geriatric vampire novel. I wrote the first chapter and sent it to her as a joke, but she told me she loved the concept and encouraged me to proceed. I'd fallen in love with the story myself, but it kept getting back-burnered by other contracts and responsibilities.

So I'm thrilled that Maureen and Gerry V and the rest of the crew have finally found their way into the world. I owe thanks to my critique partners, Alexandra Hughes and Susan Spann, for reading and encouraging and helping me keep the faith. Thanks again to Linda Grimes, who took the time to read and provide feedback on the completed manuscript. Thanks to Bill Cameron for serving as a "mystery consult" for my first dive into this genre. Thanks also to the Book Country members who critiqued the original first chapters and made me realize I needed a change of direction.

I'm eternally grateful for my Viking—who not only copes with my "present-in-body-but-absent-in-spirit" state when I'm deep in a project, but also reads and provides valuable commentary and advice on firearms and logistics.

Thanks also to the staff at Diversion Books for the lovely collaborative way they have worked with me on bringing this book to publication, and also to my agent, Deidre Knight, for believing in me.

Last, but not least, I must say thank you to my indomitable and irrepressible main character, Maureen Keslyn, who showed up on the page during revisions and told me that this book is hers.

MAY 2 6 2016

CPSIA information can be obtained at www.ICGtesting.com
Printed in the USA
BVOW05s0932120116

432588BV00004B/5/P